BLACKFOOT IS
MISSING

BLACKFOOT IS MISSING

William F. Owen

arrow books

Published by Arrow in 2004

1 3 5 7 9 10 8 6 4 2

First published in the UK by Hutchinson in 2002

Arrow
The Random House Group Limited
20 Vauxhall Bridge Road, London SW1V 2SA

Random House Australia (Pty) Limited
20 Alfred Street, Milsons Point, Sydney
New South Wales 2061, Australia

Random House New Zealand Limited
18 Poland Road, Glenfield
Auckland 10, New Zealand

Random House (Pty) Limited
Endulini, 5a Jubilee Road
Parktown 2193, South Africa

The Random House Group Limited Reg. No. 954009

www.randomhouse.co.uk

A CIP catalogue record for this book is available from the British Library

Papers used by Random House are natural, recyclable products made from
wood grown in sustainable forests. The manufacturing processes conform to
the environmental regulations of the country of origin

Typeset by SX Composing DTP, Rayleigh, Essex
Printed and bound in Great Britain by
Cox & Wyman Ltd, Reading, Berkshire

ISBN 0 099 44154 3

To my Father

ACKNOWLEDGMENTS

The vast majority of this narrative is based on the activity of CCC Kontum, from late 1969 to August 1970. Certain events are a matter of historical record and, however dramatic other events may appear, almost all are based on actual incidents that occurred during, or near, this time.

To my knowledge there never was an RT North Dakota at Kontum. All persons described in this work are fictional, and are not based on the men who held the appointments at the time.

The lion's share of gratitude must go to John L. Plaster (CCC '69–71) for his hours of interviews, hospitality, patience and suggestions.

Next I would have to thank Bryon Loucks (CCC '67–68), Luke Dove (CCC '68–69), Gerald Denison (CCC '68–69 and '71), Ralph Rodd (CCC '69–70), Joe Parnar (CCC '68-69), Frank Greco (CCC '69–70), Sony Hoffman (CCC '70–71), Allan Farrell (CCC '68-69), Don Dineen (6th SOS SPADS), George Boehmer (20th TASS COVEY) and Pete Johnston (219th AVC SPAF) for their many hours of interviews and correspondence. This task would have been impossible without the time and attention of these men, and I will be forever grateful for their efforts to remember things some have tried hard to forget.

I am also indebted to the writings and memories of Leigh Wade (USSF).

Men who also contributed valuable information and perspectives are James McGlon (CCC '67–68), Jay Massey (CCC '67), Alvin Briscoe (CCC '68) and David Kirschbaum (CCC '69).

For finding these people and encouraging them to talk to me, I have to thank Steve Sherman of the 5th Special Forces Group Association, Robert Noe (CCN '69–70) and Col. David 'Bulldog' Smith (CCC '67).

I must also acknowledge the encouragement and kind words of Lewis Sorley, whose book, *A Better War*, inspired me to write about the Vietnam conflict. Also David Mason, whose comments and criticism helped forge my manuscript into something people might read. Rosemary Osmond for her attempts to enforce the basic rules of grammar and her hours of proofreading. My editor, Paul Sidey, for his patience and persistence in helping me learn the craft of writing, and Jonathan Lloyd, my agent, for doing what agents do, only better.

Lastly, I must thank Julie, for all her love, patience, infinite understanding and encouragement.

PROLOGUE

The sun rose through the low cloud. Shafts of light shone out across the sodden jungle hillsides and fell on the drawn faces of the men on the ridge.

The Montagnard scout leant back against a tree, and listened to the sounds of sunrise. He wanted to be sure the jungle was at peace, before the coming storm.

The scout had been fighting this war for many years. He had experienced this situation before, waiting for daylight and rescue. He had watched many sunrises believing he would never see another. It had always been this way for the warriors of his tribe and the way of his people, the Rhade, who lived in the highlands and mountains of lands the white man called Vietnam and Laos, but to the scout were just the mountains. That was why the French had referred to his people as Montagnards, the Mountain People. The Americans just called them Yards.

The scout liked Americans. He liked men who liked to fight. That was why the American had stayed behind to let the others escape. He was a good fighter, had a hunger for danger. Not the hunger of a greedy man, but the hunger of a man who had grown used to little food. He only ate what he had to. Never too much. Always stored some of the danger for later, for when it would be needed. This man was a true warrior and a friend. If he were dead, the scout would miss him.

Another, younger Montagnard crouched close by, looking back the way they had come, down the far side of the ridge. His finger caressed the trigger of his carbine. He wanted to fight. They had run all night and now they were hiding. Hiding from the *Viet*. Hiding from the *Viet* who had killed the American. He knew the American was dead. He had heard the shooting when the American stayed behind to kill the *Viet* trackers. The young Montagnard squeezed the fore-end of the carbine in frustration. Another warrior was gone, like so many before him who had come to fight in the forbidden land of the mountains and forests where the *Viet* walked the trails and drove their *camions*. The *Viet* lived and hid in this secret land where the great American chief said there was no war, in a land where Americans and Montagnards vanished in the jungle, or were flown back dead, lying bloody and torn on the floor of the helicopters.

The young Montagnard knew there were many things he did not understand, but he felt he understood the Americans who fought with his people. You fought because you enjoyed it. You fought because it gave respect to your father and mother, and gave your children a pride in your achievement. War meant you had to care about others and care so much that you didn't mind dying for them. No man of peace would ever understand that.

The Lieutenant glanced across at the young Montagnard. At least the youngster looked awake and sharp. The Lieutenant tried to wipe the exhaustion from his own face. With the team leader gone, he was now in charge. God, what a night. They had started with six men and now there were only four and one of them was wounded. Doomed from the outset, they'd gone on regardless. The Lieutenant had suggested not going, but the team leader had pushed on, and dragged everyone else with him.

Damn him for taking the easy way out. Damn him for dying so that they could live, to fight another day. Damn him for being the hero the Lieutenant knew he could never be.

Ever since he'd been a kid, the Lieutenant had dreamt of being a soldier. Being just like his pa, and having all those stories to tell. He wanted people to look at him the same way they looked at his father, but that was all bullshit now. He could never tell anyone about this. How could he? There were no Americans where he was right now. There never had been. The President had told the people, so it must be true. The Lieutenant wore no identification or sign of rank. He had no name, or none that his family would recognise. If he died, he would die in another country, called Vietnam. If his body were never recovered, the mythical location of his disappearance, not death, somewhere in South Vietnam, would be the final deception.

The Radio Operator nursed his wounded arm. It hurt like hell, but the seriousness of the situation outweighed the pain. In the valleys below, hundreds, maybe thousands, of North Vietnamese would be beating the bushes, looking for their trail, still angry that the Americans had eluded them. They'd nearly trapped the team three times in the last two days, but every time they had failed. Christ, his arm hurt, but he felt he'd been lucky.

The little Army spotter plane lifted from the runway at Da-Nang and began to climb towards the broken cloud, heading northwest as the rising sun promised some not just a new day but a new beginning. For the pilot it only promised more daylight and more flying.

Despite his exhaustion from the previous day's sorties, he had spent the night tossing and turning; haunted by the news that another friend was missing, probably dead. In the blackness of the night he had resolved to cross the border at first light to try and see if he could help.

The pilot had witnessed, first-hand, a team huddled in bomb craters, fighting at close quarters with wave after wave of North Vietnamese who flung themselves against the guns and grenades. He had watched from the air as team members suddenly fell and lay motionless, or were dragged into cover. He had seen men expend all their ammunition and grenades, so that they had nothing more to fight with other than a knife or weapons they could take from the dead. With luck, they might still have a radio, to call in air strikes. He had often wondered what it was like to have your weapon lock back on an empty magazine and know that the only way you were going to survive was to kill someone with your bare hands. Or pray that helicopter gunships or fighter aircraft would save you, even though their rockets and napalm were so close they were just as likely to kill you as the enemy.

The Lieutenant unhooked the handset from his harness.

'Covey, Covey, this is Zulu Hotel.'

There was no reply.

'Covey, Covey, this is Zulu Hotel,' repeated the Lieutenant.

Damn them! Wasn't anyone listening? Didn't anyone know they were in deep shit!

The radio crackled and a hollow voice echoed from the handset.

'Zulu Hotel, this is November Mike One, read you loud and clear. Over.'

Inwardly the Lieutenant rejoiced but his reply did not reflect it.

'November Mike, this is Zulu Hotel. We're all set to go, no fire at this time.'

'Roger that, Zulu. Assets are about five minutes out. Confirm you are at your planned location, over.'

'Roger that, November. We can get everyone on one ship. Let's make this quick.'

A new voice came over the air.

'Zulu, this is Lima Victor One.'

'Lima Victor One, go ahead.'

'Zulu, are all Straw Hats accounted for? Over.'

'Negative, Lima. We're still one Straw Hat short. Over.'

The radio stayed silent for a moment before the spotter-plane pilot replied.

'Roger, Zulu Hotel. Lima Victor One, out.'

The Montagnard scout spoke good English, and had no problem understanding the radio conversation.

We are one Straw Hat short. We are missing one American.

The Lieutenant sat, tapping his chin with the handset. He looked round to see the Montagnard scout staring at him. The scout smiled.

'*C'est bon*. We go home now.'

'My friend is dead,' replied the Lieutenant.

'But we are alive,' stated the Montagnard.

Far away above the mist which swathed the valleys the helicopters, ten or twelve dots, were just visible. The familiar thump of the broad blades could be felt like a cautious ripple of applause offered for the first few bars of a dearly loved song.

Then the firing started. The anti-aircraft guns woke up and wanted feeding. Black puffs of smoke began to blotch the air and snakes of tracer arched up from the hillsides above the mist.

Over the radio, grimly determined voices called out warnings and spotted targets. Suddenly the gunships broke from the formation and swooped down to take on the guns.

The other helicopters split south, while a pair headed towards the team's position.

High above, November Mike One circled his aircraft, looking down at the action and co-ordinating the operation.

★

The Lieutenant fired a pen-flare to signal their exact location.

One helicopter made for a thirty-metre-wide gap in the trees on top of the ridge, while the second hung back, in case the worst happened.

Hovering only a few feet above the ground, it was impossible to land amid the shattered remnants of the trees that littered the clearing. The noise was deafening and the downdraft thrashed the surrounding vegetation into a wild gyrating dance.

The young Montagnard reached the helicopter first, launching himself at the skid, turning back to help pull the injured man up by his good arm.

The Lieutenant was the senior man and would thus be the last to leave. The young Montagnard swung himself on to the seesawing skid then reached out to help the Lieutenant. Both Montagnards grabbed him by his harness.

Before the Lieutenant was yanked into the cabin the helicopter had begun to drift forward, picking up speed as it flew out into clear air.

The Lieutenant watched the jungle slide by beneath them. Somewhere down there, among the trees and bamboo, was his friend. Dead or alive, they were leaving him behind.

1

It was hotter than he'd expected, much hotter than was usual for April. The air was still and the late-afternoon sun too bright.

How far was Ethan Lake's place?

'Quite a way, son,' the storekeeper back in town had told him.

The man had offered to drive Bobby up there, but said he'd have to wait till later since he couldn't leave the store unminded. But a fit young man could hike up there in two or three hours, he guessed.

Bobby accepted the challenge and walked east out of town on the main road, till he came to a dirt track heading up into the pines. He had been walking for at least two and a half hours, climbing through dry dusty woodland scattered with pine cones. Now the trees had thinned out he found himself just below a ridge, looking out far across Kentucky, towards the Appalachians. The tree-topped ridges were shrouded in haze. Far away he could see a bird of prey circling lazily on the thermals.

Thirsty and tired, Bobby quickened his pace, certain he would find the cabin at every turn of the track.

He didn't know how far to go and hadn't pushed the storekeeper on specifics, eager to be on his way. He could see the man was curious about him; the young stranger, in fresh new denims, cheesecloth shirt, carrying one of those fancy airline bags.

Then he spotted it. Not the idealised log cabin he had imagined. The roof was made of corrugated iron. A battered and rusty old Ford pick-up was parked out front next to a pile of firewood, which had been stacked against one of the end walls under a lean-to.

Bobby felt his pulse race. He tried not to break into a run as he strode to the door and knocked politely. No reply.

'Hello,' he called, looking through the dusty windows.

Nothing. There was no one there.

Bobby dropped his bag and sat down on the porch. He would have to wait; there was nothing else to do. Hard choices had brought him to this place and there was no point in asking himself if he was doing the right thing.

Bobby woke with a start. He must have fallen asleep against the door of the cabin. A large man was squatting in front of him.

'You OK, kid?' he asked. The man was a thickset guy with black close-cropped hair, flecked with grey, and smooth sun-bronzed skin. He had a classic square jaw, dark eyes set under thick brows. He wore a checked shirt and paratrooper's boots that, despite polish and care, were beginning to show their age.

'Are you Ethan Lake?' Bobby asked.

'Maybe. Who's asking?'

'I'm Bobby. Bobby Lake. Your nephew.'

The older man's expression didn't change. 'Eloise's kid, right?'

'Yes.'

'How's your ma?' asked Ethan, his brow furrowing.

'She's fine.'

'She know you're here?'

'I told her I planned to find you.'

'I guess she weren't too happy to hear that.' Ethan extended a hand and pulled Bobby to his feet. 'So you found me. Now what?'

Bobby shrugged. 'You said come anytime.'

'Sure I did. It's good to see you. How'd you get here?'

'I walked.'

His uncle nodded with what might have been approval.

'Well, you'd better come in. Had a fight with your ma?'

'You could say that.'

Ethan prepared a meal in silence. He figured the boy would speak when he was ready.

The cabin was one big room with a table and a few chairs. Along one wall between the windows was an open bookcase crammed full of books and periodicals and a whole yellow spread of *National Geographics*.

There was a workbench, with tools hung neatly on nails behind it. Then there was the rifle rack containing five or six weapons, none of which Bobby recognised. Mom had forbidden him to own or play with anything more deadly than a BB gun.

'You hunt?' asked Ethan.

'Not really.'

'That mean yes or no?'

'I've been hunting,' said Bobby, 'but I've never shot anything.'

'Who was that with?' asked Ethan lifting the lid from the pot suspended over the fire and stirring the contents.

'Uncle Jay.'

Ethan chuckled.

Bobby smiled. Uncle Jay may be a great attorney

but he was a poor hunter. A physically clumsy man, he seemed ill at ease in the woods, and unskilled in the use of firearms. His intellect and refinement seemed at odds with the very act of hunting, but he persisted regardless.

'You've got to be eighteen, right?' asked Ethan.

'Nineteen.'

Ethan paused and counted silently. 'Shouldn't you be at college? Your ma wrote something about Harvard.'

'I quit.'

'Is that right?' asked Ethan, not looking up from the cooking.

'I don't want to be a lawyer,' said Bobby, sounding more petulant than defiant. 'I want to join the Army. I want to go to Vietnam.'

'Lot of good men dying over there,' said Ethan after a while.

'I know.'

'So why you want to go?'

'You were in the Army,' said Bobby.

'That's not an answer and you know it. Sure I was. So was your pa and he's dead. Can't be easy on your ma having her son want to go and get in a war and get himself killed.'

'You didn't get killed. Uncle Jay didn't get killed . . .'

'Your Uncle Jay was in goddamn' Naval

Intelligence in Washington and then the Philippines after the fighting was over. He's never heard a shot fired in anger, and I didn't get killed because I was lucky.'

Ethan spooned the stew into the bowls and gestured for Bobby to sit.

'If you don't like it, you're out of luck. That's all I got, save for some jerky.'

Bobby took a mouthful and savoured the rich, wood-smoked taste. 'It's good,' he said, surprised that it was.

'It ain't like in the movies, Bobby. There isn't any glory. There sure as hell isn't any point to what's going on over there in Vietnam, not that I can see anyway. If you don't have to go, then don't.'

'So why did you and Dad want to fight?'

'Your pa was already in the Army. I volunteered because I didn't know any better.'

'So everybody gets to go to war except me?'

'Listen to me, kid. I bet you, right now, there's some poor son-of-a-bitch bleeding to death in a ditch who would give anything not to be there.'

They ate for a while in silence.

Bobby finally put down his fork. 'I can't run away from this war,' he said. 'A lot of kids have got no choice. Ten years from now I'm going to have to work with those guys. Mom always says it's people like us who run this country. Well, if that's true, shouldn't we fight for it as well?'

Ethan sniffed and pulled his pipe from his shirt pocket.

'Can I stay here, with you, for a couple of weeks, just till I join the Army?'

'You can stay tonight. I'll have to think about you staying any longer.'

Ethan lit his pipe while Bobby finished his stew.

He longed to tell his uncle how he had hated the smug self-satisfaction of Harvard. According to his classmates there Vietnam wasn't their problem. Everyone had seen the Tet offensive on TV, the US Embassy in Saigon overrun by Viet Cong sappers, and the Marines besieged at Khe-Sahn, but to them it seemed like a world away. To Bobby it was wrong not to care or want to help.

One night in Boston he had confronted a group of out-of-town students collecting money for medical supplies to send to North Vietnam.

'What the hell are you doing?' Bobby asked the two girls who were taking the collection.

'Standing up against American aggression! Supporting the freedom-loving people of Vietnam.'

Bobby had been unable to believe his ears. 'You're helping kill Americans! You're cowards and traitors.'

'Hey, back off, man!' The girls' boyfriends stepped in. 'Get lost before we kick your preppy ass.'

Bobby had never been in a serious fight in his life, but it seemed to come as naturally as breathing. He felled both men, with furious and unskilled blows. A bystander, sympathetic to the students' cause, backed off, proclaiming his adherence to non-violent resolution of disputes.

At that moment, Bobby felt as if he had been set free from a spell that had held him in check for far too long.

His professor was not impressed.

'That's no way for a gentleman of the law to behave, Mr Lake,' he said when he heard of the incident, third hand. 'If you want to do things like that, then perhaps you should go to Vietnam.'

Late that night, with Bobby asleep on the floor, Ethan stole quietly out of the cabin and walked down the hill, to the edge of the clearing. He sat down, looking out over a range of hills bathed in the light of a three-quarter moon.

Physically, Ethan could see more of his mother than his father in Bobby. At five foot ten he was taller than Eloise, and still sort of skinny, but he had a look in his eye that indicated a deep-seated determination.

Allan, Bobby's father, and Eloise had made an odd but fine couple. The strong, square-jawed infantry officer from Kentucky, and the diminutive, pretty heiress from Washington, turned heads wherever they went.

After Bobby's father died in Korea, Ethan took it upon himself to try and look after Eloise. The problem was, she didn't need anyone to look after her.

He pulled his pipe from his top pocket. To preserve night vision, he closed his right eye while he struck a match. For years after returning from Korea, he never lit his pipe outdoors at night. Eventually he'd got back into the habit. Lighting up in the dark wasn't going to get him killed. No snipers here, in Kentucky. Well, none who would care about Ethan Lake anyway.

It was a sniper who had got Allan. Head shot at three hundred and fifty yards. He had been dead before he hit the ground.

If Bobby wanted to go and fight, thought Ethan, then there was nothing he or Eloise could do to stop him. The boy knew his own mind. Just like his father, and just like his mother.

To Ethan's way of thinking, Bobby's biggest disadvantage in life was not having had a father while he was growing up. Eloise was smart, loving and sophisticated, but taking the kid to the opera, and on holiday to France, wasn't exactly ideal preparation for Vietnam.

'Bob, you can stay, but there's a condition.'

'Huh?' Bobby looked up from under the blanket.

'Here's the deal, son. You do everything I tell you, and you learn everything I teach you. Got it? You still wanna join the Army after that, then you're on your way. Deal?'

'OK, I guess.'

'You guess?'

'OK. It's a deal.'

After breakfast the pick-up bumped its way down the track to town.

'So what sort of things are we going to do?' asked Bobby.

'Things that'll help keep you alive over there.'

'Like what?'

'You'll see.'

'Won't the Army teach me all that?'

'The Army is gonna put you through a sausage machine so you can hold your own amongst a bunch of guys with the same training. That ain't enough.'

The boots Ethan bought for Bobby took about ten miles and several blisters to break in.

'I thought you said you were fit?' said Ethan as Bobby hobbled to the top of the hill where Ethan was already sitting.

'I said I ran track in school.'

'This ain't track.'

Bobby sat down heavily on a rock and began to tighten his laces.

They were alone in the middle of nowhere, high up on the ridges where a constant breeze blew through the pines.

'Have you decided what you want to do in the Army?' Ethan asked, lighting his pipe.

'I want to be a paratrooper, like you.'

'Know a lot about paratroopers, do you?'

'I read this book, called *The Centurions*, about French paratroopers. They seemed pretty cool.'

'Do you know why paratroopers are pretty cool?'

Bobby thought for a moment, then ventured an answer. '*Esprit de Corps*?'

Ethan shook his head. 'You got to volunteer for it. Not everyone can be a paratrooper. It's hard and it's dangerous. You'll always be where the fighting is thickest. That means the guys who are there want to be there a whole lot. They'll care more about each other. So you're less likely to die because someone wasn't doing their job. It means there's pressure on you to be good at your job to keep the others alive, and if you're good at your job, you won't die not knowing why.'

'Was my dad a paratrooper?'

'No, he wasn't, but that ain't why he died.'

'So why did he die?'

'Bad luck, I guess.'

'That's not what I meant,' said Bobby. 'How did he die?'

'Don't you know?'

'Mom says he got shot by a sniper. She says she doesn't know any more and she doesn't want to.'

'Well, she's certainly right about the sniper.'

'What happened?'

Ethan was surprised Bobby's mother had never told him, but then maybe she didn't know. 'The story is that your pa tried to fetch back some kid who had been hit. He was lying out in the open, the kid I mean, and one guy had already died trying to do the same thing. No one else was too keen on going, so your pa went.'

'Why did he do it?'

Ethan knocked out his pipe. 'When you're with a bunch of guys and you're having to fight every day, just to stay alive, they become like family. Sometimes you'd rather die than see them get hurt or die alone. OK, that's enough rest, Bob, let's get going, double time.'

★

Bang.

'Fuck!'

'Kicks, don't it?' laughed Ethan.

'Sure does.' Bobby grimaced as he lowered the Garand rifle, applied the safety catch.

'You got seven shots left. Shoot them all off. Don't worry about hitting the target. Just get used to the weapon.'

By late that afternoon, three grocery crates and a hundred-odd rounds later, Bobby could hit the target at a hundred yards nine times out of ten.

A couple of days more and he could group five rounds into the cut end of a six-inch-diameter log at the same distance – a target much smaller than the grocery crate.

Ethan could group three inches and do it standing, rather than lying down or kneeling, but he had been shooting for over thirty years.

Bobby learned to strip and assemble the Garand blindfold. Ethan didn't bother to time him. That wasn't the point. The boy probably wasn't ever going to see a Garand in the Army. The weapon was obsolete. The idea was to get Bobby used to handling it. Learning the feel and sounds that said a weapon was clean and functioning well, to understand how it worked, and how to maintain it. At the end of the week, Bobby knew as much about the M1 Garand as he would ever need to know, and that lesson was good for all weapons.

The deer froze and stared. Bobby and Ethan froze also. They had stalked it for an hour, looping around in the trees getting downwind and then walking up in the cover at the edge of the scrubland where the animal grazed.

It was a young whitetail buck. This time of year it was out of the question to shoot a doe, which might have fawns. They shouldn't have been shooting deer anyway, Ethan had no permit, but he had never been too concerned with rules and regulations.

The deer lowered its head back out of sight. Delicately Ethan used the toe of his boot to move away loose twigs, and Bobby followed precisely in his uncle's footsteps as they moved to a position about seventy-five yards from their intended prey.

Bobby felt the sun-warmed wooden stock against his cheek and a sudden twinge of pain as he pulled the stock into his bruised and tender shoulder. His body had not yet become accustomed to the powerful 30.06 cartridges of the Garand. The hunting rifle however was a finer, lighter weapon with a telescopic sight, and a joy to shoot.

Bobby's finger pushed the cross-lock safety on

the trigger guard and his eyes found the focus of the scope.

The deer looked up, alert but unaware, lazily chewing in the mid-morning sun. Bobby quietly exhaled and held his breath ready for the shot. His finger gently squeezed the trigger, feeling the millimetre or so of movement prior to the point where any more pressure will release the shot.

The deer looked straight at him. Bobby felt the significance of the moment wash over him. He was about to take a life, the only purpose of which was to prove that he could.

Crack.

Bobby heard the bullet hit the deer.

'Did I get him?' he asked, starting forward, but Ethan placed a hand on his shoulder. 'Stay put,' he said.

'Why are we waiting?'

'He may not be dead,' explained Ethan. 'We'll just wait a minute or two, to make sure he ain't gonna get up and run off somewhere. If he does, we'll trail him.'

Bobby did what he was told.

'By the way,' said Ethan, after a moment, 'the same's true of people. You ever shoot a guy, over there in Vietnam, don't be running over to see if you hit him. Stay where you are and wait for him to die or stick his head up again.'

★

The deer lay on its side, eyes open.

'See where you hit it? Good shot,' observed Ethan.

'Yeah, I see.' The competition he had just won seemed both unfair and one-sided to Bobby.

The deer moved its head and one of its hooves twitched.

'Oh, God! It's alive!' gasped Bobby.

'So kill it,' said Ethan.

Bobby cycled the bolt, putting another round in the chamber.

'Hey! Bullets are expensive.'

'I don't know how . . . I mean, you haven't told me how.'

'Relax, Bob. It's dead. It just doesn't know it. You heard of the headless chicken? Well, this is the same thing.'

Bobby nodded, considering the fact that killing was something best done with a hard heart.

Ethan hung the animal up from a branch of a tree. There, Bobby helped gut and butcher the carcass. He worked silently. He didn't like doing it, Ethan could tell, but he never complained.

'That the first thing you killed?' asked Ethan later, as they sat on the hillside below the cabin.

'Except the odd bug, I guess it is.'

'Well, it's no big deal, is it?' Ethan gulped his bottled beer.

'It was a big deal for the deer,' replied Bobby.

For a while the two men just stared out over the densely wooded hills, bathed in the soft evening light.

'You think you ought to call your ma and tell her how you're doing?' Ethan had talked to Eloise the morning after Bobby had arrived, and had managed to prevent her from driving down to fetch him on condition that Bobby telephoned her soon, to explain what the hell he was doing. The call was more than a week overdue.

'Nah.' Bobby took a long sip. 'I'm fine.'

Two crows took off from the tree line, calling out as if in agreement.

'Well, your ma might not be. She might be worried.'

'Mom's always worried.'

'About what?'

'Oh, you know. What people think, what I do and what I might be going to do. I swear she already knows who I'm going to marry.'

'Do you have a girl?'

'No one steady. Mom sort of scares them off.'

'You don't have to tell me. I remember her as having quite a temper.'

'Yeah. She scares a lot of people. It's like she's

always worried I'm going to get hurt or something.'

'Well, that's what moms do. Worry about their kids.'

'I'm going to go some day, and then she'll just have to get used to it.'

'Your mom lost your dad and now you want to run off and join the Army. It can't leave her with a very warm feeling, thinking you might not make it back. A lot of people are just scared of being lonely.'

'Mom? Lonely? You must be kidding.'

'Does she have someone special?'

'No, but she could, if she stopped being so uptight and pulled that rod out of her ass.'

'Are you sure you should be talking about your ma like that?'

Bobby felt a flush come to his cheeks.

'Can't have been easy for her, bringing you up alone,' said Ethan.

'She had a maid, a cook and a gardener.'

'You know what I mean.'

'It's what she wanted.'

'How do you know?'

'Whenever I asked if some guy was going to be my new dad, or if I would ever get another dad, she'd say I didn't need one.'

'Does she have a lot of gentlemen friends?' Ethan tried to make the enquiry sound casual.

'None that stick around. I mean, there was this one guy,' said Bobby, pausing for another mouthful of beer, 'guy called Jed. He was in the Air Force. Used to fly jets. He was OK.'

'And?'

'One day he didn't come round any more.'

'What did he do wrong?'

'Said he wasn't going to leave the Air Force and become a lawyer.'

'You know that for sure, or you just guessing?'

'Apparently it was leave the Air Force or go to Vietnam. Mom's never going to end up with anyone who could get themselves killed in a war.'

A silence fell between them.

'Did you ever get scared in Korea?' asked Bobby, desperate for a change of subject.

'If you got any sense you'll be scared all the time,' said Ethan. 'Being scared is good, but you have to learn to control it and make it your friend, so you can still do stuff, even when you're real scared.'

'Mom said that the people who are scared are the bravest people, and those that aren't are too stupid to be scared.'

'She's got that right.'

'Is it easier to kill people than deer?'

'Well, I shot a few critters before I ever got my first man.' Ethan's tone was matter-of-fact. 'Main difference is critters don't shoot back.'

★

They stopped outside the store where Bobby had asked directions when he first came into town.

'Stay with the truck,' said Ethan as he went off to pick up some supplies.

Bobby got out to stretch his legs, then stood for a while, leaning on the wheel arch and enjoying the early-morning sun on his face.

He glanced up to see a girl approaching along the sidewalk. She looked about sixteen. She was thin and had dark reddish-brown hair and a pale complexion. She was pretty in a delicate way, with large eyes and flawless skin. She walked with her hands plunged deep in her coat pockets. When she noticed Bobby, she nodded a greeting and then stuck her head back down and kept walking.

At that moment, Ethan came out of the store. 'Hey, Rachel.'

The girl stopped. 'Howdy, Mr Lake. How are you?'

'Good. How's your pa?'

'He's just fine, thank you.'

'Can I give you a lift home? I got the truck here, and I'll be done shortly.'

'If it's no bother.'

'It's no bother. Here, meet my nephew, Bobby. Bobby, this is Rachel Penny.'

'Hi,' said Rachel quietly.

'Hi.'

'I just got to get a few more things. You kids wait here,' said Ethan striding off down the sidewalk.

Rachel stared at her feet while Bobby contemplated her heavy coat, hockey boots and dungarees. In spite of the less than appealing outfit, he found himself strangely drawn to the young girl. He spotted a paperback in her pocket and seized the opportunity. 'What are you reading?'

'*Valley of the Dolls*.'

'Any good?'

'It's OK,' said Rachel. 'You ain't from around here, are you?'

'I'm from up north. I'm a damn' Yankee.'

Rachel smiled. 'What you doing down here?'

'Staying with my uncle. I'm waiting to join the Army.'

'You've been drafted?'

'No. I'm going to volunteer.'

'Why?'

'I want to go and fight in Vietnam.'

Rachel looked away. A chill seemed to descend upon them. Vietnam was obviously a conversation stopper.

'A guy from these parts got killed at Khe-Sahn the other day. He was a Marine,' said Rachel, not looking Bobby in the face.

Some part of him suddenly wanted to justify the

man's death by saying it was war and the Marines got the tough assignments, but he didn't. 'I'm sorry.'

'I didn't know him, but I guess someone I know will get killed in Vietnam, sooner or later.'

2

The buses pulled on to the hard stand. They were full of another hundred-strong class of Airborne school graduates who thought they had what it took to be a Special Forces soldier.

The doors hissed open. A well-turned-out Sergeant wearing a Green Beret appeared in the doorway. 'OK, ladies, off the bus. Get fell in outside,' he said in a matter-of-fact voice.

The assembled passengers stared back amazed. This was not what they were expecting. Where was the shouting and harassment they had become used to at Fort Benning?

Tired and weary after the long bus journey, the soldiers formed themselves into three ranks, but no one screamed at them, or urged them to move faster.

A Sergeant Major brought them to attention, gave his standard welcoming speech, and left the Sergeant to march the group off.

'Airborne!' yelled the men in unison, just as they had been taught at Fort Benning.

'Whoa! Hold up there, what the hell are you

boys doing?' laughed the Sergeant Major. 'Airborne? What the hell does that mean? Airborne is just a method of transportation. You don't yell "truck", do you? You don't yell "helicopter". I need smart men here, not dummies. You men need to knock off all that regular Army rah–rah crap right now. You're here to become Special Forces.'

'Yes, sir!' yelled the soldiers automatically, just as they had done at Fort Benning.

The Sergeant Major rolled his eyes. It was the same with every new course.

The swamp at Camp Mackall was always uncomfortable regardless of the time of year. It was either cold and wet in the winter or hot and damp in summer.

Bobby looked out through the trees and shivered. The fading winter light added to the bleak vista of leafless trees, jutting skyward from the frozen ground. He knelt closer to the embers of the cooking fire and watched the steam rise from his sock as he held it over the glowing coals. Of all the comforts he had ever experienced in his life, nothing compared to dry socks. He'd just spent twenty minutes cleaning his heavy M-14 rifle, and now it was time for some luxury. Dry socks were as good as it got.

Rest periods were rare, and an instructor

announcing that the enemy was bearing down upon them meant they would have to move fast. Bobby's squad had been on a reconnaissance patrol for most of the day. What should have been a simple task was complicated by the fact that the soldier designated to lead the patrol had failed to find the target. The instructor decided that their poor navigation had led them into a minefield and designated several members of the patrol as casualties. These men now had to be carried back to the base camp. It had been a long hard day; one of many long hard days they had endured already. There seemed no end in sight. The normal soldier's desire to fantasise about sex had been replaced by dreams of food and sleep. To get food and sleep, all you had to do was quit. For many the sustained hardship and privation was too much. Soon only the committed were left.

If Bobby had simply joined the 101st Airborne, he'd probably be in Vietnam right now. As things stood, it was going to take at least another six months, maybe more, to complete his Special Forces training.

It had all seemed like a good idea at the time. Bobby had been shocked at the level of delinquency amongst his fellow recruits in both basic and advanced infantry training. The draftees didn't want to be there and the volunteers didn't have anywhere else to be. An infantry posting in Vietnam was seen as a death sentence and the fact that Bobby was a volunteer, and had openly expressed a desire to serve in Vietnam, caused his fellow recruits to view him with both suspicion and contempt.

'What the fuck is up with you, man? Your girl leave you?' was a standard question. Behind his back, Bobby's fellow recruits called him 'Captain fucking America'.

Going Airborne at least meant you wanted to fight, but it didn't follow that you were smart. Bobby had learnt to keep his mouth shut, act dumb and go with the herd. But deep in his soul that grated. It grated that his fellow recruits had to be shown how to do everything and, in the opinion of the Army, seemed incapable of thinking for themselves.

One day, a guy turned up and asked if anyone wanted to try out for Special Forces. Bobby jumped at the chance.

'Everything copacetic, Lake?' Sergeant Kramer was two months back from Vietnam. Two months that seemed like a year, and all he wanted to do was go back. Back to Central Highlands and his A-team border camp, where he was pretty much his own man and no one screwed with him. He just did the job he'd been trained to do. OK, so that wasn't much of a life but it was his life and he enjoyed it. Now he was stuck at Fort Bragg, training the next generation of Special Forces soldiers.

'You look all done in, Lake. Why don't you quit?' he said.

'No thanks, Sergeant.'

'Look, I've got a big jug of fresh coffee and some real hot beef stew over there. Quit now, you can have as much as you want.'

Bobby hadn't had a decent meal for days. The last thing he had eaten was some of an under-cooked goat he had helped slaughter. But he knew that if he accepted this invitation, it was instant failure. 'I'm doing just fine, Sergeant,' he said, mouth running with saliva.

'Sure you are,' goaded Kramer. 'How about that coffee, though? Lots of sugar, lots of cream. Mmmm, it sure tastes good.'

'No offence, Sarge, but I think I'll give it a miss.'

'Hell, Lake. I don't take offence. It's all the same to me. We got some barbecued chicken later. It's got to taste better than that goat, boy. I mean, that must have been like having a bear shit in your mouth. What's an Ivy League boy like you doing here anyway?' Kramer crouched down and poked at the embers of the fire with his combat knife.

'I want to be a Green Beret, Sergeant.'

Kramer laughed. 'How the fuck are you going to become a Green Beret, son? A Green Beret ain't done shit! Ever! 'Cept sit on some fucker's head. Green Beret is just a hat. Truth is, it ain't even a good hat. It don't keep the sun off your head or the rain out of your eyes. It's too hot in summer and too cold in winter.'

'I want to be a Special Forces soldier, Sergeant. I want to go to Vietnam and fight for my country.'

Kramer prodded at the fire some more. 'Well now, that seems real noble and all, but I still can't figure why some rich white kid like yourself should wanna do this. I've seen your file, son. I know where you're from. That you dropped out of some fancy Yankee college.'

Inwardly, Bobby groaned. Why did he always have to explain himself? 'I always wanted to be a soldier,' he said.

'Why?'

'My dad was killed in Korea.'

'So why'd you go to Harvard? Don't sound much like you wanted to be a soldier to me.'

'My mom wanted me to go to Harvard. I stuck it as long as I could and then took off, joined the Army, and I'm never going back.'

'You one of these kids with a conscience, eh? "Why all those black kids got to go die in the 'Nam and you be safe and well?"' mimicked Kramer.

'You a Crusader, son?'

Bobby checked his sock was dry.

'I don't give a fuck about the black kids, Sarge. I just want to fight. I've got my own reasons and they're pretty good reasons. The guys at Harvard didn't want to fight. Maybe that's why they were there. I want to fight in Vietnam. That's why I left.'

'This is a lot tougher than college, Lake. Special Forces ain't no place to hide from the real world. You hear me?'

'Loud and clear, Sergeant.'

Kramer stood up and slid his combat knife back into its scabbard. The rest of Lake's squad was huddled under their ponchos trying to get some sleep and keep warm. Lake, on the other hand, was sitting up, drying his socks and cleaning his weapon.

'What if you don't go to Vietnam? What then?'

'Why wouldn't I?'

'Not everyone goes. You speak some French and you done some skiing. They could send you to Bad Tolz. Could be you'll go to the 10th Group in Europe.'

The fact he might not go to Vietnam had never seriously occurred to Bobby. 'I want to go to Vietnam, Sarge. I want to fight.'

Kramer walked off to where the Captain had his

campfire. He didn't know what to make of Lake. Maybe he really was a kid with a conscience who just wanted to serve his country. Kramer wasn't overly cynical. He'd seen enough bravery to know that true selflessness existed, especially in combat. But he'd also seen enough to know that Special Forces wasn't a place for those who believed they had to prove something. People who needed to prove something could go and prove it somewhere else.

'How're your boys doing, Sergeant?' asked the Captain.

'They'll be OK, sir,' said Kramer, accepting the proffered canteen cup of coffee.

'Was that Lake you were talking to?'

'It was.'

'Think he'll make it?'

'I reckon he might.'

Rachel Penny looked around the coffee shop for a friendly face. She spotted Nadine sitting in a booth by the corner and slipped on to the bench opposite. Nadine was a few years older than Rachel, but she worked at the library where Rachel liked to go. The library was empty most of the time, so the two girls would gossip and giggle, much to the disapproval of the few older people who came in occasionally for the periodicals and the quiet.

'Gee, it's freezing out there.' Rachel pulled off

her woollen sweater. 'What's up?' she asked, sensing Nadine wasn't happy.

'You hear about Arty Fisher?'

'The guy you were at school with?'

'Right.'

'He get married?'

'He got killed. Vietnam. About a week back. I didn't even like him that much. Now I feel sort of guilty,' mused Nadine. 'You heard anything more from mysterious Bobby?'

'He's not mysterious. I got a letter from him the other day.' Rachel scrabbled in her purse. 'You want to hear it?'

'Sure.' Nadine lit a cigarette. She only half listened to the letter, feeling envy and some pity for little Rachel. She was a strange girl. Every word she spoke had a breathless innocence, yet there was an innate instinctive wisdom in her approach to people that made her seem older than seventeen.

Nadine had met Bobby only once and still found it hard to believe that he and Rachel had become so close. Bobby was a handsome, smart-talking boy from a wealthy Washington family. What did he see in some flat-chested little girl who hung out at the town library? Who was still saving herself for Mr Right. Maybe Bobby had got lucky . . . but Rachel would never tell.

Nadine had been pretty sure that Bobby was

going to forget about Rachel in a heartbeat, but the letters kept coming. Maybe this guy really was different from all the rest . . .

'Isn't that great?' asked Rachel, folding the letter and placing it back in her purse.

'He sounds real sweet. When does he get sent to Vietnam?'

'Not for a while. He's doing some special training. He said it might take a year. I hope it does. Perhaps the war'll be over by then.'

Eloise Lake parked her car in front of the garage and then walked swiftly towards the front door of her large Maryland home.

Maria the maid appeared at the top of the steps. 'Good evening, Signora Lake.'

'Good evening, Maria.' Eloise smiled. Maria beamed back. This was a relief. Mrs Lake was in a good mood. 'You are staying in this evening, yes?' Maria, took Eloise's coat.

'Yes, I am,' said Eloise, pulling off her gloves.

She picked up the morning's mail from the hall table and went through to her writing desk in the front room. Neatly, she slit open every letter and after a quick glance arranged each on the table in order of priority. To be read later, dealt with at some other time or dropped straight into the waste-paper basket.

The last letter was from her son. It contained a photograph of Bobby posing with a rifle, looking all fit and grown-up in his Army uniform, highly polished jump boots and Green Beret. The picture had been taken in front of the new memorial that John Wayne had dedicated at Fort Bragg.

Eloise glanced over at the table by the window where she kept all the other snaps of herself and Bobby. She missed her son; or rather she missed the boy she had brought up. She didn't know the young man in this new picture.

He was her last link with Allan. She remembered thinking she couldn't live without her husband, but she had. She had got used to it and had concentrated on bringing up their son as best she could.

Bobby had come home briefly on leave after Fort Benning. All he had talked about was Special Forces. He seemed to have an almost irrational desire to be in the midst of the action. Sitting with him, watching the war on TV every evening, had been almost more than she could bear.

Lately, Eloise had wondered how she would cope if the worst happened. Could there be a God so cruel that he would take her husband and her only son?

The Instructor sucked on his cigarette, and surveyed the students who were taking a break between classes. 'You have another test tomorrow morning, ladies, so get at those books this evening.'

The soldiers he was addressing were partway through the sixteen-week radio operator's course, or the Didi-dum-dum-didi school as some called it, because of the emphasis on Morse code.

This course, in fact, was academically tough, and few people's first choice. On Phase two, the Special Forces students had to complete one of four specialist qualifications. Engineering and Weapons were the most popular, Medical and Communications the least.

'Man, I bet they don't get these fucking tests on the Weapons course,' said one of the students who was finding the academic work hard going.

'What's that, Carter?' asked the Instructor.

'Nothing, Sarge.'

'You putting my school down again?'

'No way, Sarge. I love this shit!' The class laughed, well aware of what Carter really thought.

The Instructor shook his head half in real and half feigned sorrow. 'I've told you people before, any sorry-ass fucker can fire a gun or blow some shit up. You gotta have brains to do what we do. Imagine you're twenty-five clicks inside the bad guys' back yard, and they're all around you. The only way you're gonna get help is to get that radio fired up, get it tuned, get the message coded up and get it out there, loud and clear. I no bullshit you, GI. I've been there!'

'Was that on the Projects?' asked Carter bluntly.

'What you heard about the Projects?'

'Just stuff.' Carter shrugged his broad shoulders.

'Well, un-hear it. I hear any of you talking about the Projects, you'll be in a world of pain.' The Instructor ground his cigarette out with his heel. 'OK, break's over. Get your asses back in that classroom.'

'So what exactly have you heard about the Projects?' asked Bobby, putting his tray down next to Carter's.

'Just the normal BS that goes around,' replied Carter, picking half-heartedly at his food.

'Like what?'

'It's all real "secret squirrel" shit. Commando raids into North Vietnam and China.'

'Yeah?'

'Yeah, and I'll tell you what else I heard. They carry no US equipment. The Air Force has a special Squadron just dedicated to getting these guys in and out. Anything these guys want, you know, like foreign weapons or high-speed commo gear, they get. They're real head hunters,' said Carter. 'Why you asking?'

'No particular reason.'

'Think you've got a shot?'

'Maybe,' Bobby grinned. 'Maybe.'

'What the fuck is up with you anyway, Lake? This is dangerous shit.'

'It's where the action is. How do you get into Projects?'

'You don't,' said Carter, 'they come looking for you.'

'I heard you can volunteer. Something about SOG, Special Operations Group.'

Carter grimaced. 'Then you know a shit load more than I do.'

The class was breaking up. Bobby waited until the room was nearly empty. Master Sergeant Dawson was thirty and a very different character from Sergeant Kramer. A family man, he was a no-nonsense professional and took care that his lessons got learnt. He could share a joke, but when it was time to work, it was time to work hard.

'Sarge?'

'Yeah, Lake, what is it?'

'I need to ask your advice.'

'Marry the bitch. That's my advice.'

Bobby grinned.

Dawson looked up from his paperwork. 'I'm just kidding with you, son. What's the problem?'

'Well, Sarge. I really want to go to 'Nam.'

'Don't worry, soldier. Your turn will come.'

'I speak French and I've done some skiing, so I've been told I might have to go to the 10th in Europe. But I want to go to the 5th in 'Nam.'

'Who said you'd go to the 10th?'

'One of the instructors on Phase one.'

'He was screwing with you. Where you been skiing?'

'Aspen and one time in France,' said Bobby, feeling embarrassed that his privileged upbringing had to be mentioned yet again.

'Well, I'll be!' exclaimed Dawson. 'First off, holiday skiing ain't military skiing. They're two different things. Second, they speak French in Vietnam, OK?'

Bobby remained standing in front of the desk.

'Something else?' Dawson had gone back to marking test papers. 'Make it quick.'

'I want to go to the Projects.'

Dawson's pen seemed to skid to a halt. 'Oh, yeah. Why?'

'It just seems that's where the action is.'

'And what action might that be?'

'The type of stuff you were doing.'

'You don't know shit about what I was doing, and if you did what makes you think you would want to do it?'

'I'm Special Forces qualified, or I will be by the time I get there.'

'You married?'

'No.'

'Got anyone special? Any folks that care about you?'

'There's just me, Sarge,' lied Bobby.

Dawson pulled a small notebook from his pocket and scribbled a number on a sheet of paper.

'When you get out of Phase three, call this number. You speak to Mrs Billy Alexander and you tell her that you want to go to Command and Control in Vietnam.'

'Who's Mrs Alexander?'

'Army Personnel in the Pentagon. She'll get you all the action, pain and sorrow you're looking for.'

'Sure. Thanks,' said Bobby.

'One more thing,' said Dawson. 'We never had this conversation, and I never gave you that number, OK?'

The C-123 climbed out of Pope Air Force base and headed off into the night, towards the drop zone.

Private First Class Lake wriggled in his canvas seat in a vain attempt to get comfortable. The T-10 parachute on his back and the rifle slung at his side all conspired to increase his irritation. On his knees, the heavy aluminium-framed rucksack, packed out with a radio and extra batteries, added to his burden. The temperature inside the aircraft was sweltering, but Bobby knew it would get cooler the higher they went.

All around faces were blank, bathed in the red light of the aircraft interior. Each man lost in his thoughts. Prior to boarding, a few cracked bad jokes in an attempt to relieve their own tension.

This was the last hurdle of Phase three, Exercise Robin Sage. Notionally, Bobby was part of a Special Forces A-team. An A-team comprised twelve men whose job it was to organise guerrilla forces at the enemy's rear. It was, in fact, the *raison d'être* of Special Forces, and the mission around which all training had been concentrated.

Sitting next to Bobby in the C-123 was Carlos Nunez. Carlos was from El Paso. He had completed the thirty-nine-week-long Special Forces Medics course, which meant he was only just short of being a qualified doctor. It was quite an achievement for a kid from a poor family, living just north of the border.

On first meeting Bobby, Carlos had dismissed him as some rich white Anglo boy who had thrown away a first-class college education. How dumb was that? Carlos would have killed to go to Harvard, and here was some snot-nosed Ivy League boy who just walked away from it. Like it was worth nothing at all. Carlos was more than aware that education was his ticket out of poverty and second-class citizenship. But you needed money to go to college and he had none. The Army offered the chance of improving himself, and if Vietnam didn't sound great, it had to beat the hell out of El Paso.

One evening, in a bar on Combat Alley in Fayetteville, Carlos was drinking with a small group of Special Forces.

They decided to move on, but Carlos had gone back into the bar to use the men's room. He said he'd catch them up.

Standing between Carlos and the men's room were four or five black soldiers from 82nd Airborne. Carlos asked them to move but they stayed put.

'Gonna cost you ten bucks, motherfucker.'

'I ain't got ten bucks.'

'Then you'd better go borrow some off your white friends!' Stories about disproportionate losses among coloured soldiers were breeding resentment, and each ethnic group tended to stick to their own.

Carlos wasn't ever going to pay to use the men's room. He wasn't going to go outside and ask for help either. Then a voice behind him said, 'I've got ten bucks.'

'I can handle this and I don't need your money,' replied Carlos.

'I just said I had ten bucks.' Bobby stood beside Carlos. 'If they want it, they're going to have to take it.'

The blacks looked a lot tougher than the Pro-Hanoi students back in Boston. Bobby's instinct had told him to move first. A bottle to the side of the head took one out of the fight. Carlos overturned a table, creating time and space to retain the initiative. Bobby threw a punch at the closest man, but the guy just sniffed and kept coming, his return punch knocking Bobby flat on his back. Imagining he was out of the fight, Bobby's assailant turned to Carlos. Struggling to clear his head, Bobby saw that Carlos was pinned to the wall, by two of the paratroopers. He clambered to his feet, grabbed a chair, and swung it at the back of the man who had punched him. The chair worked better than the fist. The man went down. Another swing of the chair connected and freed Carlos. Bobby delivered a kick to the back of the man as he crumpled to his knees. He raised the chair to complete the victory but was charged from the side, and fell across the other tables, scattering glasses, bottles and onlookers in all directions. He wrestled his assailant round to pin him to the floor, before pulling the man up to head butt him. Bobby felt the man's blood splash across his face and heard him cry out in pain. He repeated his action, and the man fell silent. Bobby got to his feet and stepped over the upturned tables, to help Carlos.

But Carlos didn't need any help. A wild swing connected with his adversary's stomach, and the man folded up, gasping for air.

'Let's get the fuck out of here,' panted Bobby. Carlos nodded his agreement, his nose pouring blood.

'I don't like running, man.' Carlos spat out a tooth as they staggered out into the street.

'We're not running,' said Bobby. 'We're just getting reinforcements.'

After that, Bobby and Carlos had teamed up, both knowing that neither would back down without a fight.

Carlos wasn't quite sure what he was letting himself in for, but he went along with Bobby to the payphone near the PX where they called Mrs Billy Alexander.

It had to be Command and Control. Everyone knew it was dangerous. If you were going to risk everything, you might as well risk it doing something big. If he was going to die in Vietnam, Bobby didn't want to die a statistic. He aimed to die a hero, or not at all.

★

The paratroopers stood in unison, hooking their static lines on to the overhead cable.

Each signalled his equipment checks complete and the loadmaster spread his arms, telling the first men in line to stand in the door. The sound of rushing air and the roar of the twin-piston engines filled the cavernous interior of the C-123.

Christ! I have to go through this again, Bobby cursed to himself. I know my drills and I've done this before, but I still don't have to like it.

The red light was on. The first man was waiting for the command to go, feet on the edge, hands outside the aircraft, ready to throw himself into the darkness, twelve hundred feet above the Uwharrie National Forest.

Green on! GO!

The first soldier lunged out into the void. Behind him the stick of troops shuffled forward, spewing a man a second from the plane.

Bobby reached the door and stared into the blackest night he'd ever seen. With no urging or encouragement bar the obligatory smack on the shoulder from the loadmaster, he hurled himself forward.

3

Nha Trang was the headquarters of the 5th Special Forces Group in Vietnam.

Bobby and Carlos dropped off their 201 files, changed their money, were issued an M-2 carbine and some web gear. Bobby was deeply conscious of being a freshman. His beret was pristine, and newly issued tiger-stripe fatigues had a cleanliness that broadcast his lack of experience. Tiger stripes were a garish, intricate black and green pattern, and were synonymous with Special Forces.

Sitting in the club that evening they met a Master Sergeant called Boxer, going back on his third tour.

'Where you been posted?' he asked casually.

'Command and Control,' said Bobby.

Boxer looked up from his beer.

'Well, I guess this is the last time I'll see you alive. Good luck, son.'

Bobby had been expecting to go on the Special Forces Combat Orientation Course that was held on Hon-Treh island just off the coast, but as soon as he and Carlos said they were going to Command

and Control, the course was forgotten. If you were going to Command and Control, you didn't need Orientation, apparently. Maybe nobody there lived that long?

A C-130 flew Bobby and Carlos from Nha Trang to Camp Fay at Da-Nang. Their assignment was Command and Control Central, CCC, Kontum. They took another plane out the next day. Kontum was up in central Vietnam, to the west of the mountains that formed the spine of the country. At the airbase they were met by a tired-looking clerk in a jeep who drove, without a word, out of the airfield and through the town before turning south, on to Highway 14, over the Dak Bla river and up through a shantytown village called Plei Groi. The camp lay at the far end of the village, a ramshackle collection of huts with corrugated-iron roofs and heavily sandbagged cinder-block walls. The camp actually straddled Highway 14, which ran right through the centre and was lined with barbed wire. A large earth bank with built-in fighting positions and a minefield made up the rest of the camp perimeter.

'Glad to see you, boys. We're always short-handed around here,' said the Command Sergeant Major, quickly scanning their paperwork.

'Glad to be here, sir,' they replied in unison, just as they had rehearsed.

'Oh, great. A couple of wise guys,' the Sergeant Major sighed, 'Someone else will explain more about what we actually do here. What I need you to understand is that you are now part of what is called MAC-V SOG, Military Assistance Command, Vietnam, Studies and Observation Group. Though we come under the 5th Special Forces Group for administration and support, operationally we ain't part of it. We talk direct to MAC-V in Saigon. This means that you never discuss any of this with anyone outside of this camp. However, you'll wear 5th Group Beret flashes, and act like any other SF guys in the country.'

'Yes, sir.'

'OK. Now which one of you is the medic?'

Carlos was assigned to work in the dispensary. If he did OK there, he could be posted into Recon when another medic turned up.

Bobby was sent straight over to Recon Company and told to report to the S-3.

The S-3 was the epitome of a seasoned Special Forces officer, a tall, wiry man and lifetime soldier. As the S-3, he was responsible for all operations at CCC.

'We run cross-border recon missions into Cambodia and Laos. All you can see here is the Ho

Chi Minh Trail.' The S-3 gestured to a large wall map. 'As you know, it ain't really a trail. It's more a huge network of roads and footpaths. They're adding to it everyday. We also got a lot of stuff coming up here from the port of Sihanoukville, down there in Cambodia. Our job is to locate targets for the Air Force to bomb. If we need to really fuck something up, then we've got a Hatchet Force company here, and they'll go in and kill anything they see.'

The Major looked at Bobby who nodded that he understood.

'For political reasons, we can only operate within twenty kilometres of the Vietnamese border. These areas are called Prairie Fire in Laos and Salem House in Cambodia. You'll be on a recon team. The teams are made up of three US personnel and nine indigenous. We got Vietnamese and Yard Indig here. There are also some ARVN-led recon teams but they won't concern you. We got about twelve teams in all. Right now, we've got two on the ground. You'll probably see one come back in this evening.

'Now here's the deal, son,' continued the S-3, changing his tone. 'What we do here is not for everyone. It's real hard work, and once in a while we lose folks. Laos and Cambodia are the North Vietnamese Army's back yard. It's their home and they don't like us snooping around. They got anti-aircraft guns, more trucks than you can count and whole companies just dedicated to hunting recon teams. If you find this ain't your thing, then you gotta say so. I know a lot of brave men who just weren't cut out for recon. Got it?'

Next was the S-2. He was responsible for Intelligence and Security.

'The 1961 Geneva Accord makes Laos and Cambodia neutral. We shouldn't be there, nor should the NVA. That means that all our operations are deniable. If we reveal any overt presence, so can the Russians and Chinese. Washington doesn't want this war getting any bigger, so we keep it that way. When on missions, you will not carry any identification or personal items of any sort. Everything you carry will be sterile. Any equipment of US origin will be deniable. Once over the fence in Laos, you do not exist. Roger so far?'

'Yes, sir.'

'Like you've been told already, you tell no one what you do here. Not family, not girlfriends, not no one. You don't mention it in letters and you never ever discuss it outside of the camp. If asked what we do here, our cover story is that we train Montagnards for the Mobile Strike Force.'

He paused.

'You're gonna need a codename.' The S-2 opened a file. 'You can suggest something, as long as it's simple and not already taken.'

'How about Hiawatha?' Bobby said after a moment. He remembered the endless Longfellow poem from his school days, and it didn't seem inappropriate if he was going to be scouting around in the woods or jungle.

'Taken.'

Damn!

'OK, what you got?' asked Bobby.

'Grommet, Plastic, Blackfoot . . .'

'Blackfoot.' It wasn't exactly near the shores of Gitche Gumee, but it was close enough.

'Welcome to North Dakota, son.' Big Jack was the One-zero or team leader. All the teams working out of Kontum were named after US States.

Sergeant First Class Jack Nightingale had twelve years in Special Forces under his belt. Thirty-three years old, he stood six foot three and had a powerfully muscular build, close-cropped receding hair and an easygoing mid-western manner. People treated him with respect. Slow to anger and amazingly patient, Big Jack told it like it was, and stood his ground because he had nothing to prove to anyone.

His second-in-command, or One-one, a guy called Rhett Simmons, couldn't have been more of a contrast. He was about five foot eight, with pepper-blond spiky hair and a carefully groomed moustache. Rhett had spent the first eighteen of his twenty-five years on a ranch in Arizona and, unlike Big Jack, oozed determination and aggression. No one had ever given Rhett Simmons goddamned anything.

'You just out of Bragg?' asked Simmons.

'Sure am,' Bobby replied.

Simmons didn't look impressed.

'So what brings you to Recon?' Big Jack pulled a crate of beer from under his cot and passed a can to Bobby and Simmons. They were sitting in North Dakota's team room, or hooch, where the three of them, regardless of rank, would coexist.

'I heard this is where the action is,' said Bobby, trying to sound cool and businesslike.

'Oh, fuck,' Simmons groaned. Big Jack just smiled.

Bobby felt himself go hot around the ears.

'The kid you're replacing said the very same thing,' said Big Jack. 'Sat right where you are now.'

'What happened to him?' asked Bobby, fairly certain that he knew the answer.

'He was a gutless pussy. We ran him off,' growled Simmons.

'He decided running recon wasn't for him, and the Yards weren't too happy with him either.' Big Jack adopted a more conciliatory tone.

'The Yards get a say in running the team?' Bobby was surprised.

'Not exactly,' replied Big Jack, 'but they do have influence. If you don't measure up in the Yards' eyes, then you're a risk, plain and simple. The Montagnards are smart people. Not smart like us, they're smart in a different way. They are basically tribal like the Apache or Sioux back home. Be aware, the Yards do not see themselves as Indians. They see themselves as cowboys. The NVA are the Indians. John Wayne is a cowboy and he is a member of the Rhade tribe, so if you got any Indian blood in you, keep it quiet. Our Yards are Rhade.

'Yards are the bravest people you will ever meet. You will never see a Yard beg and you will never see a Yard whore. These are a proud people, and we treat them with respect. So here's the deal, kid,' said Big Jack. 'If you're up to it, then you're on the team. If you're not, or the Yards aren't happy with you, then you're cut. Someone else might take you but I doubt it. Chances are you'll be re-assigned out of CCC.'

That seemed fair to Bobby.

'All we ask is that you fight when we have to

fight, and you run when we need to run. If someone gets hit, and we can't carry them, we stay and fight and hope the Cavalry gets to us in time. We never ever leave a live body.

'Now, if the worst happens and you don't make it, we'll try and get your body out. But we ain't gonna risk any lives trying, so, if we have to leave you, we will. That means you'll be posted MIA. Your folks won't get anything to bury, but don't worry. If we know you're dead, we'll make sure your family gets to know. OK?'

'Sounds great,' said Bobby with a rueful grin.

'We'll start you tomorrow,' continued Big Jack, 'get you down on the range and see what you got. We average about one mission a month. After each mission we get about five days off. Then we're back into training. We usually get a warning order about five days prior to the launch date. That's when we start the mission cycle.'

The Huckleberry Inn was the all-ranks club at Kontum, and was used by all the fifty or so US personnel that made up the unit. Like the rest of the facilities in the camp it had been constructed with great care. Special Forces had a homesteader attitude towards life in Vietnam. They had been here longer than anyone else. It was their war. The camp had flushing toilets and the club had real bar stools and booths. The regular Army could shit in cans and live like animals if they liked, but not the SF, who always aimed to leave a place better than they had found it.

It took Bobby only minutes to appreciate that the club also doubled as the real headquarters and training ground of CCC. It was where policy was made, lessons learned, disputes settled, ideas formulated, and praise or damnation awarded. Unless you were somebody, you kept your mouth shut and your eyes straight. If you needed to say something, then you'd better be someone who had earned the right to say it. If you wanted to tell a war story, then you had better be someone the gunfighters would listen to. Big Jack was a gunfighter. They were the Command and Control big dogs, who had run recon over the fence in Laos. If you hadn't run at least three missions, folks wouldn't even notice you existed.

Earlier that evening Bobby, along with the rest of Recon Company, had assembled on the helicopter pad to welcome back RT Vermont, after they'd done five days in Laos. The men climbed from the helicopters looking haggard and exhausted; their faces were streaked with camouflage greasepaint, their green jungle fatigues blotched with black spray paint, the belts around their waists crammed with ammo and canteen pouches. Heavy-bladed K-bar combat knives were taped inverted to their shoulder harnesses. They laughed and joked with their well-wishers and immediately cracked the cans of beer forced into their hands. These men bowed to no one. To be like them, Bobby felt, was a goal worth dying for.

Next morning he was introduced to the Montagnards.

The senior man, or Zero-one, was called Loc. He thought he was about thirty-four and spoke good French and almost as much English. He had been educated at a Catholic mission and had fought with the French back in the early fifties, before returning to his tribe. In many ways, he acted like the French soldiers he had known as a young man. He had a side-shaved military haircut, and still swore using French military expletives. His proudest possessions were a .45 Colt automatic with hand-carved rosewood grips, and a Seiko watch.

Next in the chain of command was Bluh, who wore a constantly startled expression. He also had a small moustache, but in stark contrast to Loc's military neatness, his appearance was wild and unkempt. A little younger than his Zero-one, Bluh was supposed to be the interpreter for the Montagnards, though he seemed to speak less English.

The other seven Montagnards on the team were all young men. And some of them seemed very young indeed.

Later that morning, Rhett Simmons started to school Bobby in his equipment.

'OK, as the One-two, you'll carry the radio. Know what this is?' Rhett tapped the radio set with the edge of his foot.

'PRC-25 FM radio, 920 channels. Weighs 25 pounds, transmits 1.5 to 2 watts in high band and low band.'

'OK, Mr smart-ass College Boy, who exactly can we talk to on the PRC-25? Tell me that, what with you being an expert and all.'

'I don't know. You tell me.' Bobby felt his smug certainty washed away.

'Damn' right. Listen up and keep your yap shut.' Rhett cleared his throat and began again. 'We can talk to other ground units, and we can talk to the choppers. We can talk to some aircraft. We can talk to Covey, and we can talk to the A-1s. We cannot talk to the fast movers, the jets. Jets ain't got FM. They've only got UHF. If we need to call in an air strike, we have to talk to Covey, and Covey talks to the jets.'

Bobby nodded.

'When we're over the fence, in Laos, we're out of

range of everyone. Down in the south, there's a radio relay site, actually in Laos, callsign Leghorn. We've got a bunch of guys on a 3,000-foot peak, and they can pick up and talk to anyone within about twenty miles, assuming you're up on a ridge or high up. Down in a valley, you're fresh outa luck. If we're in the north of the area, we might talk to Hillsboro. Hillsboro is a C-130. It acts as airborne command post. At night Hillsboro becomes Moonbeam. Most of the time, though, unless Covey is overhead, we're on our own.'

'What if we get hit and can't get anyone on the radio?' asked Bobby.

'Then we fight, numb nuts.'

The more Bobby discovered about his equipment, the more daunting the job became.

'We carry at least four hundred rounds. That's twenty magazines of twenty,' Big Jack explained. 'I'll try and find you one of them thirty-round mags, but they're kinda rare. I also want you to pack at least four grenades.'

He pulled a magazine from one of the pouches on his belt. 'See here, where we got this loop on the end of the mag?' Big Jack indicated the string taped to the bottom of the magazine. 'I want you to do this to all your magazines. It means you'll be able to pull them out even when your hands are shaking and covered in blood.'

He picked up a grenade. 'OK, here's what we do to even the odds a shade,' he began. 'Normally, you pull the pin and throw. So, from the time you throw and the fly-off lever comes away, you got four seconds.'

Bobby had learnt this back in infantry training.

'That's OK for your regular Army, but we need more of an edge. What I want you to get used to doing is pulling the pin, and when you're ready, letting the lever go, real slow, so as it don't make a noise. You'll hear the percussion cap fire. Soon as you hear that, count to two, then throw it as far as you can. Chances are, the grenade will detonate in the air, not on the ground. In the jungle that makes a real difference, and it scares the crap out of the bad guys. Don't bother trying this with CS or white phosphorous.'

'That's pretty risky, isn't it?' said Bobby. 'I mean, you've only got to get it slightly wrong and you collect a face full of frag.'

'Everything we do is risky. That's why we train the way we do. You got to understand – there aren't any rules out here. Forget everything you ever learnt about being safe. This is all about doing what works. The way you walk, the way you pack your equipment, the way you fire your weapon. We got the best ways to do it all. We do them our

way because we all seen other guys dead because
they did it wrong.'

Two days later, Bobby was sent down to Long
Thanh, near Saigon.

Long Thanh was where they ran the 'Recon
school' or the 'One-zero course' as it was often
called. Over three weeks they aimed to train a
Special Forces soldier in every aspect of running
recon.

This was no-shit hands-on training, given by
men who had done the job for real and survived.

'It takes approximately ten to fourteen choppers to
get a recon team on the ground. The bigger the
team, the more choppers we need,' began the
Instructor. Bobby noticed the man was missing two
fingers from his left hand, and one side of his neck
was a sheet of scar tissue.

'Because most of Laos is high up, we need to
keep the Hueys lightly loaded, so as they can still
hover and do all that good stuff Hueys do. Which
means no more than six guys per aircraft. An eight-
man team will split between two Hueys. A twelve-
man team split between two Hueys is getting close
to the limit.

'If a Huey goes down, and everyone is OK, we
might have six guys and four crew that we've got to

pull out. That means we got to use another two choppers at least. We always take enough choppers to pull out all the team and the crews. If you include the Spads, Coveys, Cobras, and every other swinging dick in town, that's near enough fifty guys working to get you either in or out. Now that's a lot of folks risking their lives. Don't forget it.'

The class was standing next to a Huey on the helipad at Long Thanh.

'This is a STABO rig.' The Instructor held up what looked like a parachute harness, minus the canopy container. Essentially, the rig was a very strong nylon harness which supported the wearer's equipment belt. Two straps could be pulled through between the legs and snap-hooked on to two V-rings below the belt. Also prominent on the shoulders were two other V-rings.

'This is the rope bag.' The Instructor hefted a heavy canvas bag from the floor of the Huey's cabin. 'Each aircraft carries four of these. Each contains one hundred and forty-five feet of nylon rope. The bags are kicked out and pay out the lift lines. They are weighted to get them through the trees, but it don't always work.' He dropped the bag to the floor and tugged out the lift bridle. 'You clip these to the V-rings on the shoulder rings. You are then ready to lift. Be aware,' the Instructor raised his voice for emphasis, 'if anyone gets caught in the trees, the crew chief will cut the ropes and you will either die from the fall or be trapped hanging in a tree, which is where the NVA will find you. This is dangerous shit, gentlemen! The Huey has to hover, and when it does that it is a stationary target. Search your soul before trying this. It is no fucking fun flying out of Laos on the strings. We've had people fall when the ropes got shot through, and we've had people bleed to death because we didn't know they were hurt and we couldn't help them. I've seen men come back covered in ice, it gets that cold up there in those rain clouds.'

The importance of a recon team being able to communicate or signal to aircraft was driven home time and again. The use of flares, smoke grenades, ground marker panels, strobe lights and signal mirrors were all introduced and practised, but to Bobby the last method covered seemed the best.

'Every US team member should carry one of these,' said the Instructor, holding up a small flat metal box about the size of a book. 'This is your URC-10 or Urc. It's an emergency radio. It transmits on 243Mhz and all military aircraft in the theatre monitor that frequency. It is also monitored by the gooks, so be real careful what you say. If your radio is fucked up or busted, or you get separated, you should attempt to raise help using this sucker. As well as voice, it transmits a homing tone so as folks can home in on you. Remember, if we can hear you, so can the NVA. Keep transmissions short and only use it when you're sure an aircraft is close by. Gentlemen, this has saved my life more than once. Look after it.'

Next came a lesson which stuck in Bobby's mind.

The Instructor introduced Staff Sergeant William Emerson, from CCC Kontum. 'This guy has run fifteen missions over the fence,' he explained, 'and those of us who know how tough that is are still asking why he ain't dead.' There was brief rumble of laughter. 'This is right from the horse's mouth, guys, so listen to what he has to say. It could save your life.'

Bobby had seen Bill Emerson around, up at Kontum. The One-zero on RT Carolina, Emerson was a gunfighter. Twenty-five years old and from Nevada, he had a reputation for being a joker, and a man you could guarantee to push the limits of any situation.

'I ain't much for big speeches,' began Emerson, 'but I been told that you guys want to hear what it is I owe my being alive to, so here goes. Listen to your Yards. I mean, really listen. When you see the enemy moving on the trail, do not stare at him. Look at his feet, look at his equipment, but do not look at him. The Yards will tell you that if you look at him, he will know you are watching. They will tell you that if you go into the jungle with evil in your heart, the spirits will warn the gooks you are coming.'

There was some shifting of feet. Was this guy for real or was he just stringing them along?

'I shit you not, gentlemen! This is for real. If a Montagnard tells you some weird deal, then listen, 'cos he ain't telling you that for fun. If he tells you there are bad spirits in an area, then get ready for trouble, 'cos he ain't kidding. What he might call bad spirits, we might call a company of NVA.

'Now, I ain't saying you let the Yards run the mission, but what I am saying is, if a Yard tells you that there is bad shit coming down, then you got to be ready for it. You still got to do the mission, but at least you got some warning. Oh, yeah, and if you ain't already heard, running recon ain't for everyone. If you find you can't get off the chopper, then you've left it too late to quit, and you're probably going to get yourself and some other folks killed. Know when to call it a day, gentlemen.'

'Hey, man, how's it hanging? You do OK at the school?' Carlos had spotted Bobby across the crowded club.

'Sure. It was a blast. You OK?'

'Fucking great,' said Carlos, his voice heavy with sarcasm. 'I got all these big-time juicers turning up every morning saying they got the shits and they need antibiotics. Don't suppose them having the shits has anything to do with them drinking too much beer every night. It's a great job, man. I love it.'

'You get to fly Chase medic, don't you?'

'I want to be running recon. Not pulling other guys out.' Carlos sipped at his beer.

'Maybe recon's not all it's made out to be?'

'You wanna swap jobs?'

Bobby shook his head.

'Say, did you get one of those One-zero lighters?' Carlos was referring to the Zippo lighter given to every graduate of the One-zero school.

'Sure.'

'Let's see it.'

'It's back in the hooch,' lied Bobby. He didn't want it to seem as if he was showboating. The One-zero lighter was an object of beauty and pride, a polished metal Zippo with the unofficial SOG crest adorning the case. It showed a skull wearing a Green Beret, bursting forth from the darkness into the light.

4

It had stopped raining. The November sun, low in the sky, probed the clouds for breaks. All was quiet, except for the sound of steady dripping.

Each of the eight men listened in his own way. Bobby did like the others, not sure what he was listening for. He guessed he would know when he heard it.

This was recon. You walk, you stop, you listen, you walk again.

A slight breeze ruffled the trees. In the distance there was a low rumble of thunder. It would rain again soon.

The sun found a gap in the heavy clouds, casting a golden beam across the team huddled in the vegetation. Bobby enjoyed its warmth on his face.

Big Jack looked over at Loc, speaking with his eyes. *Where was the sound, the sound you heard? Do you still hear it?*

Loc glanced back. *Keep listening and you'll hear it.*

Big Jack checked his watch and looked skyward. *It's dark in three hours. We need to move.*

Loc frowned back. *Stay still a little longer. I know*

they're out there. They're tracking us. They know we've stopped. They are listening as well.

The other men could guess the thoughts of Loc and Big Jack.

If we move, they'll hear us.

Big Jack wanted to be on the move. Any time you weren't moving, you weren't doing the job. If the enemy kept you still, they were winning.

There was a soft brushing sound, far away, almost indistinguishable from the breeze, a rustle of moving vegetation out of tune with nature.

Hands came alive levelling weapons. Bobby strained to see through the brush beyond Loc.

He was walking slowly backwards guided by Big Jack's hand on his belt. Tension rose like a huge wave about to roll on shore.

There it was again. To Bobby the sound was almost drowned out by the thumping of his heart. Instinctively the whole group began to get clear of each other's muzzles, each man alternately fanning out, left and right of the game trail on which they found themselves.

Suddenly Loc's body went taut. Big Jack sensed it and let go of his belt.

The wave crashed.

A stream of brass cases spewed from Loc's weapon, and then he was gone, replaced in space by Big Jack who emptied his weapon in the same direction. Twenty or thirty rounds were gone in seconds.

The gunfire sounded like a huge roaring laugh. It broke the spell. Bobby registered the metallic clicking of a grenade's fly-off lever.

Big Jack was gone. It was Bobby's turn. The butt of the carbine found his shoulder and he squeezed the trigger. Another thirty rounds ripped out towards the unseen enemy. The bolt locked back on the empty magazine. As Bobby turned, one hand was swiping the empty magazine from the weapon and dropping it down the front of his shirt. Within another two seconds, a fresh magazine had taken its place. The repetitive drills suddenly made complete sense. Bobby didn't feel the weight of the equipment. He didn't feel the fear he'd expected and had worried might paralyse him. He just reacted as he had been trained to do.

After running for twenty minutes, the team slowed, executed several direction changes, and carefully began to sterilise their back trail. Eventually they halted and went to ground.

Big Jack glanced across at Bobby. He had kept up and done well. Maybe this guy could run recon. Big Jack thought back to Bobby's predecessor, a twenty-one-year-old kid from Illinois, who had volunteered for Command and Control because some of his buddies had persuaded him to do it.

On his first mission, he'd done fine. They hadn't run into any trouble. A bit of ground fire on the insert, but that was it. On the second mission, they had collided with an NVA company sweeping the area. The initial firefight was fast and furious. The team found itself under attack from three sides. Big Jack had broken contact and the team ran.

An hour later they stopped and made sure they weren't being followed. Big Jack waited another hour and led the team back into the area they had been searching before they encountered the NVA.

The kid had begun to shake. He became clumsy and noisy, the greatest of all sins in the jungle, but he'd pull through, thought Big Jack. They halted as another NVA patrol had passed close by. When it was time to move on, the kid just hadn't wanted to go.

'They're everywhere! This is crazy! They know we're here!' he hissed, wide-eyed. 'If we go on, we'll get fucked up.'

At that moment Rhett Simmons had whispered something in the new guy's ear, and after that things were OK. But Big Jack knew he had become a liability and the whole team extracted the next morning.

Back at Kontum, the kid didn't want to admit there had been a problem. He had just been expressing an opinion. He wasn't scared. He wanted to transfer to another team. Besides, what was the big deal? It was just one mission. It wasn't worth dying over.

Rhett Simmons had thrown him across the room and pinned him to the wall. 'Listen, chicken shit! It's about getting the job done so some other poor sap ain't got to come back and do it for you!'

That night in the club the kid approached a few other One-zeros to ask if he could run on their teams. He claimed he had a communications problem with Big Jack. First thing the next morning the kid was summoned to the Sergeant Major's office. He was never seen again.

With two missions under Bobby's belt, Big Jack invited him down to the beach club up the coast from Vung Tau. He reckoned this kid would last the course.

The club itself was really nothing more than a bar-cum-restaurant. Though it looked fairly rundown, the place was maintained to a good standard. The club was out of the way and was either unknown or unpopular with other US personnel, so it was a good spot to decompress between missions, and close enough to Vung Tau if you needed a really wild time. There was an old French-style hotel close by, and the team normally met for breakfast in the hotel restaurant, before going over to the club.

Simmons was busy devouring breakfast when Bobby showed up.

'*Qué pasa?*'

'OK, *amigo*. Where'd you get to last night?' Simmons asked, having noted that Bobby had turned in early.

'Needed sleep.'

Simmons spooned another mouthful of egg-fried rice under his well-groomed moustache.

'Hell, boy. You need to learn to drink if you want to run recon.'

'I do run recon,' replied Bobby flatly.

'Well, you ain't run enough.'

'So when will I have run enough?'

'When you're dead or fucked up.'

Bobby looked around for a waiter. 'How many times you been over the fence?'

Simmons chewed methodically. 'It ain't the number you run that counts. It's what goes down when you're out there.'

'I can dig that.'

'There ain't no doubt about it. Anyone can wander around in the woods, all fat and happy. It's what happens when the shit hits. That's when you find out who's got enough balls for the job.'

Dried blood covered the front of Carlos's fatigues and coated his forearms. A recon team had got into a bad fight. One American was wounded and two Montagnards were dead. Carlos had been flying Chase medic, trying to stabilise the casualties as soon as they got them in the air. The blood on Carlos was Montagnard.

'You OK?' asked Bobby as they wandered from the heli-pad.

'I'm OK . . . He sure as hell ain't.'

A few minutes later they sat together in the late-evening shade cracking open cans of beer. Carlos had drained half of his before Bobby even took a sip.

'Nothing I could do, man. He was too far gone,' said Carlos. 'I couldn't find any way to stop the bleeding.'

Carlos coughed, cleared his throat, and took another swig of beer, rubbing his eyes with his other hand. 'I got to get to run recon, man. I can't do this patching up shit. I want to go kill someone.'

Every morning at 08.00 Recon Company gathered in front of headquarters for morning formation. Dress regulations were non-existent. Almost everyone wore sun-bleached jungle fatigues adorned with unofficial CCC, SOG and team patches. All patches, especially team patches, were strictly illegal. But no one was about to tell Recon Company they couldn't wear them. The

Montagnards in particular took great pride in a dramatic and colourful patch. North Dakota's was a black background, crossed by a silver lightning strike, and a winged skull wearing the Green Beret flying over green hills. The words 'RT North Dakota' were stitched around the edge. It meant nothing to anybody, but it was ominous and dramatic. That was good enough for the Montagnards.

The Recon Company 1st Sergeant appeared and the chatter died away as he glanced at his clipboard and called out, 'Mr Emerson.'

'Yes, Top,' came the reply from the front rank.

'See me afterwards.'

There was a smatter of laughter. The night before an inebriated and for no good reason naked Bill Emerson had commandeered a jeep from the motor pool and, to the encouraging cries of a small crowd of equally inebriated onlookers, had attempted to drive down to the Green Door, the local whorehouse in Kontum. Luckily for all concerned, he had been unable to get the guys on the gate to let him out. Being naked wasn't the issue. It was the fact that he was unarmed.

'Take a gun next time, Bill,' someone called from within the formation.

'He did, but it was too small,' came an anonymous reply. The crowd hooted.

The 1st Sergeant smiled but wasn't going to laugh.

'OK! Knock that shit off!' he barked. 'I'm saying this too often, gentlemen. Haircuts! I see far too many sorry-ass weirdos wandering around here.' A rumble of amused protest swept through the company.

'That goes for moustaches as well,' he added. This time protest was more audible.

The 1st Sergeant ran through the rest of his notes in a loud, clear voice. He was always issuing warnings of various minor military infringements, which, back in the US, he would enforce rigorously. Here in Recon he didn't care too much, though he would never admit it.

At about 14.00 Big Jack, Simmons and Bobby filed into the briefing room in the Tactical Operations Centre. All three had brought note pads and pencils.

The room was crowded but cool thanks to the air conditioning. The Weather and Air Liaison Officers stood at the back ready to chip in when needed. The rest crowded round a table in the centre of the room.

Just like school, the S-3 checked those present against a list and then got his show on the road.

'Your mission will be to proceed to Uniform six and capture a prisoner.'

Uniform six was a six-by-six kilometre box within which RT North Dakota would have total freedom for the duration of their mission. No bombs would be dropped, or any other action taken, within that area unless the team requested it.

'Obviously,' continued the S-3, 'if you're successful, your team will benefit in all the normal ways.' He was referring to the $100 bonus that would be paid to each US team member and the Seiko wristwatches that would be awarded to the Montagnards in the event of a live prisoner being captured. There was also the possibility of an R&R flight to Taiwan.

'Back in October a team came across some new trails in this area here.' The S-3 used the tip of his pencil to indicate a point on the wall map. 'They reported fairly regular movements of small numbers of troops, so your chances of grabbing someone are pretty good.'

Simmons grunted.

The S-3 heard him, but passed no comment. He had done his time running recon and knew the score. He was one of the few men who had actually brought a live prisoner out of Cambodia.

The Intel Sergeant stood up to give his brief. He didn't look much older than Bobby and wore Army-issue black-framed glasses. He spoke in a thick New York accent. Bobby wondered if he had been given the job just because he looked the part.

Uniform six was a rugged area encompassing two small converging valleys. The average height of the terrain was between four and five thousand feet. According to the Intel Sergeant, the area itself was pretty quiet. The target boxes to the south and east, however, were hornets' nests of activity, and this was what had prompted the boys down in Saigon to want to know more.

After the briefing, Big Jack, Simmons and Bobby stayed behind to study all the patrol reports on the area and check any recent aerial photographs.

Big Jack quickly formulated a plan. The team would be the normal complement plus five Montagnards. Loc would choose which five of the team's designated nine would run the mission.

Bobby felt his body tingle with anticipation.

It was another sunny morning out on the range. Three days till the mission launch.

Big Jack dragged a stick across the dust marking the outline of a notional trail. Bobby, Simmons and the nine Montagnards looked on.

'OK. Here's the deal.' Big Jack motioned for everyone to come closer 'We're gonna use two groups of three claymores. One facing up trail and one down.'

The claymores looked like small flat television sets. The front was convex and embossed with the words 'Front Towards Enemy'. Contained behind these innocuous words were seven hundred steel balls, and behind them a layer of explosive. On firing, the balls created a sixty-degree fan of fast-moving projectiles that killed anything within about two hundred feet, and maimed anything left standing immediately beyond. The mine stood upright on two sets of metal scissor-type legs. It had a simple sight on top and was detonated either by a command wire, a time fuse or trip wire.

Big Jack took Loc and another Montagnard, Mee, and placed them about twenty-five metres up the imaginary trail.

'You guys are security one. Rhett, you're security two.'

'Sure.' Simmons grabbed Hih and led him to a corresponding position down the trail. Hih was a young wild-looking man who always seemed to be late for everything.

Jack then took Bobby and another Montagnard, Kreh, and positioned them next to the previously indicated no-kill zone.

Bobby was suddenly aware that it was going to be his job, with Kreh, to grab the prisoner.

'So you're with me.' Big Jack gestured to Bluh. 'Here,' he indicated a ten-foot-wide area directly in front of him, 'is our no-kill zone.' Loc followed, as he had done from the beginning, with his translation.

'Beside the no-kill zone will be a block of C-4,' said Big Jack, referring to the plastic explosive. 'The security groups will tell us when the enemy is coming. I'll trigger the ambush, by firing the C-4. That should knock at least one guy off his feet. When the C-4 goes, we'll fire the claymores. Lake and Kreh will assault into the no-kill zone and grab any gook still alive. Got it?'

With the translation complete, the Montagnards all grinned broadly. Though incredibly brave and tough, they had lived beyond the influence of the twentieth century and western thinking for most of their lives. Just because they nodded and smiled didn't necessarily mean they understood. Some of the more complex aspects of military operations did not come naturally to them. Thus everything had to be explained and demonstrated several times and rehearsed until the sun went down.

But Bluh still did not look happy. He muttered something to Loc that made the other Montagnards laugh.

'He say maybe he should get VC. He say Kreh too small,' Loc explained to Big Jack.

Montagnard ages were almost impossible to

judge accurately. Kreh was only about five foot two and looked about fifteen.

'I need the strong men with me,' was all Big Jack said.

It didn't sound like an adequate explanation, but Bluh seemed to appreciate the compliment.

The plan was simple, but the devil was in the detail. The claymores would need careful arrangement to ensure that there were overlapping kill zones.

The rest of the day was spent rehearsing the deployment of the ambush. They also practised recovering the equipment, withdrawing and deploying it all over again. They went on until the whole operation could be performed quickly and silently, without a word of command being given.

Big Jack had flown out over the target area the day before. He'd taken pictures of likely LZs – landing zones – and now spread the map and aerial photographs over the table to show Bobby and Simmons.

'I couldn't see any sign of a trail.' He indicated a point on the map with the tip of his pencil. 'But I guess they're down there. It's thick bush, and we got some tall trees. We got this spot here, for a high ladder insert. I can see another LZ about a click away that we'll use as an alternate, in case we hit trouble here. If we use the alternate, it'll add about another day to the mission. If we get in on the first try, we'll head in below this ridge. If we insert near dark, we'll spend the night here.'

'No problem,' said Simmons.

'Once we've done the dirty deed, we'll head north until we hit this clearing here. If we can't use that, we'll keep going north until we get to this area. It's been hit pretty hard and it's covered in bomb craters. That's where we'll get out.'

'That's a fucking long way to run, dragging a pissed-off gook,' commented Simmons.

'Damn' right.' Big Jack smiled. 'There are a couple of really tight clearings, just up here to the east. We could use those if we can blow up a couple of trees.'

They all knew that the second they started blowing up trees, the NVA would come running.

'Make sure everyone's got at least a pound of C-4,' Big Jack continued. 'And make sure you check. Don't take their word for it. Check the claymores as well. Better yet, issue everyone new ones, just in case.'

'What's gone wrong with the claymores?' Bobby asked.

'The little guys break open the backs to get at the C-4. You don't want to hit the clacker on a claymore and just hear "pop", do you now?'

explained Big Jack. 'They use it for cooking and boiling up water. I reckon it's easier just to give them a present of a pound of C-4. That way we can use whatever they might have left.'

'I done two prisoner snatches,' confided Rhett Simmons as they sat in the club later. 'First time, the guy was dead, and the second we had to kill him, 'cos he started shooting.'

Bobby took a gulp of beer.

'So when all the smoke clears, and you got to grab the bad guy, grab the first fucker you see. If he's out of it, drag him back and check for a pulse. If you find a live one, smack him in the face. Break his fucking nose. Don't go shooting him in the legs unless he tries to run. If you do that, we'll have to carry him.'

Bobby's mouth went dry at the prospect of meeting the enemy face to face. It didn't seem like an opportunity for glory any more. It seemed like a burden.

The day before the mission, everyone cleaned then test-fired their weapons. In Big Jack's opinion, a high percentage of weapon jams could be traced to magazine problems. Any magazine found to cause jams was dropped to the ground and shot through, to prevent further use.

Even the weapons carried by the team were testament to Big Jack's sense of no-nonsense conservatism. C&C had access to almost any form of exotic weapon, but Big Jack kept it simple. Every man, bar one, carried a CAR-15 carbine. Which meant everyone could use everyone else's ammunition.

The only exception was Mee, who carried an M-79 grenade launcher. It fired one round at a time and broke in two, like a large shotgun. Mee could regularly hit a man-sized target at two hundred metres. He carried fifty rounds, spread between pouches and a specially constructed vest. His only other weapon was .45 pistol for self-protection.

Dak-To was about forty-five kilometres northwest of Kontum, and the airfield was situated to the west of the town itself and on the banks of the Dak Poco river. Route 512, a dead-end road to the Cambodian border, ran parallel with the airstrip to the north.

Dak-To was the launch site for most Command and Control Central operations into both Cambodia and Laos. The Hueys, carrying RT North Dakota, settled on to an airfield shrouded in early-morning mist.

Sunset came about 5.45. The plan was to insert the team within about an hour of last light, but if the aircraft were scheduled for other missions they would have to insert whenever they could.

Bobby grabbed his rucksack and walked to the small wired-off compound by the side of the runway.

Entrance to the launch-site compound was via a small footbridge over a wide drainage ditch. A sign warned that this was a classified area and visitors were not welcome.

Bobby nodded a greeting to the men in the Bright Light team standby area. They nodded back and sipped their coffee from soot-blackened metal canteen cups. The coffee smelt tantalisingly good in the cool mist-laden air. The Bright Light team had spent the previous night in the compound. They were the men who would come and rescue North Dakota if things went wrong. Every recon team did a weeklong standby stint. While it could be boring, the fact that you were only a thirty- to sixty-minute helicopter ride away from the worst situation you could imagine, kept everyone sharp and snake-eyed.

Having dropped his equipment in the isolation tent, Bobby wandered back over the footbridge and around the edge of the runway to watch the helicopters or talk to the crews. He had developed an avid interest in everything to do with helicopters. What was the smallest LZ they could use? How much could they lift? How long could they stay over the target area? Not only was it useful, potentially life-saving knowledge, it also helped take his mind off the mission.

'We don't like to hover up high,' one pilot told him, 'so don't be planning to rappel into an area or come out on strings, unless you really need to. The chopper's using a lot of power. We're a sitting duck and we're making a lot of noise. Everybody knows where to find us. We attract fire like moths on a bulb. Whatever you do, do it fast. The faster you're down the ladders or out of the door, the better. And always make sure you mark your position well. We ain't got time to fuck about trying to find you.'

On the far side of the runway stood the sleek Cobra gunships. Swarming about them, ground crew fed belts of rounds into their ammunition bins and slid fresh rockets into the launcher pods that hung from their sides.

Nearer to the compound were four squat Kingbees, large piston-engined helicopters. The Kingbees might be slower, larger and less agile than the Hueys, but everyone loved them. They were incredibly rugged, and could carry more men. Their cabins stank of fuel and hydraulic fluid. Flying in one was an assault on every sense in the human body.

*

It was time to go. Bobby tried to chew moisture back into his mouth. He checked the radio once again. It was the only item in his rucksack. His rations and sleeping gear were spread across the rest of the team. The checks complete, he swapped rucksacks with Big Jack. This enabled the team leader to have communications and control over the insertion.

The gaggle of helicopters lifted from the runway and headed west, the four Cobras nosing ahead, followed by the six Hueys, with the four Kingbees bringing up the rear.

5

Wind roared through the open doors, and Bobby tried to make himself less uncomfortable in the cramped cabin. He felt extremely vulnerable flying slowly above the forbidden land. The sun was low in the sky, bathing the cabin in a pinkish light. Below, the green tree-covered mountains of Laos looked like some far-off benign Shangri-la.

Bobby glanced at Kreh, nonchalantly huddled against the rear bulkhead. He smiled, giving a confidence-boosting thumbs up. Bobby wondered if Kreh had any sense of fear at all. He was one of the few survivors from a village that had been attacked by the Viet Cong back in 1965. His whole family had been slaughtered in front of him before he had managed to escape into the jungle. A Special Forces A-team that had taken back the village had rescued him, and young Kreh had been fighting ever since.

One of the door gunners signalled that they were almost there.

★

Big Jack had selected a patch of thick brush on the edge of some taller trees. The helicopters could not land but that was OK.

The pilot lowered the collective lever, taking lift out of the rotors and letting the helicopter descend. His co-pilot covered the controls with his own hands, in case enemy fire injured or killed the pilot.

The lead helicopter was approaching the clearing. In the back, the door gunners released the ladders.

The pilot put the helicopter into a slow left-hand turn, to give time for the lead helicopter to get his team out.

There was a solitary radio call in the pilot's ear.

'White Lead, clear.'

Now it was his turn. Tightening the turn, he lined up on the patch of brush, pulling the stick back to bleed off airspeed and lowering the collective even more.

As they got nearer he began to check the descent. He needed to be in a hover about twenty-five feet above the bushes.

'Clear on the right,' said the co-pilot as they neared the tall trees forty feet away.

The pilot pulled back on the stick, and pushed with his left foot to stop the machine swinging. Once he could see that the trees on his left were stationary, he knew the machine was hovering.

★

Bobby swung his legs out on to the skids while gripping hold of the ladder. Once established on the swaying rungs, he began to descend as fast as he could.

Suddenly he felt someone tap his foot. A few more steps and he was down, almost stepping on Simmons who was holding the bottom of the ladder.

Bobby looked up to see the door gunner's face peering back, waiting to signal that everyone was off the ladders. Then the helicopter clattered away over the trees.

Apart from the sound of other departing helicopters, all was silent. Bobby and the rest of the team crouched down among a clump of saplings.

This was dangerous. The helicopters were far from silent, and any North Vietnamese close by would be pushing towards the sound and attempting to fix the location of the insertion.

Big Jack led the team a short way through the trees and halted. Everyone fell into a defensive position, and listened. Any sight or sound of the enemy now, and it was back to the landing zone.

The team waited five minutes. Nothing happened. Big Jack keyed the handset.

'Team OK.'

★

They were huddled into thick brush just below a ridge. This was their RON position, where they would spend the night.

Big Jack allocated everyone a field of fire and each man placed his claymore mine to cover that specific part of the perimeter. Placing claymores needed a lot of care because while the seven hundred steel balls shot out one way, a considerable blast went the other. Conventional wisdom decreed that you place the claymore as far away from you as the command wire would allow. The manual said you must position it no nearer than sixteen metres to dug-in troops. In C&C you sheltered behind the meagre protection of your rucksack or placed the mine in front of a reasonably sturdy-looking tree, because the claymores would only be about seven metres away in the open, and maybe as close as four if a suitable tree could be found.

The team ate one at a time, and in silence, waiting for dark.

Overhead came the droning of a solitary aircraft. It was the sound they were expecting.

Bobby looked at Big Jack who gave him a nod. Bobby keyed the radio handset.

'SPAF, this is Lazy Shoe.'

'Roger, Shoe, this is SPAF-4. Go ahead.'

Bobby gave SPAF-4 the evening situation report, or sitrep as it was commonly called. SPAF-4 was an Army spotter plane out of Kontum. The SPAFs worked solely for CCC. Used to fly visual recon over Laos, SPAFs normally did first and last light checks with the teams, to relieve the workload from Coveys.

SPAF-4 would be back in the morning. Until then, they were alone.

The darkness fell like a door closing.

Each man lay close enough to touch the next. Circled around Big Jack, all eight men were crammed into an area less than twenty feet in diameter. No one removed their web gear, except to undo their belts. Each used his rucksack as a pillow and slept with his hands on his weapons. High in the mountains winter nights were cool, even in the jungle. For warmth, each man wore a black nylon windproof jacket and huddled beneath a poncho liner, but no one really slept and, for that reason, no one stood guard.

Bobby drifted in and out of consciousness. For all his pre-mission dread and nerves, it never seemed so bad once he was on the ground. In fact, it was sort of fun.

What was Mom up to right now? he wondered. How would she feel if she could see him? The thought of his mother's inevitable anxiety made him uneasy. It always did. Better she didn't know.

You can be anything you want to be, his mom had always said and she meant it, right up to the point where he wanted to join the Army and go to Vietnam.

Bobby tried to think of something else.

He hadn't heard from Rachel for ages. Did she still think of him? God, he hoped she did. It had been nearly two years since they had first met, but he could still see her face as if it were yesterday. He'd made a lot of promises back then, when promises had seemed so easy to keep. Neither had ever said they loved the other but they had become as close as only lovers can.

But her last letter to him had seemed more questioning of what America was doing in the war, and he found himself experiencing flashes of anger when he read her accounts of what the papers and TV were saying: reports of the My Lai massacre, stories of open dissent in combat units, and statements from serving and former soldiers condemning US involvement in the war. Who the hell were these people and what did they know? No one in CCC condemned the war and they ran more missions and took more casualties than anyone. Of course Rachel could only go by what she read in the papers or the five-o'-clock horror stories on NBC and ABC. But Bobby couldn't tell her the truth, even if he wanted to. It was classified.

Maybe he should have kept the relationship more casual, with no promises and no commitments. But he didn't believe that was what she wanted. Lying there on the unforgiving ground, he wondered if he felt true affection for Rachel or whether he had selected her as the sweetheart all soldiers had to have back home. She certainly deserved better than being a 'Goodbye sweetheart, Hello Vietnam' fuck.

A nudge to his arm quickly dispelled the reverie.

He sat up slowly, trying to make absolutely no noise. What little moonlight there was filtered hazily through the branches. Bobby felt his heartbeat accelerate. He strained to catch the slightest tell-tale sound of danger.

Nothing. There wasn't even a breeze. Slowly, one by one, each man relaxed.

The process would be repeated at least three or four times a night.

Bobby felt another tap on his arm.

His eyes snapped open. He had actually fallen asleep for a moment or two.

'OK, Lake. Let's get going,' Big Jack's voice whispered in his ear.

It was still dark. He flipped open the leather cover over his watch. It was five-thirty. Sunrise wasn't due for another forty minutes.

He was stiff and ached all over. It seemed as though no position he chose to curl up in was free from either twisted roots or bruising rocks.

Bobby stowed his sleeping gear and pulled the rehydrated rice ration from his rucksack pocket and started to eat using a small plastic spoon. He would have killed for some coffee, but once in Laos such luxuries were for your dreams. The rice was eaten cold. To add some flavour, Bobby opened a C-ration tin of meat. To a starving dog, the aroma might have been more thrilling. Bobby just swallowed it down. Food was fuel.

Next to him Simmons was massaging his neck. He had obviously spent an even more uncomfortable night.

It was SPAF-2's turn to fly the first light patrol and the team checked in soon after dawn. The claymores were safely gathered in and everyone shook themselves out into patrol order.

Loc went first as the point man or scout. Big Jack was number three and Bobby followed him. Simmons was second to last, in front of Mee, the tail gunner with the M-79.

*

The team made their way through thick vegetation. Every fifty to a hundred feet huge trees topped off what was normally referred to as triple canopy jungle, so what a team could see was usually very limited.

The pace was slow and deliberate. How slow depended on the ground and how close the enemy might be.

He who moves fastest, makes most noise and cannot hear others. Move slowly, see and hear the enemy first, was the primary survival skill for a recon team. It also reduced, but did not eliminate, their trail. The North Vietnamese made extensive use of trackers, many of whom were almost impossible to deceive. One of the tail gunner's responsibilities was to sterilise the team's trail by hiding broken or bent foliage and covering up footprints.

Otherwise they had to rely on Loc walking point. If he suggested a change of course, it was foolish to ignore him.

Every hour or so they halted to scribble notes on the terrain, topography, vegetation or soil type, any pertinent information the Intel boys down in Saigon might need. The breaks also afforded a few moments to drink some water and touch up camouflage face paint, which had been sweated off.

The lower they went into the valley, the denser the jungle grew. It was hard going but by late afternoon they were close to the first of the planned ambush sites.

Vegetation constantly snagged on packs and equipment, and men had to be carefully and quietly disentangled. The air was hot and still. Stinging beads of perspiration ran into eyes and dripped off noses. Being the middle of the dry season, there was virtually no chance of rain. More often than not, the way ahead was blocked by impenetrable bush and they would have to backtrack and find another route.

Enveloped by darkness the exhausted North Dakota was crammed into its usual small space. One or two of them manage to doze quietly.

The silence was shattered abruptly.

'Dogs!' whispered Simmons.

Without being asked, Bobby powered up the radio. They didn't have contact with anyone, but it seemed like a wise precaution.

Given the thick bush, no one could get near without making a lot of noise, but if the dog sniffed them out, the NVA could easily surround the position and wait till daylight.

'Everyone stay cool,' whispered Big Jack, leaning close to Loc.

'Dog?' he asked, wanting to make sure it wasn't a barking deer they were hearing. It was easy to mistake the two.

'Dog,' replied Loc, after listening to another bark.

'How far away, d'you reckon?'

'Don't know. Maybe he get closer.'

By now Bobby's heart was beating almost out of his chest. He had to make a conscious effort not to hold his breath and to release his vice-like grip on his weapon.

'Pack up. We're moving,' hissed Big Jack.

An NVA tracker may have picked up their trail and alerted the local sector commander that a recon team might be in the area.

They moved north and then east, putting about two hundred metres between themselves and their original position before halting to sit back-to-back facing out into the dark. The rest of the night was spent waiting for dawn.

The ambush site was on a slight bend in the trail.

Big Jack deployed the two security teams first. This meant that the rest of them were protected while actually setting the claymores. Bobby again switched rucksacks with Big Jack, so that the One-zero had control of the radio.

Bobby and Kreh lay about twenty feet back from the trail, in good cover.

They had been in position about ninety minutes when the monofilament communication cord, strung between Simmons, in his security position, and Big Jack began to twitch. Simmons was signalling that someone was coming.

Big Jack leaned forward and tapped Bobby's foot three times. This was it. He felt a current of dread and excitement pulse through him. He clenched the plastic handcuff strip in his teeth and his whole body screamed with anticipation.

Through the curtain of leaves, he saw men in khaki pith helmets and pale green uniforms stride by, bent under heavy loads. Bobby closed his eyes and lowered his head behind the protection of the rucksack.

BANG! B-B-BANG!

The rucksack Bobby was sheltering behind was hurled back against him. The air was suddenly filled with dust and leaves.

Eerily in the chaos came the crash of a falling tree, claimed by the back blast of a claymore. Someone was screaming.

'Go! Go! Go!' yelled Big Jack.

Bobby and Kreh leapt forward on to the track.

But there was no one in the no-kill zone!

As the dust began to clear, Bobby could just make out half-a-dozen crumpled bodies strewn across the track. Weapons and helmets lay unneeded and ownerless. One man, caught by the edge of the ambush, writhed in pain.

Kreh shouted. He had found someone thrown into the bushes on the far side of the track. Bobby grabbed the man's shirt and pulled him upright. His eyes were wide, dull, and unseeing. Small trickles of blood began to flow from his nostril.

'Fuck,' said Bobby.

BANG! Simmons's claymore detonated. A burst of carbine fire followed. Obviously he had company. A long rattle of enemy fire replied. Bobby could now tell the difference between the report of an AK-47 and the CAR-15.

Two shrill whistle blasts rang out. Big Jack's signal to move. No more time and no prisoner.

'The fucker's dead,' yelled Bobby above the sound of firing as he struggled to put on his rucksack.

'Yeah, OK,' said Big Jack, as if it was of no great concern. Once the shooting started, there was little point in sticking around. Big Jack keyed the radio.

'Covey, Covey, this is Lazy Shoe. Anyone copy?'

'Coming through,' shouted Simmons, as he crashed in amongst them. Seconds later Loc and Mee also appeared. 'We got a bunch of gooks coming up the trail and they're pissed.'

Big Jack checked heads. All here. Without a

word of command, the team quickly followed the point man. Behind them, long bursts of fire and shouting rang out as the enemy advanced along the trail to discover the carnage of the ambush site. They would want revenge.

Speed was now crucial. The NVA would be summoning help from all over the area. Within fifteen minutes, they could have a hundred men involved, and within an hour probably five times that number, plus anti-aircraft guns.

Loc found another trail cutting across their path. Big Jack motioned that they should cross it. He wanted to head north and there was no time to work out a better route.

With Loc covering left and Big Jack taking the right, the rest of the team dashed across the four-foot strip of hard-packed clay.

Bobby was first across into the jungle on the other side.

Crack! Crack! Instinctively, he ducked down and returned fire.

'Man down!' shouted Simmons, dragging Mee across the trail by his harness.

Bobby scrambled to help. Kreh and Hih grabbed the casualty's feet and belt. Just as Bobby got to within feet of them, he felt something wet hit his face. Simmons fell. Bobby thought he had tripped. Rounds tore into the ground around them. Kreh staggered back, reeling from blow after blow as the bullets struck him. Bobby dropped to the jungle floor, burying his face in dry leaves. He felt the shock wave of passing bullets on the back of his legs.

Big Jack, Bluh and Loc were blazing away from the far side of the trail. Bobby scrambled into cover behind a tree and let rip with his carbine. He could see fleeting shapes where the trail twisted out of view, but nothing you could call a target. Muzzle flashes blinked in the distance, and more rounds thumped into the branches overhead.

On the edge of the trail, Simmons lay sprawled, one blood-soaked hand clutching a wound on his left hip. To the right, Kreh lay lifeless, three large dark stains across his torso. Mee was also strangely still, a gaping hole where his ear used to be. Hih appeared unhurt.

Simmons was trying to stand, but his legs were useless. He had taken another round just above his right knee, and his one free arm flailed in a cloud of dust and leaves as he tried to drag himself to cover.

Loc and Bluh had taken shelter and were busy putting covering fire back down the track. Bobby knew it was up to him.

It took all his strength and determination to drag Simmons into cover behind a tree. Grabbing a field dressing from Simmons's web gear, he pressed it into the red wet gash on the wounded man's leg. The dressing soaked with blood immediately. Bobby pulled another from his own gear and packed it into the exit wound on the back of the leg. Big Jack crawled over, tearing open a field dressing with his teeth, and tried to stem the flow of blood from Simmons's hip.

'Dump the rucks!' he shouted, tossing a white phosphorous grenade down the trail. Seconds later, a truck-sized cloud of white smoke burst out, shielding them from view.

'Kreh and Mee are dead,' reported Bobby. What else could he say? He felt neither sorrow nor anger. He was functioning on instinct and training. Emotion was now a luxury or a hazard.

'Yeah, I know,' replied Big Jack, grabbing Simmons by the harness, and heaving him further into the jungle. Simmons cursed and growled in pain.

Beyond the smoke, the NVA were still firing, but firing blind.

'Can you walk?' Big Jack tried to help Simmons to his feet. He tried but his legs buckled under him.

Hih appeared carrying the now ownerless M-79 over his shoulder, and seconds later Loc followed, the front of his shirt heavy with ten or so 40mm rounds he had stripped from Mee's web gear.

Big Jack passed the radio to Bobby, and hoisted Simmons across his back. With Loc in the lead, they pushed west.

Bobby keyed the handset.

'Covey, Covey, any fucking Covey! This is Lazy Shoe, Prairie Fire. Prairie Fire. We have two Soap Bubble KIA, and one Straw Hat wounded.'

Covey took the call, and the words 'Prairie Fire' flashed across the communications net.

The gaggle scrambled from Dak-To.

At Da-Nang, the two A-1s sitting on strip alert readied themselves for take-off.

Hillsboro began to round up any airborne strike aircraft that could assist. The nearest were two loitering A-1s, waiting to cover the insertion of another team due in that morning. As soon as they heard the call, they stood on their wing tips and swung south.

Reduced to only six the team couldn't stand and fight. Running was the only option. With Simmons wounded they couldn't run fast.

Big Jack could only carry his One-one so far. Eventually he would have to have help. Bobby and he exchanged loads and kept going. Bobby was sure his lungs were going to explode. His thighs felt as though they were on fire and sweat poured down his face and stung his eyes. He couldn't carry Simmons for long.

Staff Sergeant John Pasco was a gunfighter, an eighteen-mission veteran of recon, and an accomplished One-zero. Slackening his seat straps, he peered through the canopy down into the jungle.

A small bright Sparking flare sailed up from the trees, and then slowed to a stop before falling back to earth.

'I got 'em. Four o'clock low.'

'Roger that,' called the Captain, banking the OV-10.

A new voice came on the UHF radio set.

'Covey, this is Spad Two-one.' A-1s were checking in.

'Roger, Spad. Go ahead.'

'Covey, Spad Two-one and Spad Two-two. We have you visual. We are packing nape and CBUs.'

'Roger, Spad. We have friendlies running. Hold high and dry at this time, we're still trying to sort out where our boys are at.'

Below their position came shouts and a burst of fire.

'They're on to us,' exclaimed Bobby.

'Let's slow them up then,' grunted Big Jack as he laid Simmons against a tree. Bluh, Loc and Hih immediately took cover.

Bobby grabbed his weapon and looked at Big Jack, aware that his eyes were probably wide with terror.

'Wait for them to get real close,' whispered Big Jack.

Heads and faces bobbed into the swaying undergrowth.

Big Jack released the fly-off lever of a grenade and counted to two before lobbing it out towards the enemy.

There was a shouted warning, but it was cut short as the grenade detonated some three feet above the ground.

The team opened fire. Streams of spent brass glittered in the shafts of sunlight.

'Let's go!'

Bobby and Big Jack reloaded and, grabbing Simmons by the harness, dragged him behind them. Loc, Hih and Bluh fired a few more bursts and followed. After sixty metres they stopped. The NVA were still shooting but the rounds were all high and wild.

Big Jack fired another pen-flare.

The Captain had taken the plane down to about twelve hundred feet, and had spotted the flares marking the near-exact position of the team.

'Spad Two-one, this is Covey. Watch my mark.

Target elevation is 2700 feet. Run in north to south to start with. If you get hit, head for the fence. Call FAC in sight.'

Bobby had heard Covey's approach, but hadn't taken his eyes from the direction he expected the enemy to materialise. The rockets caught him completely by surprise as they smashed through the trees and exploded. Bobby felt the succession of shock waves ripple over him.

Big Jack hoisted Simmons on his back and the team set off north, across the slope of the ridge.

Twenty seconds later, Spad Two-one pulled out of his dive, the tubes under the wings disgorging their payload of baseball-shaped cluster bomb munitions.

Bobby heard the reverberating detonations as the team made its way north. The wild firing of the NVA ceased immediately.

I hope we killed them, thought Bobby. I hope we killed a lot.

6

Up in the OV-10, Pasco checked out the LZ. It was still about a kilometre away. The team was running in thick bush and hard to follow.

'Where are the choppers at?' asked Pasco.

'About ten minutes out,' replied the Captain. 'They ain't gonna make it in time, are they?' he added.

'It's gonna be close,' agreed Pasco. If the team wasn't at the LZ by the time the gaggle got overhead, the choppers could only hold for so long before they'd have to go back to Dak-To to refuel. That could take another hour, and this team had a wounded man.

The enemy was sweeping towards them, deliberately clacking bamboo poles together to try and provoke them into careless movement or to push them towards an ambush.

Breathing heavily, Big Jack lowered Simmons to the ground and consulted the map. North, and the route to the LZ, was blocked. South lay the enemy, and east would take them back down the slope and towards the trails. The only direction left was west.

The ground was less steep towards the top of the ridge. The trees were shorter and the terrain more open. Immediately beyond a well-worn footpath, the ground fell away down a small cliff face. From there, they had a grandstand view over western Laos and the higher mountains on the other side of the valley.

Simmons lay semi-conscious, still gripping his carbine which they had been unable to take from him. Bobby spoke into the radio.

Big Jack walked to the edge of the cliff and waved a marker panel.

'I see you,' said Pasco, spotting the flickering orange panel on the ridge.

Thank God for that, he thought to himself.

The ridge extended north for about another thousand metres, before dropping back down into the jungle. There was a small clearing about seven hundred metres north, just big enough for a helicopter.

'Shoe, this is Casper. I need you to move north about seven hundred metres. There's a real tight LZ. We can try and get you out from there.'

'How you doing?' whispered Bobby, applying

another dressing to Simmons's leg wound. He looked pale and drawn. Unless he literally couldn't bear the pain any longer, no morphine would be administered. A wounded man could still fight, but a man full of morphine couldn't.

'I'm fucked, but you're doing good,' croaked Simmons.

With those words, all fear and fatigue seemed to leave Bobby, like smoke blown on the wind.

Simmons groaned in pain as Big Jack again hoisted him on his broad shoulders. With Loc as usual in the lead, they set off along the path. They'd reach the LZ in about ten minutes.

The Captain briefed the two loitering A-1s on the new plan, and wheeled the aircraft round to get a closer look at the clearing.

Muzzle flashes blinked from shadows under the trees. Tracer flashed past the canopy.

'Gun on the ridge!' called the Captain, as he swung the aircraft away.

High above, Spad Two-one had been watching the OV-10.

'I see it, Covey. FAC in sight. On my way.'

Easily portable by three or four men, the 12.7-millimetre anti-aircraft gun could be set up anywhere to lie in wait for the slow and vulnerable helicopters. Its thumb-sized rounds could easily tear through any aircraft it found, seeking out engines, personnel or any other vital equipment. It paid not to get hit.

Spad Two-one throttled back and nosed into a dive. Eighteen hundred feet short of the ridge, he flattened out and fired.

The gun team had jammed their weapon firing an overlong burst at Covey. As the A-1's 20mm cannon shells tore into the ground and the trees around them, the pilot could see men running along the top of the ridge, stumbling and falling in clouds of dust and clumps of earth thrown up by the fire. Then he saw the gun fall on its side, and one man topple backwards over the cliff. Releasing his finger from the trigger, he pulled back into a climb.

'Shoe, hold where you are. Stop moving, we got guys on the ridge,' called Pasco, peering back over his shoulder as Spad Two-one pulled off target.

The enemy came racing along the footpath. Loc's burst ripped through the first man's chest and he fell, dead before he hit the ground.

North Dakota opened fire in unison, killing at least five more and wounding several others. One man stood his ground, returning fire from a semi-crouched position, his shooting wild and inaccurate. Rounds tore into him, and he died where he fell.

Cordite fumes swirled around them as Bobby and the others quickly and methodically swapped their spent magazines for fresh ones and waited for new targets to appear.

Enemy fire slashed through the branches above their heads. Big Jack grabbed the M-79 from Hih, and using rounds passed to him by Loc, fired three times in quick succession.

'Covey, we got guys on the ridge, due north. They're close!' yelled Bobby above the firing.

Big Jack snapped the M-79 shut with a fresh round and laid it beside him.

'You OK?' he asked, with almost fatherly concern.

'I'm good,' said Bobby, feeling so scared that he doubted he could stand, his legs were shaking so much.

Desperate yelling and gunfire erupted in front of them.

Another group of soldiers came rushing along the path, their mouths wide open in screaming aggression.

No one fights like this, thought Bobby, but he was already firing.

Some men ran headlong. Others dropped prone behind the bodies of their fallen comrades and attempted to return fire. Loc and Bluh, who had been checking the rear, swung round and opened up at the charge. Barely conscious, Simmons levelled his weapon and prepared to fight hand-to-hand if necessary.

Bobby's carbine ceased to vibrate in his hand. Empty! An NVA soldier was closing on him fast. Bobby rolled back behind the tree, expecting at any second to be bayoneted in the neck. He tore the magazine from his weapon, and pulled another from his ammo pouch. Please, God, don't let me fuck this up. Someone kill that guy! The magazine on, Bobby's hand slammed the bolt release. The NVA soldier fell dead beside him, his face slick with sweat, creased in fear and surprise.

'Cease fire! Cease fire!' yelled Big Jack. Bobby looked to his left to see Hih standing there, his carbine smoking in his hand. He flashed a nervous grin at Bobby before retreating to the cover of his tree. Lifeless or dying bodies littered the path.

'Everyone OK?' shouted Big Jack.

Before anyone could reply, Spad Two-two laid another carpet of cluster munitions a hundred metres to the north, and the staccato crackle of detonations made the air vibrate.

Instinctively, the whole team ducked, all except Big Jack who knew when to duck and when not to.

'Hey! Simmons. You OK?' Bobby asked.

He had lost a lot of blood and was in shock. The normal solution would be to get a drip of serum albumen into him, but that had been dumped with the packs.

Big Jack crawled over and checked the dressings. They were sodden but seemed to have stopped the bleeding.

'I'm OK,' insisted Simmons, his voice weak.

Behind them, Bluh started firing again.

'Fuck! They're behind us,' spat Bobby, more in irritation than fear. He pressed the handset. 'Covey, we got them to the south now!'

'Roger, Shoe. Spad's on the way.'

Twigs and small branches fell like snow as hundreds of rounds ripped over them.

'Covey, this is Shoe. We need nape, as close as you can get to our south,' yelled Bobby, pressing one finger into his ear as Hih returned fire over his back.

Bobby never heard Spad Two-one rolling in. He never saw the two large silver pods tumble from the wing of the plane and burst, impacting on the lip of the ridge barely twenty metres from the team. The huge wave of gelled fuel ignited and blazed through the trees, engulfing the enemy.

Whoosh!

The air was sucked from everyone's lungs. The

flash painted the jungle a bright golden-white. Sound evaporated for an instant. Bobby's fingers clawed into the soil.

He felt the immense heat on the backs of his hands and forearms as he covered his head. There was a suffocating smell of gasoline. The air itself seemed to be on fire. After a few seconds the heat eased and Bobby dared to look up. The leaves on the ground in front of him were blazing. Beyond was a wall of flaming jungle. A huge, dark pall of smoke momentarily obliterated the sunlight.

Off to his left, Loc was beating at flames on the sleeve of his shirt. All around them, burning leaves and debris drifted earthwards.

'Jesus Christ, Spad! You nearly fried the whole fucking team,' screamed Bobby into the handset, unable to contain both his anger and his relief.

'Understood, Shoe. Any casualties?' asked Pasco calmly.

The rest of the team were staring, open-mouthed, at the conflagration.

'Yeah. We're all OK. That sure was close.' He coughed dryly as smoke billowed over them.

Out in the flames someone was screaming, in agony. A dull explosion, as the man's ammunition exploded with the heat, ended his misery.

Bobby pulled out his canteen and gulped down the warm plastic-tasting contents.

If the gooks don't kill us, the Air Force will, he thought to himself.

'This is Panther 37 and Panther 39. We're over the ridge.'

'Roger that, Panthers.' Pasco gazed down to see two Cobras breaking into a turn below him. The fast, menacing gunships were always the first to arrive, so the gaggle would be about two minutes away.

'Covey, we're moving north. Can you guys see us?' Bobby was on the radio again.

The Captain reversed the aircraft's turn so that Pasco could look back at the ridge. In the shadow beneath the trees, an orange marker panel was waving vigorously.

'Roger, Shoe, we got you.'

Lifting Simmons once more by the shoulder straps of his harness they dragged him off. Bluh, Loc and Hih led the way, ready to shoot anything that moved. They passed bloodied bodies, scattered weapons and equipment, ditched by fleeing and wounded soldiers.

The cluster bombs had shredded the jungle. The ground was strewn with freshly fallen branches and the air was thick with the smell of burnt explosive, dust and fresh wood.

Emerging into a patch of open ground, the team came under attack again. They returned fire while Big Jack crawled to the edge of the cliff and threw out his marker panel.

The Cobras rolled in, their .30-calibre mini-guns acting like an invisible saw on the jungle, high explosive rockets whooshing from their pods.

The rockets slashed through the trees and slammed into the jungle floor, detonating with dazzling flashes followed by thick black clouds of smoke and dust that rolled up through the trees. Bobby watched one large branch spin lazily in the air, almost in slow motion, before crashing to the ground.

Spad Two-one came on the net. 'Guns on the ridge. We got guns on the ridge.'

Intermittent flashes coming from under the trees told Pasco there were more 12.7s. Without any bidding, Spad Two-two dived into the attack. Cluster munitions straddled the gun positions. To the east Pasco could see the gaggle circling, waiting to be called in.

'Shoe, can you guys get moving?'

There was a pause and then Bobby's voice crackled back over the sound of gunfire. 'Negative, Covey. We still got a lot of fire down here.'

'Roger, Shoe. Understood.'

'What have we got left?' Pasco asked the Captain.

He consulted the grease pencil notes on the side of the canopy where he tracked what loads the A-1s still carried. 'About half left,' he replied. 'I don't know where the hell the next two Spads are, but we should have some Fox-fours with us any minute.'

The team was still about five hundred metres short of the LZ and the NVA was going to fight them every step of the way. It was time to do something radical.

Spad Two-one dropped his last pair of napalm tanks across the ridge about seventy-five metres to the north of the team, while Two-two dropped another load of cluster munitions just down the slope to the east. The Cobras worked in close, and the fire directed towards the team subsided into the occasional inquisitive burst.

'What's the story, Casper?' asked Bobby mopping his face and coughing again from the smoke.

'Er . . . Choppers are running in, Shoe.'

'Roger. Drop the strings right on us. Our wounded guy will be on the first ship out, so make sure he gets some help, OK?'

'Roger, Shoe. Make sure everyone's ready to go. Casper out.'

Bobby reached between his legs, pulled the straps through and clipped them off on the V-rings. He signalled for the team to do the same.

'He ready?' asked Bobby.

Big Jack pulled tight on Simmons's harness.

'He is now.' Big Jack turned to Loc. 'Rhett, Hih, Bluh and you will go out first. We'll go out second. Understood?'

'I stay and . . .' Loc began.

'That's an order,' snapped Big Jack.

Loc nodded and moved over to tell Hih and Bluh.

'You OK, buddy?' Simmons nodded and winced in pain. Big Jack pulled one of Simmons's canteens from his gear and wetted his lips for him.

'Well, any moment now we're gonna have you out of here, eh? Pleiku. Think of them nurses, man. Great big round-eyed gals. This time tomorrow you'll be in Japan. You're one lucky cowboy.'

'Yeah. Great,' said Simmons weakly, but he smiled all the same.

To the south there was another muffled whoosh as Spad Two-two's napalm impacted the ridgeline, the thick smoke mushrooming skyward.

'White Lead is inbound to you. He'll be coming in from the west on to the northern panel. Roger that?'

'Roger that,' confirmed Bobby.

The Huey turned left and flew towards them. Zooming past the Huey came two Cobras, dropping down to prowl the ridge for targets.

The downdraft from the Huey waved the branches back and forth and rolled the smoke into tumbling waves.

The two rope bags dropped from each side of the helicopter, paying out the lift lines as they fell. The bags slammed to the ground right on the edge of the ridge. If a bag snagged in a tree, or went down the cliff, one less man would be able to leave.

Big Jack and Bobby grabbed Simmons between them and dragged him to the nearest rope bag. The Montagnards each got hold of a set of lift lines.

Snap hooks clipped on to V-rings and hands tugged vigorously to check they were secure. It took less than five seconds.

'Good luck, man,' said Bobby, as he secured Simmons.

'Thanks, Lake.'

'White Lead. Go! Go! Go!'

The helicopter accelerated vertically upwards. The loops of rope still in the bags paid out until no more slack was left. The four men suddenly shot skyward. As soon as they were off the ground, the Huey backed away from the ridge, swinging them out over the cliff and clear of the trees. Bobby watched them grow smaller and disappear. Relief swept over him. It was just him and Big Jack now, and no one was going to get them. They could run along the ridge or jump down the cliff and continue all night if they needed to.

The next helicopter began to run in towards them.

Away to the south the rapid chatter of heavy machine-gun fire began. There must have been one gun the Cobras hadn't spotted. The helicopter seemed to buck and sway in time to the sound of the firing. Tracer flashed past its nose. A puff of black smoke belched from its side and a panel fell fluttering towards the ground. The engine note surged, screamed and then died.

'Mayday! Mayday! This is White-two. Engine's out. We're going in.' The voice on the radio was strangely calm.

Bobby watched transfixed as the aircraft flashed twenty feet over their heads, its skids dragging in the trees.

The blades smashed through the foliage and the sound of rending metal filled the air.

'Covey, this is Pintail 1, checking in. We're at the RP.'

The F-4s had arrived.

'Roger, Pintail. Hang high and dry. We've just

lost a chopper down here. I'll call when I need you.'

'Roger, Covey. Pintail out.'

Bobby and Big Jack charged down the slope, expecting to receive fire at any moment.

The helicopter was lying nose down, half on its side. The tail had broken off and dangled from the branches that had caught it.

One of the pilots was climbing out through the cabin. Seeing two men running towards him, his adrenalin-swamped brain sensed danger and he scrabbled for his pistol.

'I'm American! American! It's OK,' Big Jack shouted.

The pilot said nothing to express his relief, merely turned back to the cockpit in an attempt to help his co-pilot.

'Bob, check out this guy,' said Big Jack, pointing to a body lying beside the wreck.

One of the door gunners had been thrown out on impact. Bobby rolled the body over and felt for a pulse. Nothing. The man's face was still and he was obviously at peace. Bobby noted to himself that he felt nothing, but that he would remember the moment for the rest of his life.

'He's gone.'

'OK. We're gonna have to leave him. We ain't got the time to spare.'

From farther down the slope came shouting and the odd burst of fire. The enemy was close by.

'Covey, this is Shoe . . .'

Bobby's words were interrupted as a Cobra gunship thundered overhead and began shooting at the ridge.

He tried again. 'Covey, we're at the chopper. We got bad guys close to the east of the crash site.'

'Roger, Shoe. Stand by.'

Big Jack scrambled back, dragging the three surviving flyers with him.

'Welcome to Laos,' said Bobby, amazed at his own sense of levity.

'Very fucking funny,' sneered the second door gunner, flinging away his helmet and cocking an M-16 that he had pulled from the cabin. 'What about . . .'

'He's dead,' Bobby said.

Rockets and mini-gun fire from the Cobras shredded the trees just beyond the wreckage.

'Stick with me and do what I say and we'll get out of this mess,' yelled Big Jack, above the sound of a volley of rockets.

He led the men a short way up the slope into some thick bush. He corralled the chopper crew into the cover. The co-pilot was badly hurt. His left arm was lacerated and he had dislocated his shoulder.

★

'OK, Shoe, get ready and dig in. The fast movers are gonna go to work.' Pasco's voice was as calm as ever over the radio.

'Get ready,' warned Bobby as Big Jack and the chopper crew pressed themselves on to the ground, clamping their hands over their ears and opening their mouths.

As the roar of the diving jet became deafening, Bobby yelled, 'Now!'

Everyone closed their eyes and screamed as loud as they could.

The first pair of 500-pound bombs landed just under two hundred metres away, just below the ridgeline. The concussion wave enveloped the team like an express train speeding through a station, ripping the air out of the jungle. Screaming prevented burst lungs and eardrums. The team stayed hunched on the ground as yet more debris thumped into the earth around them.

Big Jack was the first to recover, pulling the dazed crew to their feet. They dashed back to the ridge and struck out along the path towards the craters. Any NVA between them and their destination had very little chance of surviving. The Cobras circled overhead, just in case.

It took them less than five minutes to reach the two twenty-metre wide craters. They scrambled down into the bottom of the first, glad of the cover it provided.

The next bombs went in on the ridge, a hundred metres short of the proposed LZ. Huddled in the crater, the team repeated the same protective drill, feeling the bomb detonations hammer through their bodies, then they were up and moving.

'We're on the LZ. Covey, we're on the LZ!' screamed Bobby as the group found themselves in a small semi-circular clearing of waist-high elephant grass.

Out towards the west a Kingbee began its approach while the Cobras headed south to exterminate any pursuers.

'Kingbee running in,' crackled a voice on the radio.

Clang. Ping. Clang. Rounds started to hit the aircraft's side, but the Kingbee kept coming.

Bobby emptied a magazine into the jungle, then dropped to his knees, slapped in a fresh magazine and fired again. He was now into his last pouch of ammo with only four magazines remaining.

The jungle on the ridge began to disintegrate under the hail of fire from a Cobra's mini-guns. Meanwhile the Kingbee rolled into the clearing, half its fuselage suspended in space over the edge of the ridge.

Big Jack pushed the helicopter crew towards the cabin door. Bobby was still firing.

'Lake! Let's go!' Big Jack shouted. Bobby lunged at the open cabin door, followed by his team leader.

The pilot brought in the power and reversed the chopper back out over the cliff before tilting into a falling turn, letting the machine pick up speed as it flew off northwest.

One dull metallic thud was followed by another. Sunlight gleamed through bullet holes in the side of the darkened cabin. Everyone dropped to the floor. They took two more hits on the airframe, but then no more.

'We OK? Everything cool?' shouted Bobby to the Vietnamese crewman, who seemed distinctly unworried by the enemy fire. He grinned and gave a thumbs up.

Bobby eased himself up off the cold aluminium floor and slumped into a canvas seat. He ran his hand through his sweat-flattened hair. His clothes reeked of smoke and cordite. He felt as if he was going to vomit. Leaning forward he waited for it to happen, but the nausea passed. Bobby pulled his one full water bottle from its pouch and drank. He felt weak and hungry. He emptied the remaining water over his head, and fell back against the side of the cabin. He didn't think he could go through all that again if he had to.

7

The Kingbee touched down at Dak-To. As the others started to get out Bobby remained in the cabin, not sure if he was just very tired or beginning to experience mild symptoms of shock.

'OK, Lake. Let's go,' Big Jack called from outside.

Gripping both his knees to try and stop his legs collapsing beneath him, Bobby climbed out into the sunlight.

The pilot was already on the tarmac. He was a dapper-looking Vietnamese Captain, wearing a tailored black flying suit, and camouflage neck scarf.

'That was a heck of a job, man. Thanks. We owe you one,' said Bobby.

'No problem. Anytime you need, we fly,' he said, shaking Bobby's proffered hand.

Captain Gillman greeted them outside the launch-site compound.

'What's the word on Rhett?' asked Big Jack.

'Chase medics lifted him out to Leghorn,' said Gillman. 'He'll make it. He may lose the leg, but don't quote me.'

★

That evening, a Huey took the team back to Kontum.

Recon Company were on the helipad to meet them. The HQ, Communications and TOC staff swelled the numbers. A homecoming was even more poignant when the team had lost people.

Bobby and Big Jack walked through a sea of well-wishers. This was the kind of adulation Bobby had dreamed of, but it didn't seem to mean much now.

Back in the hooch, he dropped his rucksack and web gear and flopped down on his cot. There was no euphoric sense of relief, just a nagging emptiness.

Simmons's bed space looked abandoned and forlorn. Simmons was done running recon. He'd made it.

The debriefing lasted two hours. There was no point in running recon unless information was gathered.

'How high were the trees?' The Intel Sergeant spoke with a flat New York drone.

'How far apart were they spaced?'

'What was the slope of the ground?'

Bobby took it upon himself to decipher Simmons's scrawled words. Despite assertions that he was just a poor cowboy with no education, the

One-one's notes were concise and detailed.

'Could the trail be seen from the air?'

'How wide was it?'

'Were there any bicycle tracks?'

By the time the debriefing ended, it was dark.

'You did good,' said Big Jack, as they strolled over to the club.

Bobby shrugged.

'Now we've just got to get the next guy up to speed.'

'Next guy?'

'Yeah, the next guy. You're the One-one now.'

'Thanks,' said Bobby, walking again, 'but I never wanted to get the job this way.'

'Yeah. Well, that's the way it goes.'

Bobby patted his pockets for his chit book, and was irritated to discover he'd left it back in the hooch. The chit book was used in place of cash.

'No sweat, I'll get this one.' Big Jack patted him on the back.

'Forgot your chit book? That's pretty fucking irresponsible, Lake. Totally unprofessional,' said Doug Webber from his usual bar-stool perch. After nearly twenty trips over the fence and two tours, Doug had been persuaded to take it easy and he'd accepted the post of Launch-site NCO. He was a fount of knowledge on all things recon and on anything to do with alcohol. It was also rumoured that he had once shot someone's pet monkey while drunk and claimed self-defence as justification, even though the animal was chained and, unlike Webber, had a reputation for being generally docile and good-natured.

'Put your money away, Jack. I'll get these.' Doug indicated two vacant stools beside him. 'Hey! Barkeeper guy! Three whiskeys.' The ever-tolerant Vietnamese bargirl looked up from her magazine and did as she was told.

Bobby didn't like whiskey but he wasn't about to argue. Gunfighters didn't often buy him drinks, so this was a moment to be savoured.

'A toast,' said Doug. 'Fuck the gooks, and the horse they rode in on.'

Bobby had hoped for something a little more profound but he tipped the spirit down his throat and tried not to shudder.

'We gotta get you some drinking practice, son,' laughed Doug, seeing Bobby's eyes water. 'This guy any good?' he asked Big Jack.

'He's the One-one on North Dakota. I only got good men on North Dakota.'

'Ain't that the truth? That calls for another drink! Go get your chit book, son. It's your turn next.'

Bobby was glad for the temporary reprieve.

Doug played with his empty glass. 'You hear about Cooper?'

'What about him?'

'He quit.'

'Damn.'

'Up at the launch site. He just walks into Captain Gill and says he's aborting the mission.'

'Rough on the other guys.'

'He should never have come back.' Cooper had returned to CCC after being wounded on a previous tour.

Both men contemplated their glasses in silence. No one would ever criticise Cooper for quitting.

'Three more large whiskeys,' said Bobby slapping his chit book on the bar.

Big Jack retired early. For Bobby the rest of the evening became a blur of Scrabble and whiskey.

'B-A-D-I-N-A-G-E. Badinage! It's a fucking word, man!' he protested.

'It fucking ain't. What sort of word do you call that!' snorted Doug.

'It's more of a word than Snafu. It's like talking shit. You know, badinage. French originally.'

Challenging Bobby to Scrabble, in the full knowledge that he had been a Harvard man, wasn't perhaps the smartest move Doug had ever made.

'You like shit, kid?' asked Doug, as he totted up the score.

'Huh?'

'Do you like shit?'

'What do you mean, shit?'

'There ain't a fucking right or wrong answer here, Lake. Do you like shit or not? Yes or no.'

'You mean drugs?' asked Bobby.

'What are you, some sort of dope-head? You a fucking hippie, man? You into all that free love and shit?'

'If it's free, I am!' Bobby beamed.

The small crowd of Scrabble experts, watching the game, cracked up with laughter.

'Fuck! You are one dumb college boy!' declared Doug, wiping his eyes. 'I mean human shit. Do you like it?'

'Do you?'

'Sure! Down in Saigon they got this team of doctors who analyse NVA shit. They can tell what the gooks are eating, if they got any disease or stuff. One day they're gonna send you out on the trail to pick up shit.'

'That's bullshit, Doug,' called a voice from over his shoulder.

'No, it's North Vietnamese shit!'

It wasn't that funny, but Bobby thought he would die laughing.

★

Bobby knew he looked ridiculous wearing his OG cut-offs, Hawaiian shirt and Ray-bans. The world was just too bright that morning, and there was a dull throbbing from behind his eyes.

The mess hall was almost empty. Most people had already had breakfast and gone to work, but Bobby had time off and time to kill.

Carlos wandered in. 'Thought I'd find you here. I thought you'd want to know, Simmons's OK.'

'That's great. How's his leg?'

'He'll walk. He ain't gonna run no more recon.'

Carlos got himself some coffee and joined Bobby, who was hoping that the caffeine would jolt him from his hung-over daze.

'I was Chase medic yesterday. Saw the whole thing. The bombing, the chopper getting shot down. Talk about wild.'

'Believe me, you don't want any part of it.'

'Aw, come on, Bob. You got a spare slot on your team. You could put in a good word for me.'

'I don't run the team. Big Jack's got his own ideas.'

'C'mon, man. You gotta do this for me,' said Carlos. 'What do you say? You and me, man. We could be a great team.'

'OK, I'll talk to Big Jack, but if I get you in, I get to fuck one of your sisters. Deal?'

'Get me on recon, man, and you can fuck my whole fucking family.' Carlos grinned from ear to ear.

Head still throbbing, Bobby drifted back to the hooch to find Big Jack packing up Simmons's kit, separating the military equipment from the personal stuff. Simmons didn't seem to have much in the way of belongings.

There was a knock at the door.

'We go now?' Loc asked.

'Back in four days, OK? You understand? Four days,' said Big Jack, holding up four fingers. 'And take it easy, you guys. Get some rest.'

Loc, Bluh and Hih would go back to their village to see Kreh and Mee's families and tell them how their men died.

Bobby hauled Simmons's kit bag over to the supply room, while Big Jack took the personal belongings over to the HQ building.

'Beach club?' Big Jack asked.

'Sure. As long as we take it easy on the whiskey.'

Bobby changed into his regulation fatigues. Unlike those that he used for training, or ran recon in, these fatigues sported all the badges and name tags you'd expect to see on a normal 5th SFG soldier serving in Vietnam. Big Jack did the same.

They found a jeep and a driver who drove them north down Highway 14, through the village of

Plei Groi and over the river into Kontum. It was the capital of Kontum province. The centre of the town was lined with old French colonial buildings, and looked little different from how it must have done twenty years before. To the northeast of the town was the airbase. After visiting the PX, and putting their names down on the list for a flight down to Saigon, they found a bar that claimed to be a restaurant by virtue of having a few tables away from the bar and a hand-written menu.

The meal was fairly disgusting. The rice tasted musty and the fish soup was mainly water. Bobby had made a serious effort to embrace Vietnamese culture, but at times like this he found it hard going. For example, instead of keeping beer in an icebox, the Vietnamese served beer with the ice floating in it. There was no hope for this country.

Bobby pushed his bowl away. He used his chopsticks to drum on the greasy tabletop. 'I know this guy who works in the dispensary. He's a buddy of mine. He really wants to run recon.'

Big Jack stared dolefully at the contents of his bowl. 'Good for him.'

'I know him from Bragg. He's a medic.'

'Medic's good but we need a gunfighter.'

'Sure, I know that, but . . .'

'No buts. I know this guy's your buddy and all, but you got to be certain he's the right man for the job. We ain't got time to experiment. Think you could trust him on a team?' asked Big Jack.

'Sure.'

'What's his name?'

'Nunez, Carlos Nunez.'

'He's a Mex?'

'From El Paso.'

Big Jack took a long swig of watery beer.

'I'll have a word with the Sergeant Major,' he said, 'but if this guy isn't up to speed within a week, he's off. I'm cutting him no slack. OK?'

'OK.'

The two men sat in silence for a while. A slight frown from Big Jack suggested to Bobby that he should quit playing with his chopsticks.

'When did you first come here?' he asked eventually.

'Did my first tour back in '63.'

'So, what's different between now and then?'

'More than you can imagine.' Big Jack leaned back in his chair. 'In those days, it was our war. We were the only guys here doing any fighting. We had a bunch of Marine and Army helicopters, but that was about it. It was a real sweet deal. Some guys got Yard wives. No one was on our backs. We've gone full circle.'

'Full circle?' Two fresh glasses of beer arrived.

'Sure. We were just here as advisers. Now we

got a couple of hundred thousand guys in the country and half the damn' Air Force, and what does Nixon want to do? Send them all back home, and let the Vietnamese do the fighting. That's a mistake waiting to happen.'

'Worked for the Koreans.' Bobby was repeating received wisdom he had heard from elsewhere.

'Took those guys ten years and the war was over for most of that time. The Vietnamese ain't the Koreans. First, we got to win the war, and then we train them to win the next one.'

'How the hell are we gonna do that?'

'Same way you win any war, son. Look, the VC are screwed. They've pretty much ceased to exist since Tet in '68. The NVA are a conventional army. There's no way they can win while we're here. They're gonna have to wait till we've gone.'

'And by then we'll have trained ARVN up,' said Bobby, as if delivering the punch line.

'No way we can do that in two or three years. Nixon wants us all home in time for re-election. The only thing that's gonna save this country is a real solid peace treaty, and the NVA don't honour treaties.'

'So what are we doing here? Are you telling me this is all bullshit?'

'It ain't bullshit. It's just war. Don't take it

personally. The boys in Washington are trying to do their job, and we're trying to do ours. The best we can.'

'The sooner people wise up and recognise we've lost this war, the better,' said Seth.

'Why do they have to lose? Why can't they just leave?' asked Rachel.

'If they don't lose, the Generals will just start another war. We've got to pull with our North Vietnamese brothers to stop that happening,' explained Seth, as though it was all too obvious.

The students nodded in agreement, but Rachel didn't look convinced. She didn't like Seth. She didn't trust him. She knew a small-town hustler when she saw one, and Seth was just another snake-oil salesman with a better line of merchandise. Anti-war was a big thing on campus and that made Seth a big man.

Rachel had a straightforward view about Vietnam. She wanted the US out of the war and for Bobby to come home.

Seth wanted military victory for the North, not because he was a Communist, but because that would tell the world that his parents and all their friends were wrong, and he was right.

'Rachel, babe. You've got a friend over there, right?'

'Yeah. I know someone in the Army,' Rachel replied.

'He's a Green Beret, right?' said Seth. 'Well, those Green Berets are like the Gestapo. Do you actually know what Green Berets do?'

'They're like commandos. They work with partisans,' said Rachel, repeating the explanation Bobby had given her.

'That may be what they tell you, but that ain't the truth,' Seth sneered. 'Forget all that John Wayne movie shit. They're bad people.'

'You don't even know my friend. He's not a bad person. He just wants to serve his country.'

Seth sucked on his cigarette and blew smoke into the air. 'He may not be a bad guy, but I'll tell you for free, he's doing bad things.'

'Like what?'

Seth looked around the table, as if waiting for some of the other students to volunteer a reply, but none came. 'Like torture. Like rape. Killing kids.'

'Bobby would never do anything like that!'

'Fight terror with terror, babe. That's what they do, Rachel, even your little friend. They'll get him so psyched up, he'll do anything they tell him to. He'll rape, torture . . .'

The slap nearly knocked Seth off his chair. Rachel snatched up her coat and bag and stormed out.

*

Rachel seemed to have grown up a lot, yet she still looked the same. She had told Bobby she hated having her picture taken, but he had begged for a photograph. It showed her sitting on the porch of her father's house, staring self-consciously at the camera. Her attempt at a smile hadn't quite succeeded and she looked as if she would be having more fun at the dentist. Was there a deeper message in her expression? Had she found someone else?

It's just a picture, Bobby reasoned. She'd tell me if there was something wrong, wouldn't she? I tell her the truth, don't I? Well, I tell her the truth about how I feel.

Maybe Rachel had grown up too much, become too cynical to believe the promise Bobby had made not to die in Vietnam, to come back and see her. Two years later, he knew now that it was a naive promise made by a naive young man. But it was a promise he intended to keep.

Back at Kontum, training began again.

While everybody respected the fact that even as a new guy you had skills and training, no one was going to trust you till they knew you could do the job under fire. If Carlos didn't make the grade in training, he was off the team. It was nothing personal; it was just how things worked.

The Yards seemed to like Bobby's friend. They even forgave him for being a *Bandito*. Carlos looked Mexican, and the often-shown US Westerns usually depicted Mexicans in a less than favourable light. Mexicans weren't as bad as Indians, but they certainly weren't John Wayne.

The Montagnards loved Westerns so much that they were banned from carrying weapons when they attended camp movie nights. There was always the danger that they would get so excited they would completely lose their cool and join in any gun battle on screen.

The Westerns usually depicted Mexicans as either vicious and often cowardly thugs or helpless dirt farmers and peasants. The Montagnards were curious to know which stereotype Carlos fitted. Farmers didn't seem too good with guns or fighting, so it was probably better to be a *Bandito*.

Christmas came and went, and 1970 dawned without much comment from anyone.

The next One-zero course at Long Thanh wasn't due to be run for a while, so Carlos would get all his training on the job.

'What we have here is a claymore, with a forty-five-second pull igniter.' Bobby demonstrated to Carlos the contents of the pocket sewn on to the top flap of his rucksack. Every member of North Dakota carried a claymore in the same fashion.

'If we're being chased, someone will pull this out, tug on the fuse, and leave it pointing down the trail. The bad guys should run right into it. If you ever need to dump the radio, then you'll need to destroy it. That'd be another good use for this baby.'

'Cool,' said Carlos.

Some men claimed it was enough just to leave a burning pull fuse lying in the bushes by the trail. The enemy would recognise the smoke and retreat in terror.

Bobby went on to explain about the M-14 toe-popper anti-personnel mines, and the self-destruct kits that destroyed the mine, anywhere from several hours to several weeks later. This was pretty important stuff to know, as at least two recon personnel had trodden on mines laid earlier by other teams.

The sun began to get low in the sky, casting long shadows across the range. North Dakota had spent the day training.

'Can I get a group picture of you guys?' Carlos produced a camera he had bought at the PX in Da-Nang.

Big Jack didn't raise any objection, and the

Montagnards were always keen to strike heroic poses.

The team hammed it up while Carlos tried to frame the picture.

Bloop!

Everyone froze. Hih, who now carried the M-79, had accidentally fired a round straight up into the air. It would take only three or four seconds for it to fall to earth and detonate.

The team dropped to the ground and prayed.

The round landed harmlessly about fifty metres away. Loc was first to his feet and immediately set about the offender with a torrent of French military abuse followed up by a succession of kicks and slaps. Hih, knowing himself to be in the wrong, didn't even try defending himself.

'Hih, how much you wanna pay?' asked Big Jack. Hih was going to have to be fined.

Loc translated for both men. 'He say one hundred piastres, *Trung-Si*.' One hundred piastres being the normal fine for the accidental firing of a weapon.

'One hundred piastres is good for one shoot carbine. M-79 not same-same. Much bigger.'

Two hundred piastres was Hih's next offer, which represented a substantial portion of his monthly pay cheque.

'Can we try that again without any firing?' Carlos asked, aiming his camera

★

The life of a tribal mercenary wasn't an easy one and the Montagnards had a tough time of it. Often, they just decided they needed a break and would wander up to the One-zero and say something like, 'Brother die. I go now.'

What they were really saying was, 'I've been fighting since I was fourteen or fifteen. I'm twenty now, and I want to have some time off.'

To Bobby it seemed as if they lived in a dark and fearful world of war without end. He would go home one day. They'd still be here, either fighting for or against the South Vietnamese and desperate to protect their homes from the Communists.

Replacing Kreh and Mee were Rah and Truc. Rah had been recruited on Loc's recommendation. This was his first mission. Loc had declared him ready and Big Jack needed no other seal of approval. Truc had run recon before. He was the sole Montagnard survivor of a group recruited on to his original team back in 1968. Weary of combat, he had gone back to his village. It was only Loc's insistence that Big Jack was a good man that had persuaded him to return.

8

After two weeks they pulled another mission, an area recon on a suspected enemy base area, just inside Laos. Highway 968 ran across the north of the area. Other teams had worked the area on a regular basis and most had hit trouble. Practice was over. It was game time.

For the first day they moved slowly. Big Jack's plan was to criss-cross the target area in a Z-pattern looking for signs of trails or camps. As always, they stayed clear of the ridges and the valley floors. The enemy frequented both. Despite the fact that Loc found numerous tracks or signs that small groups were patrolling the area, for all of the second day they saw and heard nothing.

On the morning of the third day, they stumbled across a well-worn trail. Only about four to six feet wide, it exactly followed the contours of the hillside, weaving its way through the trees so as to be invisible from the air. They noted its position and took cover to watch for a couple of hours.

Thirty minutes passed. With the team hardly daring to breathe, over three hundred men marched past them, no more than twenty feet away. Immediately they coded a message and tried to pass it to Covey, but no one was listening. Another twenty minutes dragged by before they managed to make contact, but by then the target had melted away.

They hung on a little while longer, then altered their position.

Late-afternoon the next day, the team worked its way carefully down a thickly wooded slope, towards a position where they planned to cross the stream marked on the map and then to move south along the side of the valley. About three hundred metres short of the crossing point, they found themselves overlooking two bomb craters.

It seemed like a good spot to take a break. The nearer they got to the stream, the thicker the jungle would become, and the crossing would be dangerous. Resting up for five minutes would ensure everyone was fresh again.

Bobby scribbled a few observations, and took a gulp of water from the canteen that was passed around. He was just putting away his notebook when something made him jump.

Clack, clack. The sound of two bamboo poles being banged together. Very close.

Clack, clack. This time further away and slightly to the north. Another group of trackers was closing in to cut them off.

Carlos had never heard the sound before, but like everyone else he knew what it meant.

Big Jack led the team quickly down towards the stream. If they were being followed, then it was better to trade speed for caution.

The idea was that the enemy would figure they were going to try and lose their pursuers in the thicker bush at the bottom of the valley. But just short of the stream, North Dakota would loop back on their own trail and ambush the trackers. The technique was called fish hooking.

Shafts of sunlight shone through the high tree canopy, casting jagged shadows across the team. There was neither sign nor sound of the enemy. If the trackers were using dogs, then there was always a chance that the ambush could be detected. Big Jack had sprinkled CS gas powder on their back trail. The howl of a dog in severe discomfort would at least give North Dakota some warning.

The silence was palpable.

Thirty long minutes passed, and Big Jack decided that if they stayed put any longer the trackers had won.

Bobby felt drained. As he rose slowly to his feet, a hand fell on his shoulder.

Carlos pointed his weapon back down towards the stream.

'Someone's there,' he mouthed silently.

Bobby listened intently. Nothing. He looked over at Loc, whose expression confirmed his worst fear. There were bad guys down there.

What should they do? Stay put until it got dark and try and break out? That would allow the enemy a couple more hours to bring in extra troops, and while it wasn't totally impossible for aircraft to support the team in darkness, it would be difficult, especially in thick jungle where the team's infrared-covered strobe lights might not be seen.

Doing nothing was out of the question. Big Jack made a signal for Loc to lead off, very quietly, back the way they had come.

Everyone expected the silence, at any moment, to be ripped apart by gunfire. Bobby found himself almost wishing for anything that might break the tension.

Eventually, they made it back to the lower edge of one of the craters. It was beginning to get dark. They warned Covey that they could get hit anytime, and he'd better have some air support stood by.

As the dull light seeped away, they slipped from

the jungle into the craters. They afforded good cover and the opportunity for short ladder LZ.

The team checked their pen-flares and strobe lights. They placed the claymores out beyond the rim of the crater. Magazines and grenades were laid out, ready and within easy reach.

Bobby awoke with a start. He looked at his watch. It was only 21.00 hours. To the north, he could hear the intermittent rumbling of the nightly American effort to thwart the movement of supplies down the trail.

A few of the men had heads nodding with fatigue, but most lay still, weapon in hand, listening for any sign of movement from the jungle beyond. Both Big Jack and Carlos were wide awake, making Bobby feel guilty at having dropped off.

The night was cool and clear. Above, the stars were as bright as they were in Kentucky. At any other time and in any other place, Bobby knew he would love to be out on a night like this, but right now, here, he wanted the dawn and extraction. Down by the stream, the enemy had been able to get very close, and if Carlos hadn't noticed them, North Dakota might have blundered straight into the ambush.

*

Tension tightened like a noose. All the men were sure they heard the swish of a branch and the crack of a twig. Then nothing. It could have been an elephant. Despite their size, wild elephants could move with incredible stealth, and at least one member of CCC had been badly injured by a stampeding pachyderm that had been surprised by a recon team.

The rest of the night passed fitfully as a series of unidentifiable noises kept everyone on edge.

Just before dawn Covey was overhead, and glad to hear the team was alive and well. The dawn's soft half-light revealed a group of dust-coated men looking tired and drawn.

'We'll try and get out of here and continue with the mission,' Big Jack explained to Covey.

Bobby's heart sank. He was sure they'd be extracted at dawn, but he knew they'd only done half the job.

After repacking the claymores and magazines, Big Jack climbed from the crater first and made his way to the tree line. The rest of the team covered him, anticipating enemy fire at any moment. Bobby was conscious he was a witness to an act of pure bravery.

One by one the rest of the team followed until everyone was huddled into the bushes above the crater. They'd made it.

A single shot rang out from below. It was impossible to tell how far away. There was another shot. Bobby ducked instinctively. This one came from the south, as if answering the other. Maybe the trackers had been alerted by the sound of Covey passing overhead or maybe they'd spent the whole night out in the jungle and needed to check where they were. Either way it was bad.

The team pushed up the slope, again trading speed for stealth.

A night out in the cold mountain air had left muscles stiff and tense. Hih lagged behind. Bobby stopped and pushed the young Montagnard forward.

The team crashed through the undergrowth, constantly changing direction and pace. After some ten minutes they slowed and regained the security of silence and the anonymity of stealth.

The water was cold. Only knee-deep and a couple of feet across; in the rainy season it would be a torrent. Having pushed on up the far slope, they followed the contour of the valley before taking up a defensive position. The only sounds were the breeze in the trees and the occasional call of birds.

Twenty-four hours later, Bobby scrambled up the ladder and into the cabin of a hovering Huey.

'Why didn't they attack?' Carlos asked as he and Bobby strolled into the launch site.

'Fucked if I know,' said Bobby.

'Is it always this much fun?'

'Right up to the point where someone gets their head blown off.'

Back in the hooch, they began the post-mission ritual of cleaning weapons and checking equipment. Every magazine had to be emptied, to rest the springs. Every item needed constant checking. It could be as mundane as sharpening your knife or as vital as checking all the radios. Bobby found his strobe light didn't work, and went to the supply shed to get a new one. Big Jack came along, to pick up a new canteen cover.

'So did Carlos do OK?' asked Bobby.

'You ran the same mission I did. You tell me.'

'I think he did good. We'd have been in the shit if he hadn't heard those guys down by the stream.'

Big Jack nodded in agreement.

'That was scary, wasn't it? Down by the stream.'

'You were scared?'

'Well . . . I mean, I wasn't . . .'

'I was scared,' said Big Jack. 'Don't confuse being scared with being a coward. Ain't nothing wrong with being scared. In fact, if you ain't scared, I don't want you on the team. You know what? Most guys are scared of being scared. They're more scared of that than they are of the gooks. I seen men hardly able to walk with fear, climb on Hueys and run missions. We got guys here that would rather die than admit they're scared.'

Bobby stayed silent.

'One day you could be a One-zero, and you don't want to be one of those guys who'll get a bunch of folks killed trying to prove that you're not scared. Balls ain't nothing without judgement, son. Day you forget that, then you'll buy the farm, for sure.'

It was early evening in the club, and Bobby sauntered over to where a small group of gunfighters were huddled around a Staff Sergeant he hadn't seen before. Some looked up and nodded, acknowledging Bobby's presence. The Staff Sergeant went on speaking.

'All I'm saying is, the overnight team positions are passed up to the STD, and fuck knows who gets to see them after that.' Staff Sergeant turned out to be a former recon team member, now working at MAC-V Headquarters in Saigon.

'You can't trust those fuckers in the STD,' remarked a gunfighter.

The STD was the Vietnamese equivalent of SOG. It was well known that the Vietnamese military was vastly corrupt at all levels, which made it a breeding ground for betrayal. Most people believed that the North Vietnamese Intelligence agency, the Trinh Sat, had infiltrated the STD.

Bobby vividly remembered the day RT Maryland disappeared off the face of the earth, somewhere in Laos. He had only been at Kontum a month when it happened. Maryland had checked in as 'Team OK' after they were inserted and no one ever saw or heard of them again. The Bright Light had gone in to search for them. No bodies, no equipment, no nothing.

'So what do you suggest?' asked a gunfighter.

'Be fucking careful. Code up your position three hundreds metres away from where you actually are. Do whatever it takes,' said the Staff Sergeant.

'Just another thing we got to deal with,' said Bobby.

Hearing what Bobby said, the Staff Sergeant looked up.

'Oh, yeah? And who the fuck are you?'

'Bob Lake.'

'It's OK. He runs recon. North Dakota,' added one of the gunfighters.

'Well, you sure got that right, Lake,' said the Staff Sergeant. 'It's another thing you got to deal with.'

★

Much later that evening, Bobby was laughing so much he thought he would bust. Bill Emerson was recounting the story of a friend of his who had been a One-one on prisoner snatch in Laos. 'So they get his hands tied, and figure that's it. Time to go home,' explained Bill, 'when suddenly the little fucker is up and off down trail.'

Bill stood with his hands clasped behind his back and ran vigorously on the spot.

'So the team's just sort of standing there thinking, How the hell did that happen? And John's telling the Yards, "For fuck's sake, don't shoot!" and takes off after the guy. Next thing you know there's all this shooting, and everyone figures John's bought it. Then back round the corner he comes, running like hell. He goes straight past the team, and Luke yells after him, "Hey, John. Where's the prisoner?" '

The audience collapsed in laughter.

'You ever get one?' asked Bobby, wiping the tears from his eyes.

'Yeah,' said Bill, 'but it didn't work out so good.'

'In what way?'

'I shot him,' came the matter-of-fact reply. 'After I grabbed him, he just kept screaming. I didn't have anything to gag him with, and I'd used my last field dressing on one of the Yards, so when he wouldn't shut up, I shot him.'

★

Big Jack, Bobby, Carlos and Bill stayed late in the club, and after it closed, they decided to try the Covey riders' bar.

'Jesus Christ, Covey, you almost burnt the whole fucking team!' said John Pasco from behind the bar, in what was supposed to be an imitation of Bobby's radio call after the A-1 had dumped napalm close to the team.

'Yeah, well, I forgive you,' said Bobby.

'That's mighty big of you. We got you out, didn't we?' said Pasco.

'So what are you drinking?' asked Bobby.

Around three in the morning, someone produced a Berretta pistol with a silencer. It was kept around the Covey riders' club for vermin control. There was an absolute rule that you never fired a weapon in camp. The camp could come under attack at any time and even a single shot would bring everyone out on to the wall, ready for action.

The silencer made it almost inaudible and ideal for an impromptu beer-bottle competition.

No one seemed too worried that they were all too fucked up to handle firearms safely, or that they stood little chance of hitting anything. The beer bottles were placed on top of a fifty-gallon drum by the fence and the competition began.

Two problems immediately became apparent. The first was that if a bullet hit the drum, it made a very loud noise, and the second was that any bullet that didn't hit the drum or the beer bottle went straight through the fence and into the latrine block wall beyond. Each time a round struck the drum, with a resounding and gong-like clang, there was a drunken 'Shhh', followed by stifled laughter and the pistol was passed to the next man to try his luck. Every other round, the Berretta jammed and finally the competition was abandoned.

Some time before dawn, Bobby crawled into bed.

'I need every swinging dick! Get your shit and get out to the pad, we got guys in trouble,' roared the Recon Company First Sergeant from the door of his office.

'What's up?' asked Bobby, as he broke open a box of two hundred linked rounds for the M-60 machine gun.

'Carolina's been hit, and are running. The Bright Light needs help, and there's no one left up at the launch site,' said Mitch Barker, fusing grenades.

At Dak-To a sad-looking Captain Gillman met the ragtag band of fifteen men. 'Stand down, guys. We've got them out. They're on their way back.'

Relief swept over the team.

'They're coming in on strings. We've lost someone, but I don't know who.' Gillman scratched his chin. 'We'll just have to wait and see.'

No one liked waiting to find out which of their buddies hadn't made it.

The late-afternoon sun cast long shadows, and the men shielded their eyes as they squinted into the west for the first sign of the Hueys. Bobby almost wished they wouldn't come.

A shout went up as the gaggle appeared from the haze. Two dark clumps of bodies hung on hundred-foot ropes below the aircraft. A body bag and stretcher were brought over to await the casualty. The group fell silent and cigarettes were extinguished in respect.

The men on the ropes were clinging together to form a bundle, which was lowered gingerly on to the runway. Hands reached up to help as the haggard men of RT Carolina collapsed in a heap, their legs drained of blood and sensation from the STABO rig straps which cut into their thighs.

Men moved quickly to help unclip the snap links, and the ropes twirled and danced in the downdraft.

Some of the arrivals were wounded. All were dazed and in shock, but one lay still amongst the other moving shapes.

The stretcher was carried over to the second

group. Carlos was hunched over the figure making absolutely sure that the man was dead. The others helped the living. A medic unrolled the body bag, which flapped in the rotor wash.

'Who is it?' called Bobby.

'It's Bill. Bill Emerson.'

A cold hand gripped Bobby's heart.

Not Bill, he thought. Please God, not Bill. I liked him. He was better at this than I was. If they can kill Bill, they can kill me too.

9

It was nearly a month since Bill Emerson had died.

Bobby, Big Jack and Carlos were using the late afternoon to make final adjustments to their equipment. The hooch was littered with claymores, blocks of C-4, CS gas grenades and ammunition boxes.

This was going to be Carlos's third mission and Bobby's sixth. Their last trip over the fence had been 'a dry hole'. The team uncovered a few discarded ammunition crates and signs of human habitation but, by the time the North Dakota arrived on the scene, everyone was long gone.

The Intel Sergeant turned up with a small wooden crate. 'This is for you,' he said, dumping the crate at Big Jack's feet. 'Three rounds of Eldest Son, 82mm,' he declared. 'There's some reported ammo caches in the area you're working. We'd like you to try and slip this in.'

Eldest Son was the codename for carefully doctored rounds of ammunition, which, when fired, blew the weapon to pieces, usually killing the soldier holding it. The mortar bombs killed anyone standing close by.

'Take it away, son,' said Big Jack, kicking the box dismissively. 'We ain't taking it. You want to go get us some of that AK ammunition, we'll be glad to see what we can do, but I ain't humping that across Cambodia for you. Give it to a Hatchet Force platoon. You can't slow down a recon team with stuff like that.'

Without a word, the Intel Sergeant picked up the box and walked out. The One-zero's word was law and you didn't argue. He came back about twenty minutes later with two AK magazines. Loaded into each was one doctored AK round.

'Here's your money, Bob. Thanks,' said Carlos, dropping a wad of grimy dollar bills on Bobby's cot.

'That's OK,' he said, pocketing the cash Carlos had borrowed earlier. 'You rob a bank?'

Carlos splayed his poker winnings out on his blanket. 'Sure did,' he chuckled. 'Five aces.'

'Are you still saving for a car?' asked Bobby.

'Got to get back home first.'

'Well, just make sure you don't piss it all away.'

'Thanks, Pa. What are you? My father? It's not like we're talking big bucks here, Bob,' said Carlos.

'Yeah, but the money helps.'

'You'd be here even if they didn't pay you a cent, wouldn't you?'

Bobby looked up from his book. 'Why do you say that?'

'I know you got your reasons, man, but you ain't ever been poor.'

'Sure I have.'

'When?'

'When you had my fifty bucks.'

The launch site for the next mission was Plei Jerang, a Special Forces camp forty-five miles south-southwest of Kontum.

MAC-V was increasing the intensity of operations in Cambodia. Two CCC teams were due to insert that day, and North Dakota was going to be the second.

Bobby and Doug Webber watched the first team walk out to the choppers. They were dressed in NVA uniform and all carried Soviet or Chinese weapons.

'I don't trust that little fucker,' said Doug, referring to the other team's former NVA scout, 'I don't trust any fucker who changes sides.'

'Hell, Doug, he didn't get fed for nearly a week. All his buddies got killed, and he never got re-supplied. Defecting was the right thing to do,' said Bobby. Thousands of former VC had surrendered under the 'Choi Hoi' or open arms programme. Subsequently, many NVA had started to do the same. Food shortages and the general hardship of life in the NVA convinced a whole bunch of people that they were not going to emerge on the winning side.

'I had another one on my team back in '68,' said Doug. 'We never gave him any ammo, and we made him walk point.'

'He must have loved that,' said Bobby.

'He was a smart little fucker. Warned us about an ambush once and showed us all sorts of stuff.'

'Well, that takes balls,' said Bobby, 'I can't imagine running recon with no ammo.'

Doug nodded. 'He had balls, all right.'

'So what happened to him?'

'Got his balls blown off.'

The team burst from the door of the Kingbee into a clearing of elephant grass and lay still.

The big helicopter clattered away.

Welcome to Cambodia, welcome to Salem House, Bobby thought to himself as he tagged on to the second-last place in the column. The mission was a point recon, ten kilometres inside the border. Unlike Laos, the area was flat, low-lying and heavily forested. If Laos was bad, Cambodia was worse. Only recently, Salem House operations had claimed an entire CCC team, RT Pennsylvania. An

RPG had struck their Huey just as it lifted the team out of the LZ. No bodies had been recovered.

To make matters worse, politics meant no team could be supported by fast movers or A-1s. Their only support was Cobras.

As if the job wasn't tough enough, mused Bobby.

They snaked slowly north through the forest. It was hot and dry, and careless steps caused leaves to crackle underfoot.

Close to last light they found a good overnight position. The claymores were positioned and the check in with SPAF-4 completed.

Bobby looked up through a latticed tangle of branches to the stars, the only points of light in a stygian world. He brought his knees up, folded his arms on top, and let his head rest against them, his carbine cradled against his chest.

A faraway squeak of brakes cut through the still night, followed by the slamming of a door.

For the next twenty minutes they all listened to the sound of trucks arriving and departing. They were being driven slowly and in a low gear.

'Shall I see if I can get anyone?' whispered Carlos, powering up the radio.

'No point,' replied Big Jack, 'Cobras can't work at night.'

Big Jack had laid down clear instructions on the

subject of enemy night sweeps. You didn't move or fire until they were so close that the next thing they would do was step on you. The logic was simple. A great many NVA night sweeps relied on spooking the teams into moving, then driving them towards ambushes. If you stayed put and sweated it out, you had a reasonable chance that the troops would just move past, oblivious to your presence. The downside was that the enemy might have followed your trail and would then use the night to truck in more troops and surround you.

Was that what had happened to RT Maryland? The thought that the NVA might creep up in the night and slaughter them as they slept meant Bobby was inclined to castigate himself for losing consciousness, but you had to sleep or else you were no good to anyone.

Bobby awoke several times an hour, almost expecting to see an NVA soldier standing a few feet away. For a while he had fixated on a curious, dark shape among the trees that seemed to move the more he stared at it. He knew his eyes were playing tricks, but that was little comfort. Daybreak confounded his dark imaginings.

The next morning Carlos looked wiped out. Bobby was sure he looked just as bad. Big Jack seemed as fresh as normal.

Covey checked in and picked up the truck report. The morning routine complete, North Dakota went to work.

Loc sniffed the air almost like an animal. After a frozen minute, he started to walk backwards slowly. Big Jack covered him until he had passed, and then followed the Montagnard's example. All the team retreated into a defensive position.

Big Jack signalled to Bobby. 'Bad guys up ahead. We're gonna try and work round them.'

They stopped again, all straining to hear any tell-tale signs of danger.

Here we go again, thought Bobby, smiling at Hih. Bobby had developed a habit of smiling at the Montagnards during moments of tension. You can't be scared if you're smiling. Smile and the whole world smiles with you. Smile and . . .

'*Dia, Mau-len, eh*,' an unseen Vietnamese called out. Bobby jumped, and swung his weapon towards the sound.

The voice called again, this time further away, and someone else replied.

Much to Bobby's surprise, instead of moving back the way they had come, Big Jack slowly led North Dakota forward.

He waved Bobby over to join him.

About fifteen metres away, above the bushes, was the canvas tilt of a truck, which had been expertly reversed under a tree and could not be spotted from the air.

Big Jack pointed to his eyes then pointed back at the truck. Carefully both men dropped their rucksacks and inched their way forward.

A figure walked round the back of the truck, pith helmet just visible above the undergrowth, the rest of his body partially obscured. Big Jack and Bobby crouched down, their weapons trained on the figure. The soldier took a few steps nearer to the Americans, then stopped and started fiddling with his trousers. There was the sound of water trickling on to the ground.

Bobby found himself trapped partway between terror and hysterical laughter.

After what seemed like an age, the man zipped up and wandered away.

Big Jack signalled a retreat. It was obviously too risky to advance any closer.

The team made its way west again, but, with the enemy so close, they barely covered fifty metres during the next hour. Each step was a carefully planned operation. Once more Bobby felt tension gnaw away at his resolve.

Loc pointed out another truck, also parked carefully to take advantage of natural cover. They crept about twenty metres past it, until they came to a track.

They had to cross it.

Big Jack checked his watch. It was nearly midday, Poc time, the noontime break that most Vietnamese observed. So ingrained into the culture was Poc time that at least one recon team, who were certain they were being followed, had actually run down Highway 110 during Poc and not encountered another living soul. It was the sort of trick you only got away with once, but it made a great story back in the club.

Loc checked left, followed by Big Jack who looked in the other direction. Carlos waited like a sprinter in the blocks. Big Jack held a white phosphorous grenade, with the pin straightened, so that he could pull it with his teeth. If they hit trouble, the smoke would provide near-instant cover.

He signalled and Bluh leapt across the track, disappearing into the bushes on the other side. After a suitable pause Carlos followed. Then the rest of the team did the same, each man taking care only to step once on the packed dirt between the tyre ruts. Big Jack joined them last, using his bush hat to brush out the single smudge of footprints.

North Dakota pressed deep into the bush and stayed put while Big Jack, Carlos and Bobby checked the exact location on the map and scribbled in their notebooks.

Carlos coded up a report on the truck park and tried to raise Covey. No answer. He and Bobby double-checked the frequencies. The radio appeared to be working fine, but no one was listening. Yet again, they had found a target and couldn't raise Covey. It was frustrating as hell.

'What about laying some toe-poppers?' whispered Bobby.

Big Jack shook his head. Sure, it would be nice to take out one of the truck drivers but it would alert the NVA to their presence. If the driver got out of his truck, then came back an hour later and got his leg blown off, the first thing the NVA would do would be to check for signs of a recon team. Besides, it was always better to save toe-poppers for trackers.

The desire to fight and kill the enemy had to be resisted constantly. The mission came first. Big Jack was sure that one or two of his lost friends had been unable to resist the impulse for action, and landed themselves in more trouble than they could handle. There was a popular cartoon pinned on almost every noticeboard in Special Forces showing a gnarled old vulture perched on a tree. 'Patience my ass,' read the caption. 'I want to go out and kill something.'

Satisfied they could do no more, Big Jack led the team away from the truck park and pushed further west to get round it.

Bobby always saved a small amount of his bland morning rice ration for the midday halt. Eating little and often was a good way of maintaining energy levels. In the evening he would have his cold gourmet C-ration tin of meat. There were very few overweight men running recon.

This was now the height of the dry season, and the forest was bereft of even the slightest breeze. In the briefing, the men had been told to carry a lot of water. The area didn't have any notable streams or rivers, and every water source was carefully watched. The team only ever drank at rest halts, first from the canteens carried in the rucksack pockets, the logic being that if you had to dump the sack, you still had water on your belt. Big Jack insisted that team members pass around canteens until they were empty, so as not to risk the noise of individual, half-filled canteens.

Later that afternoon they came across two large pits, about twenty feet long, ten feet wide and six feet deep. The dugout earth had settled and small tufts of vegetation had begun to grow there.

Beyond the pits, a narrow footpath ran back to the trail.

After taking photographs the team withdrew a short way while Big Jack made notes and checked the map for their exact location.

'Looks like burial pits,' he whispered.

That's good, thought Bobby. If the NVA are digging mass graves in Cambodia, we must be hurting them.

Ahead of them the brush had been cleared and there was open ground between the trees.

Loc halted, and motioned Big Jack forward. Wisps of grey smoke drifted through the jungle in front. A faint smell of cooking permeated the air. Loc was angry with himself for not having noticed it sooner, but there was no wind.

About fifteen metres away, an AK lay propped against a tree. Against the trunk, but with his back to them, was a man. He was smoking, one arm propped on his knee, oblivious to the proximity of his enemies. If he was a sentry, he wasn't doing much of a job. Beyond him sat another soldier, rummaging through the contents of his pack. The soldier by the tree muttered a few words and the other man tossed him something he'd just picked out of his pack. It wasn't a good throw. The book-shaped object, wrapped in canvas and bound with string, flew past the soldier's right shoulder and fell in the leaves behind him. If he turned to fetch it, he would almost certainly spot them.

Off to the right, someone coughed.

Big Jack and Loc watched in total amazement as the soldier with the cigarette lazily crawled from behind his tree, picked up the package and returned to his position without noticing anything untoward.

Big Jack considered attacking and taking a prisoner. But it was getting close to dark, and extraction would have to wait till morning. He signalled to the team to retreat.

Two hundred metres away and with the claymores out, the night sitrep sent and everyone fed, Big Jack conferred with Carlos and Bobby.

'At first light, we'll go back and see if we can grab one of those guys. Think you boys can handle that?'

Carlos and Bobby exchanged glances.

'A prisoner is worth a point recon,' said Big Jack.

'There could be a whole bunch of NVA out there,' said Bobby.

'Loc thinks there was only one fire. That's not enough for more than maybe ten guys. Besides, if there're more, I've got that covered,' said Big Jack. 'We'll move up on them, exactly the same way we did today. I'll either grab someone or try and wing him. Once I've got hold of him, I want you to let rip with everything else, CS gas, Willie Pete, the lot. We'll move back, blow a couple of claymores, and run. Any questions?'

Bobby and Carlos shook their heads.

As usual, no one really slept, but Bobby tried to let his body relax while his mind raced. Was this a chance worth taking? A prisoner would mean bonuses for the team and a week off in Taiwan for the three Americans. Bobby knew Big Jack wanted to take a prisoner. He'd never managed to get one although he'd been close twice. No one at Kontum had brought a single prisoner out of Laos in 1969, and the same was probably true of Cambodia. This would be a big feather in the team's cap.

In the darkness before the dawn, North Dakota prepared for the fight. Leaving their rucksacks, they donned their gas masks and crept forward, with CS gas and white phosphorous grenades held ready.

Bobby pulled off his gas mask and looked around him. Nothing. The soldiers had gone. Relieved, he folded the lightweight mask in his hand and packed it back into the pouch on his harness.

The fire still smouldered, only recently extinguished. Loc signalled that there must have been about twenty to thirty guys. It certainly wasn't the ninety or a hundred Bobby had imagined, but it was more than the ten Loc had estimated. You guessed the odds and played your hand.

For the rest of the day, North Dakota had little sight or sound of the enemy. Big Jack stopped regularly to check the map. In the flat, heavily wooded terrain, navigation was a significant challenge and the detours to work around the various NVA positions had introduced a certain margin of error into his planned route.

Then, late in the afternoon, the team chanced upon a foot trail that was covered in leaves, which indicated it had not been used for some time. They decided to follow the trail through some thick bush and it seemed to head in the right direction. After only a minute Loc suddenly froze.

About eighteen inches above the ground was a wire.

Back in January, RT Vermont's point man had found a similar wire on a recon mission in Cambodia. Instead of treating it with suspicion, the point man had, for reasons known only to him, yanked on it, causing an explosion, which had wounded four men. An NVA squad then launched an attack.

The word was now out: never mess with wires.

Big Jack crept up to take a closer look. It was a thin green wire. He touched it very lightly with his finger, gauging the tension. No one lays hair-trigger wires in the jungle, for the simple reason that wind or rain can set them off. To left and right, the wire disappeared into bushes. It was quite possible that the enemy might have anticipated the wire being spotted, and have laid mines immediately beyond it. That was what Big Jack would have done. Cutting the wire was not really a very good idea. Releasing the tension might detonate something. Secondly, if the cut wire were discovered, it would alert the enemy to their presence. He signalled to Loc that he was going to step over.

A lesser man might have had Loc go first, but that was not how you gained the trust and respect of the Montagnard.

Big Jack stepped gingerly across. Nothing. He advanced a few feet, stopped, then signalled the rest of the team to follow.

A short way beyond the wire, they heard the dull throb of a vehicle being driven slowly towards them. It sounded too light to be a truck as it passed by.

They waited five long minutes for any more traffic, then moved forward. They soon discovered a trail with fresh tyre tracks, which suggested a command car of some sort.

Big Jack didn't want to hang around. He had his target and they were only a couple of hundred metres away from where he'd expected to find it.

10

Loc always found it amusing that Americans, who were not used to Montagnards, were so impressed with what he considered to be basic hunting and tracking skills. They could do the same, if they wanted to. All they had to do was ask and he would teach them.

Beyond the brush which concealed their progress the ground rose suddenly in a bank about two feet high. Loc paused and tested the earth with his foot. This was not a natural feature. This was man-made.

Big Jack stepped past him and mounted the bank. He found himself on top of a large flat rectangular mound, maybe thirty by fifteen feet and two feet above the jungle floor. It was made of hard-packed earth and had little in the way of leaf litter on it.

'We got a bunker complex here,' whispered Big Jack, returning to the team. 'Looks like it could be a big one.'

Bobby's mouth went dry, anticipating yet another large concentration of enemy troops.

North Dakota deployed quickly past the first

bunker and then crept up along the rear edge of a second to discover another track.

The bunkers had been built without disturbing the surrounding trees, which provided good cover from the air.

The NVA built thousands of bunkers like these to protect personnel from bombing, but there was always the possibility that supplies or ammunition might be stored inside and they could be worth booby-trapping.

'I'm going to take Loc in for a closer look,' Big Jack said, after they were satisfied the place was deserted.

'I'm coming too,' mouthed Bobby.

Big Jack frowned. He wasn't asking for volunteers. Bobby didn't have to prove himself to Big Jack. But if he wanted to join them, that was up to him.

'OK.'

Bobby couldn't just sit and wait. He had to be doing something. If he lay still with the team, he would have to endure the same gnawing anxiety that plagued him whenever he expected imminent contact with the enemy. He had observed that when he was scared, his judgement began to slip away.

Outside the first timber-framed bunker, Bobby and Big Jack positioned themselves to left and right of the entrance while Loc knelt by the track covering forward.

Bobby sniffed the air. It smelt cool, dry and dusty with the faintest odour of fresh-cut wood.

Bobby indicated to Big Jack that he was going in. Big Jack gave one nod. Silently, Bobby wished himself good luck and jumped down into the entrance, stepping quickly to one side so as not to silhouette himself against the light.

The afternoon sun laid a golden path up the centre of the floor, revealing that there was nothing there. It was pleasantly cool. From the inside, it was obvious that the bunkers had been constructed like log cabins, then covered with the soil that had been dug out of the hole. It was simple, effective and ingenious.

Bobby went back outside.

The three men checked two of the remaining bunkers, both of which were empty and showed the same signs of having been recently completed. Big Jack pulled out his camera and started photographing the area.

They were ready to check the fourth when the sound of voices drifted towards them through the trees. They could also hear the metallic chinking of tools, perhaps someone tinkering with an engine.

Every bone in Bobby's body yelled that they should get the hell out of there, but Big Jack stayed put.

Go get the rest of the guys, he signalled.

In a clearing, the top of a man's head bobbed into view, then disappeared from sight. Loc could only detect three voices and seemed convinced there were no others.

The boys in Saigon really wanted to get their hands on a truck driver. Drivers knew all the convoy routes, and other secrets of the trail.

Big Jack turned to Bobby, clenching his fist as if grabbing at thin air, and then pointed to the voices.

There wasn't time for anything elaborate or sophisticated. This was going to have to be done the old-fashioned way.

Ten feet away, three NVA were grouped around the open hood of a small canvas-tilted Russian-built jeep. One was under the vehicle, his legs sticking out from under the door. Another stood casually with one foot on the fender. The third was lounging against the side of the vehicle.

'Hands up. Stand still!' barked Loc in Vietnamese. A second later, he broke from the bushes with Bobby and Big Jack to either side of him.

All eyes met for a second. Two of the NVA exchanged glances. Then everything happened at once.

The man standing at the front of the jeep made to draw a pistol while his comrade grabbed for the rifle which lay against the side of the vehicle.

Loc and Big Jack dropped the first man before he could even get the leather holster flap clear. Bobby's fired a quick three-round burst, and the other man slid down the blood-smeared door to the ground.

I just killed a man, noted Bobby. The thought took less than a hundredth of a second to register. He had fired at the enemy before, but never been sure he'd killed anyone.

The third man took advantage of the mayhem. Having frantically crawled under the vehicle, he dashed into the jungle.

Loc fired a quick burst but Big Jack knocked the muzzle to one side.

Ditching his rucksack, Bobby set off in pursuit.

In his panic to escape, the soldier didn't see a fallen branch. He tripped and fell heavily among the leaves that littered the forest floor.

Bobby grabbed the dazed man by the collar and tried to pull him to his feet. The man struck out wildly with his arms and legs, but fear and the effects of poor nutrition quickly sapped what little natural strength he had.

'Give up, man! You're mine, OK? Give it up!' yelled Bobby, but his captive continued to lash out, yelling all the while. One blow caught Bobby's lip. He dropped the soldier back to the ground and slammed the stock of the carbine into the man's face. The yelling stopped.

'Now shut the fuck up!'

Bobby dragged the semi-conscious soldier to his feet and frogmarched him back to the vehicle.

'Well done, Bob. Outstanding.' Big Jack smiled as Bobby threw his prisoner against the vehicle and bound his hands with plastic handcuffs.

Yanking the captive's head up by his hair, Loc warned him that if he even tried to speak again or made to escape they'd kill him. The man nodded his head violently, and soiled himself where he stood.

Carlos ripped the magazine off one of the dead men's weapons and tossed it into the jungle. He then replaced it with one containing the Eldest Son ammo.

A satchel of documents was discovered in the jeep. Big Jack strapped it across the top of his rucksack while Bobby took the camera and quickly photographed the vehicle and its dead owners.

Seconds later they set off at the run.

It had only been two minutes since the first shot was fired.

'Covey, Covey, this is Blind Rock,' hissed Carlos into his handset.

'Rock, this is Covey.'

'Covey. We've done the dirty deed. We got a package. We need a ride ASAP.'

'Roger, Blind Rock. Be advised that we've other

friendlies in contact. We're trying to pull them out right now. I don't think we can make it tonight. Can you hide up till morning?'

Big Jack cursed. This was how the god of war repaid you for improvising and not sticking to the plan.

'Roger, Covey. Blind Rock out.'

The team changed direction. No sooner had they done so than a shot rang out, and someone shouted. It was too far away to tell if the enemy was on their back trail, but they had to assume the worst.

Big Jack's plan was to head for a small series of bamboo groves about 1,800 metres to the north. It was the area he had intended to use had they completed the original point recon. From the air, the groves looked like a series of gashes in the jungle. Using their banana knives, the team could cut an area large enough for the choppers to get them out, but it would have to be with the ladders.

Another shot rang out behind them. A few seconds later, from their right, an answering shot replied. Two groups of trackers were attempting to co-ordinate their sweep.

Bobby pulled a plastic bottle of dog repellent from his pocket and squirted a liberal amount of the CS powder across their trail.

Twenty minutes later a single shot was fired, but

this time it was close, maybe less than a hundred metres behind them. The team stopped quicker than a dog running out of leash. The prisoner was forced flat on the ground, a boot across his neck and the muzzle of a carbine in his ear.

Big Jack gestured for everyone to take cover. They were going to let the trackers walk right into them.

There was a soft rustling then the swish and thwack of a branch swinging back on their pursuers.

These guys are clumsy, thought Bobby. It'll get them dead.

As if from nowhere, the head and shoulders of an old dark-skinned man materialised about twenty-five metres away. He wore a faded, torn green shirt and loincloth. He carried no weapon and was probably a local Cambodian hunter. An NVA soldier appeared behind the old man, and then another. All of them peered at the ground for traces of North Dakota's trail.

The hunter's head disintegrated. An invisible gust of small arms fire flattened the others.

A volley of grenades, arced over the bushes and into the jungle beyond, detonated in a sharp series of bangs, drowning out the ongoing hail of fire that was scything through the undergrowth.

Big Jack tapped Loc on the shoulder and pointed

to where he wanted to move next. Bobby ripped open the pocket on Hih's rucksack flap and pulled out a claymore on a time fuse. He placed the mine and jerked the igniter. Smoke confirmed the fuse was burning. Pushing Hih in front of him, he raced to catch up with the rest of the team. The claymore blew, but there were no cries.

Again they switched direction before slowing to a more deliberate pace. Big Jack stopped to consult the map. As he did so, more shooting broke out to the south. All except Big Jack ducked instinctively. There was some shouting and blowing of whistles, then the firing ceased. It sounded as if two NVA patrols must have walked into each other and opened fire. Bobby hoped so.

They set off north for about five minutes. A shout in Vietnamese away to the left of the team made them come to an immediate halt.

The voice yelled again, urgent and desperate.

'He see us!' hissed Loc to Big Jack. 'He say we here.'

Then silence. Whoever had seen them hadn't fired.

Another voice called out, very near.

Truc and Rah saw the enemy first and fired. The rest followed suit, and then moved off swiftly, their speed only checked by the prisoner who tripped and fell every few steps.

Bursting out of the thick brush, they found themselves running headlong into several NVA, who were completely unprepared for the encounter.

Loc felled the first man with one burst, delivered on the run. Big Jack killed the next. Carlos took aim at a man who still had his back to him and put a burst between the soldier's shoulder blades.

Hurdling the fallen bodies, they headed for an area that had been cleared of ground vegetation.

They could make good speed through this type of ground but they could easily be spotted.

A rocket-propelled grenade shot between them, and slammed into a tree trunk about eight feet away.

The blast blew Big Jack off his feet, and flattened the rest of the team.

Bobby's head hit the hard earth, temporarily stunning him. He felt a burning pain above his eye, and shook his head to regain his senses. The world sounded muffled and looked blurred, as though he was seeing everything from inside an old glass jar. The prisoner, his arms tied behind his back, was running desperately towards his friends. Two rounds struck him. He fell, and didn't get up.

Blinking furiously and not sure how badly wounded he was, Bobby struggled to his knees and returned a few bursts towards the sound of firing.

As if in slow motion, two grenades sailed through the air towards the enemy. Bobby flung himself flat, to avoid collecting any fragmentation. The sharp detonation broke the spell and he suddenly found himself functioning as normal. One of the grenades had been white phosphorous and the spreading thick white cloud screened the team.

Bobby felt his face. His hand came away with blood on his fingers. He had been hit, but there was no time for that now. The Montagnards were keeping up a steady stream of fire, but Big Jack was still on the ground, trying to crawl to cover.

Oh, shit! He'd been hit!

Carlos reached him first. One side of Big Jack's face was covered in blood. More blood was starting to soak through the sleeve of his jacket.

Rounds slapped into the foliage overhead. Bobby spun round and returned fire.

'I'm OK, goddamn it! I'm OK!' Big Jack yelled as Carlos struggled to drag him into cover with one hand, while firing his carbine with the other.

The Montagnards fell back, firing short bursts. Bobby crawled over to Truc, unhooked another white phosphorous grenade from the back of his rucksack, yanked the pin free and hurled it towards the enemy.

'We gotta go,' shouted Bobby.

Rah and Bluh appeared, dragging the escaped

prisoner between them. The man's eyes were half closed. He knelt, twitching and wheezing, between the two Montagnards. One side of his head was slick with blood.

Rah tried to pull him to his feet.

'Leave him,' ordered Bobby.

Loc repeated the order. Rah dropped the man to the ground and shot him in the head. Bobby stood stunned for a second. He hadn't meant for that to happen.

'Can you stand?' he asked Big Jack. The whole left side of his head and torso was soaked with blood.

Big Jack struggled to his knees. 'Son of a bitch!' He grimaced. His left arm appeared useless and he gripped the elbow in an attempt to alleviate the pain.

'Let's move,' said Bobby, suddenly realising that with Big Jack hurt, it could be down to him to lead the team.

Big Jack could walk, but for how much longer nobody knew. Loc had shrapnel wounds in his arms and on top of his shoulder, but he continued as if nothing had happened. Bobby had sustained a bad cut above his right eye, which he bandaged as best he could.

After fifteen minutes, pain and blood loss were starting to get the better of Big Jack. He vigorously refused help, but eventually took a stick Bobby cut for him. Carlos did his best to dress the wounds, but Big Jack insisted they kept going. There could be no thought of stopping yet. They had to find an LZ or good cover.

After another three-quarters of an hour they could see a bamboo grove up ahead. There was no way of telling if it was the one they had planned to use, but it seemed to be in the right place.

They moved past the grove and looped back, so anyone following the team's trail would be obliged to pass the clearing and thus reveal their presence.

Toppled by either age or lightning, a large tree lay along the far edge of the grove.

Big Jack sank against the three-foot-diameter trunk, and forced a grin. 'Circle the wagons.'

The Montagnards didn't need a translation. There was a flurry of activity. Within a minute Bobby had assigned fields of fire and fine-tuned the position of each claymore.

Carlos had no luck trying to raise Covey.

The sun was dipping low in the sky. Sunset was less than an hour away.

'How you doing?' asked Bobby, hearing Big Jack gasp as Carlos examined his arm.

'I'll live,' replied Big Jack, sounding more his old self.

'Think they'll get us out before dark?' Carlos

hoped his nervousness didn't show.

'If they don't, they'll get us out first thing,' Big Jack replied.

Bobby was desperate to get on the radio and ask when the hell the choppers would be there, but he resisted. It was impossible to believe that the pilots wouldn't give a hundred percent to get them out even if there was only the slimmest chance of success.

Carlos shifted the radio to another position and tried again. Something as simple as a tree trunk could sometimes block the signal.

This time he got a reply.

'You guys OK?' asked Covey.

'Could be better, Covey. What's the news?'

'We're losing the light fast. You're gonna have to wait till morning. We're just pulling the other guys out. They've been mauled pretty bad.'

Carlos coded up the situation report and passed it to Covey, then set about trying to splint Big Jack's arm. With the utmost care, he and Bobby removed Big Jack's rucksack. Cutting a twelve-inch section of relatively straight branch and using further triangular bandages, Carlos managed to immobilise the arm, which would relieve some of the pain. Morphine, as always, was out of the question.

Next they took the six-inch-thick pile of documents out of Big Jack's rucksack and stuffed as much as they could into Carlos's. There was no question of ever jettisoning the radio, so the documents would be the last thing to get dumped. Whatever couldn't be crammed in with the radio, Bobby took.

Just my luck if this turns out to be the unit's medical records, he thought. The rest of Big Jack's equipment was distributed around the rest of the team, and the empty rucksack hidden under a pile of leaves.

Quickly the team cleared the ground of all the other branches and leaves so they could move about the small space without making too much noise. It also made it easier to find any items that might be dropped in the dark.

Carlos cleaned the wound over Bobby's eye and dressed it. He also attended to the handful of minor wounds that had been incurred by the rest of the team.

They changed the radio battery and waited for dark.

11

Bobby looked about him to see who was awake. It was unlikely anyone had fallen fast asleep, but the team was tired, and the down after the adrenaline rush could hit like lead flowing through your veins. Big Jack's head was lolling and Bobby wondered if they should make use of the Green Hornets or amphetamines. Only the One-zero could give the order to issue them.

Bobby shook Big Jack gently.

'Huh?'

'You OK?'

Big Jack winced. 'Never better. What's up?'

'We need to break out the Green Hornets. The guys are beat.'

Big Jack nodded his agreement. Bobby found the pills and gave them to Carlos to distribute, with the warning that they should not be taken unless absolutely necessary.

Suddenly there was a flash from the jungle. Involuntary reflex made Bobby duck, but nothing happened. The light blinked again, this time for about two seconds. It was a flashlight.

The idea of using a flashlight at night was anathema to anyone in the US Army, let alone the Special Forces, but this was the NVA's back yard. They could do what they liked. They might be using the flashlight to try and flush North Dakota or draw fire.

It flicked on every twenty or thirty seconds. Meanwhile the team pulled on their rucksacks and prepared for action.

Bobby touched Carlos on the shoulder almost causing him to jump out of his skin. 'Try raising someone. This could get messy,' he whispered. Despite the ban on air support for Cambodian missions, Bobby felt there was no harm in asking. Especially if things went bad.

The fact that it was dark ruled out the Cobras. Bobby prayed that there were A-1 drivers willing to disregard the rules. They ran the risk of a court martial, but they had done it before.

The flashlight moved past, less than twenty metres away. Bobby repositioned Truc next to Hih who was covering the sector where the enemy would arrive. Bobby cursed himself for not having laid any toe-poppers on the back trail. That would have slowed the fuckers down and given the team a good fix.

Bobby made his way back to Carlos. 'We got anyone?'

Carlos continued to hold the handset to his head with his right hand, with the other clamped firmly over his other ear. Eventually he leaned over and whispered, 'Nothing.'

The flashlight blinked on again.

Bobby knew Hih would have loaded a canister round into the M-79, giving the weapon the equivalent effect of a 40mm-shotgun. There was another flash, so close that Bobby could see the ground illuminated by the beam. He heard hushed voices, and the faint crunching of leaves underfoot. Another blink and Bobby could see a man's legs, the green fatigue material, the salt staining of sweat on the thighs, scuffed knees.

He raised his weapon, but Hih beat him to it. In his peripheral vision, Bobby saw the massive muzzle flash of the M-79. Truc immediately emptied his entire magazine towards the enemy. Muzzle flashes illuminated the trees.

The claymores all detonated in quick succession.

'Go!' yelled Bobby. Carlos heaved Big Jack to his feet, and one by one, grabbing the back of each other's packs, they followed Loc out of the clearing.

Shots sprayed the air around them.

There was a lot of shouting and the odd piercing whistle blast. Loc changed direction.

After about an hour, Big Jack collapsed unconscious and North Dakota came to a halt.

Carlos fingered vomit from Big Jack's mouth so that he could breathe and also to make sure that his choking did not betray their presence.

Bobby fought to control his fear that the situation was spiralling beyond his control. Big Jack was now a dead weight. They couldn't carry him. They didn't know where they were, and the NVA wasn't going to call it quits.

Ten minutes passed while they waited in total silence. Big Jack mumbled he could go on, but go where? wondered Bobby. He had consulted the map, using a flashlight masked with a triangular bandage, but it was too dark to see your hand, let alone take an azimuth you could navigate by.

'We stay here,' whispered Bobby to Bluh. 'Tell the others.'

Like blind men, methodically they formed a circle with Big Jack in the middle. Although they still had their anti-pursuit claymores, there was no point in deploying them since they could not be command-detonated.

Far away, the sound of trucks rolled through the still night air. Bobby prayed that this was just another nightly convoy, and not reinforcements.

At 05.45 Carlos powered up the radio and made the call.

'Blind Rock, this is Covey. Good to hear you.

Been calling a while. We're orbiting just over the fence. You guys ready to come out?'

Carlos estimated that they were somewhere between two and three hundred metres to the east of last night's position.

Bobby gazed up at the fading stars, which left behind a flat grey expanse of sky. The early-morning mist hung in the jungle and gave a comforting sense of serenity and calm. It would be light soon.

He decided it would be just plain dumb to go back to the clearing. Better to push slowly northeast and see if they could find a suitable LZ. Almost immediately they came across another bamboo grove, which would be a useable short ladder LZ if they could blow two large trees. With about five pounds of C-4 and six pull-fused claymores, there was more than enough explosive to do the job.

Covey could be heard up to the north. Carlos guided him overhead. They just had to be patient a little longer.

At the first sound of the approaching helicopters Bobby fired a pen-flare. It hissed skyward, hung for a second, then dropped, bright against the morning sky.

'I see you,' called Covey.

Bobby ran over to the first tree and tugged on the pull igniter before dashing back to the team, all of whom hunkered down into what cover they could find. A loud thud shook the forest, followed by the crash of a falling tree.

'Timber!' shouted Carlos. No one cared about noise any more.

All around, the jungle reverberated with the screams of birds and animals. The tree was down, sprawled across the grove, flattening great swathes of bamboo.

To the northwest, a rifle shot sounded. The NVA was awake.

A minute later the next tree was felled.

A Huey needed about seventy feet in diameter. What they had was close enough.

'That's it. Get in here!' ordered Carlos over the radio.

Dragging Big Jack, the team scrambled to the newly created clearing, taking cover behind the fallen trees. Truc, Bluh and Rah began using their heavy-bladed banana knives to hack at any branches that might snag the ladders.

Heavy machine-gun fire cut through the still morning air.

A Cobra pilot, who had been waiting for just such an eventuality, reacted quickly. 'Panther 24, I see the gun. Going in.'

Relieved to hear the sharp clatter of a slowing Huey, Bobby looked up to see the helicopter loom into view. The leaves in the clearing were whipped into a blizzard by the downwash.

As the Huey descended, ladders unrolled. The door gunners were leaning out, checking the clearances and giving directions back to the pilots. About twenty feet from the ground, the machine stopped its descent.

Bobby snatched the handset from Carlos. 'Get lower! I've got a wounded man here. He can't climb that.'

Eight feet from the ground the helicopter could come no lower. A branch from one of the felled trees was dangerously close to the tail rotor.

'Good enough!' yelled Bobby to no one in particular.

The door gunner stepped out on the skid.

Big Jack seized the centre wire of the ladder and summoned all his remaining strength to pull himself up using his one good arm. Jamming his shoulder under Big Jack, Bobby supported his weight as best he could. Truc snap-linked his rucksack to the bottom of the ladder, scrambled past and began heaving Big Jack from above. Each step seemed to take forever. The door gunner stepped from the skid and climbed down to reach the wounded man by his harness, and pull him into the machine.

With Big Jack, Truc, Rah and Hih also safely aboard, the helicopter began to lift.

The remaining men were busy, scanning the jungle for targets.

The next helicopter lowered into the clearing, blades slicing through some of the higher foliage. If the blades hit anything thicker, that would be it. The machine would shake itself to bits.

Twenty feet from the ground, the ladders rolled out.

Bobby managed to resist the urge to scramble up until he could see that the other men had footholds on the ladders. Then he seized the highest rung he could reach, shouting, 'GO! GO! GO!'

The chopper began to lift. It was vital to reach the cabin before the forward speed of the helicopter made climbing further too dangerous. At that point, anyone not in the cabin would have to ride the ladders back to Vietnam.

Someone got a grip on Bobby's harness and hauled him aboard.

'Ha, ha. Way to go! We fucking made it!' cheered Bobby, as he collapsed on the mass of rope and steel wires that criss-crossed the floor. Carlos grinned back at him.

Chink. Clank. Crack.

The Huey lurched, taking severe ground fire. The pilot banked to the right and Bobby braced himself against the bulkhead. He looked out of the door, straight down at the jungle rushing past below them. The helicopter shuddered from another direct hit.

Carlos was suddenly face down on the floor, sliding towards the open door. Loc lunged forward, hooking a rucksack strap.

The helicopter levelled and Bobby helped pull his friend back from the edge.

Carlos's side was dark with blood.

'Jesus! What happened?' Bobby tore a field dressing from his web gear, ripped open Carlos's shirt.

The wound was massive. Carlos wasn't moving.

Loc felt for a pulse in Carlos's neck. '*Bandito* dead,' he shouted, above the roar of the engine and the howl of the wind.

The helicopter had taken a heavy burst of machine-gun fire. The co-pilot's rudder pedals were gone, along with half of the flight instruments. They were also losing fuel. But somehow the Huey made it on to the runway at Plei Jerang.

Bobby was oblivious to everything. He held Carlos close all the way back. Grim-faced, Loc and Bluh climbed out. The door gunners climbed silently from the cabin, unsure of how happy they should be at their safe landing. They inquired if

Bobby was OK, but got no reply.

'Hey, Lake.' It was Stitch Ellis, the Chase medic. 'We need to get Nunez,' he said quietly, after examining the body which Bobby still held.

He watched blank-eyed as Carlos was zipped into a body bag. His discarded rucksack lay on the cabin floor, the radio handset still crackling.

'Covey, this is Blackfoot,' Bobby said.

'Go ahead, Blackfoot.'

'Covey, *Bandito* didn't make it.'

The handset hissed for a couple of seconds. 'Yeah, we know. Sorry, man.'

No one was expecting them in back camp at that time in the morning. Teams normally stayed up at Dak-To till the evening. The Intel Sergeant told Bobby to report to the TOC, but Bobby had other priorities. He dropped his equipment back at the hooch, then went over to see if the Montagnards were OK. Regardless of whether he was the One-zero or not, Bobby intended to behave like one.

At the Recon Company office, the 1st Sergeant was surprised to see him. 'I'm real sorry about Nunez, Lake. He was a good guy. What's on your mind?'

'I've got a favour to ask, Top.'

The 1st Sergeant wasn't in the business of granting favours, but he'd hear what Lake had to say.

'I know we've been all shot up, but those guys are a great team, Top. Please don't split them up.' Bobby felt himself beginning to choke with emotion.

'I hear what you say,' said the 1st Sergeant. 'We'll do our best. But I don't make promises.'

'One more thing, Top?' asked Bobby, but the 1st Sergeant interrupted him.

'Go get cleaned up, Lake, and get something to eat. Then go get some sleep, and then go get drunk. Talk to me tomorrow. That is all.'

The S-2 looked up to see a man covered in dried blood standing in front of him. He had a dirty blood-soaked bandage over his eyebrow and his face was drawn and streaked with dirt.

'You wanted to see me, sir?' asked Bobby, his hands hooked into his pockets. He didn't even attempt a salute.

The Captain stared for a moment, then said, 'We got a report that you got a prisoner. What happened to him?'

'He's dead.'

The S2 looked up, wanting more.

'We ran into trouble. He got hit. So we left him.'

The S2 looked, as if he hadn't understood a word Bobby had said.

'Sergeant Nightingale was wounded. I couldn't

carry both, so I left him. Oh, and we got a bunch of documents as well.'

'Documents?' exclaimed the S2.

'We got a bunch of documents. We took them out of a jeep we ambushed.'

'A jeep?'

'Yeah.'

Bobby got the documents and dropped them back to the TOC, then went over to the dispensary to get the cut over his eye stitched and dressed.

Five minutes later the Intel Sergeant came running over to find him.

'You're going to Saigon, Lake. You're going to safe-hand the documents down to MAC-V. They're diverting a Blackbird to come pick you up. Get cleaned up. I've got to get you down to the field ASAP.'

An hour later Bobby was down at Kontum airfield waiting for the lumbering C-130 to taxi over. The relationship between MAC-V and CCC was classified. For that reason, Bobby travelled in sterile fatigues. Except for metal pin-on rank badges, he was devoid of all patches, nametags or insignia. Even his Green Beret had been left back at the camp. A .45 pistol was tucked into his waistband. His orders allowed him to carry a concealed weapon. He carried a B-4 bag containing a civilian change of clothes, some overnight gear, and the all-important documents.

Sitting in the jeep he felt overwhelmingly tired and empty. Carlos was gone. Deal with it and get the hell on, a voice inside him said. Don't cry. This is war. You wanted to fight. These things happen.

12

Bobby sat in a small room on the ground floor of 137 Pasteur Street, a nondescript five-storey apartment block-cum-office building. Apart from a green metal locker, there was only a table and two chairs. Bobby had dozed a little on the short flight, but he was beginning to feel distinctly groggy. The de-briefer had gone to fetch him some strong coffee.

The table was strewn with maps and papers, as well as a folder with the pictures Big Jack had taken. Carlos's bloodstained notebook lay there too.

'So what did this vehicle look like?' asked the de-briefer, flicking through the photographs.

'I can't remember exactly.' Bobby sipped the bitter brew. 'Look at the pictures we took.'

'Sure. Just help me out here. That it?' The de-briefer showed Bobby a picture in a recognition manual. The vehicle was parked in snow against a backdrop of fir trees. The title below it read: '0.5t Utility. UAZ-469/BJ-212'.

'I guess,' said Bobby. He could tell the de-briefer

was less than happy with his lack of precision, but he said nothing.

'Were there any distinct markings on the vehicle, either interior or exterior?'

'Couldn't say.'

'Look, if you're beat, we can do this tomorrow. Why not go and get some sleep?'

'I'm not going to remember stuff I never knew,' Bobby sighed. 'We weren't really looking at the fucking thing. We were trying to grab a prisoner and get the hell out of Dodge.'

'Why'd you abandon the prisoner?'

'Because we already had a casualty and I had to decide between him and the prisoner. We couldn't deal with both.'

'Do you think he's dead?'

'Don't know and don't care,' Bobby lied. 'So what about all those papers we snatched? What are they?'

'I can't say.'

'Can't or won't?'

The de-briefer looked pained. 'Security,' he said flatly.

'I lost a good friend getting that shit,' growled Bobby, 'I'd like to know it was worth it.'

'OK, OK, wait here a minute.' The de-briefer left the room, to return moments later with an Air Force Colonel.

'Relax, son, siddown,' said the Colonel, as Bobby sprang to attention.

The Colonel introduced himself as Deputy Chief SOG. 'Hell of a job, son, hell of a job. You did real good.'

'Thank you, sir,' said Bobby, as the Colonel shook his hand vigorously.

'I got good news and bad news, son,' began the Colonel, 'The good news is that the documents sure were worth whatever you boys went through to get them. Bad news, I can't tell you why. OK?'

'I guess I'll have to make do with that, sir.'

'Are we done here, Sergeant?' asked the Colonel.

'Yes, sir.'

'Well, keep up the good work, son,' he said. 'You're doing an outstanding job. Outstanding. Real honour to have boys like you on the team.' With that, he turned on his heel and left.

Bobby was dropped back at House Ten. This was a two-storey walled villa used by MAC-V as accommodation for any Command and Control personnel visiting Saigon.

Bobby went straight to one of the bunkrooms and fell asleep before he could undress. Waking with a start, he felt restless and jumpy. He found himself yearning for the familiarity of camp, the camaraderie of his team and the club. He'd got used to having Big Jack and Carlos around twenty-four hours a day. Now, one was dead and the other badly wounded.

Bobby stripped down and cleaned his .45 then timed himself reassembling it. It was a pointless exercise with no military relevance, but it took his mind off things for a while. He took a shower, then went back to sleep.

A lean, skull-faced Sergeant looked up as Bobby sat down beside him in the small upstairs bar.

'An inch or so lower and that would've really fucked you up,' he commented, seeing Bobby's bandaged head. A small amount of blood had seeped through, leaving a heart-shaped blotch.

'Yeah, well, I got lucky. Others didn't.'

The Sergeant nodded and turned back to his beer.

'My name's Lake,' said Bobby.

The two men shook hands.

'McMillan. What you drinking?'

'Beer. Thanks.'

'You run recon?' asked McMillan.

'Yeah, out of Kontum.'

'I figured. Who you know at Kontum?'

'Jack Nightingale.'

'Shit! I know Big Jack. I was at Bragg with him. How's he doing?'

'Not good. He caught a shit load of frag yesterday,' said Bobby.

'Fuck! You on Big Jack's team?'

'Yeah, I'm the One-one.'

'You're the One-zero now,' said McMillan in a matter-of-fact way.

'I guess.'

'Want some advice from another One-zero?'

'Sure.'

'Know when to quit.'

'Tell me something I don't know.'

'Better you are, the worse it gets.'

Bobby raised his eyebrows.

'The better you do, the more missions they throw at you. If you're real dedicated and get a reputation, then they're just going to keep throwing you those curve balls. All them hard targets will end up on your list, and what you gonna say? You got enough guts to say you're all burnt out and you can't run no more?'

Bobby took a long pull on his beer. He felt burnt out right now, and he'd only run six.

'And don't go back.' McMillan was about to take some leave in the US. 'No one there wants to hear about the war. You can't tell anyone about the shit you've been through. Even if they do want to hear, they won't get it.'

'Got to go back sometime,' said Bobby.

'Why? When this war is over, I'm staying here. Vietnamese women know how to treat guys right. That's the one good thing about this fucked-up little country.'

'How long you reckon ARVN will last without us?'

'You think the Dinks are gonna win? You think the NVA is going to roll into Saigon?'

'If we leave? Yeah, I do.'

'Well, I'm staying. Fuck 'em.'

'Good luck. I'm going home.'

'What you gonna tell 'em when you get back? Eh? What you gonna say you did, when you were fighting here, in Vietnam, Republic of?'

'I fought for my country. I did my duty. I didn't run away to Canada, or say I was queer to get out of the war.'

McMillan shook his head and smiled a bitter smile. 'No, man,' he said. 'You gotta tell them what they want to hear. You got to tell 'em you killed babies and raped folks. You got to be all, "Wow, man, I'm bummed out after my year in the 'Nam, man! Charlie fucked us. I took dope and partied. The war's wrong. Long live Uncle Ho." That's what they want to hear.'

'No one's going to hear that shit from me. I'm going to tell it like it was.'

'What the fuck you gonna say?'

'I'm going to say what I did, and that I was proud to do it.'

McMillan shook his head. 'It's all classified, man. You can't say shit.'

The room smelt of disinfectant and Vietnamese cooking from the restaurant downstairs.

'You very strong boy,' the girl said. 'You give me more money. I love you big time. I love you long time.'

Bobby couldn't remember her name, even though she had said it five minutes before. She was highly recommended by McMillan. She looked pretty, like a lewd doll, in a low-slung red halter-top and black mini-skirt.

'You buy me good watch, you buy me guitar, I be your girlfriend,' offered the girl, running her hand over his crotch.

Bobby didn't like the idea of paying for sex. He didn't even want to get laid that badly, but he was going to doubt his own sanity if, as a healthy, just twenty-one-year-old Green Beret, he didn't have sex at least once while he was in Saigon. He had clumsily negotiated the minimum payment for a blowjob, and now watched with almost detached fascination while the girl set to work as she had thousands of times before. Oral sex was pretty much the only option. There were some extremely nasty diseases doing the rounds. Everyone back at Kontum knew the story of the guy who had gone back on leave and infected his wife. Try running recon with that on your mind.

The girl looked up, seeking approval for her technique. There was something in her eyes that reminded him of Rachel, but Rachel would never do this, at least not the Rachel he thought he knew. Bobby remembered the smell of her hair and the gentle way she held his hand. He wanted to be back in Kentucky, right now. The girl was becoming irritated that she was getting no reaction at all from her client. Bobby told her to stop, gave her a good tip and left.

Saigon's dust-filled streets were choked with traffic and people. Bobby was finding that loud noises made him uncomfortable, and that being jostled by people on the sidewalk was making him angry. The air was thick with smells that either promised all the mystery of the Orient or warned of all its squalor and degradation.

Bobby stopped into the Morning Star, a bar on Tu Do Street. McMillan had told him that it was a Special Forces hangout and always worth visiting on the off chance you might run into old buddies. But Bobby had only been in Special Forces eighteen months. He didn't expect to know anyone.

Standing at the bar he nursed a beer. It was early-afternoon and the place was almost empty.

'Hey, fucker! You Special Forces?' A large blond-haired man lounged on the bar next to him.

'What's it to you?'

'I don't see no SF flash or Green Beret on you, boy.'

Bobby ignored him in the almost certain expectation that the encounter was about to become physical.

'Hey, I'm talking to you!' The man jabbed him in the arm.

'What about, cocksucker?' Bobby pushed his beer away and turned to face his aggressor. For a moment, the blond man looked surprised, but then quickly recovered himself and threw a punch. He was clumsy and slow. Bobby dodged the blow, and jabbed hard at the man's throat. Two men grabbed hold of him as he reeled backwards, while a third stepped forward and placed a hand on Bobby's chest.

'Stay cool!' he said.

'I'm cool,' replied Bobby. 'It's shit for brains that's got the problem.'

'Why, you little fuck!' The man made a lunge for Bobby, but his friends kept hold of him and led him back to their table.

'You don't wanna get old Lew upset. He's a bad guy to lock horns with,' warned one of the men.

'I didn't start it,' said Bobby, turning back to his drink.

'Who you with?'

'Who wants to know?'

'Hey, troop. We're all on the same side, right?'

'C and C, Kontum,' said Bobby.

'My name's Neilson. You want to join us?'

Bobby looked over to where Lew glowered back at him.

'Thanks, but I don't think so.'

'Aw, c'mon. Don't let old Lew scare you. He's a sweet guy really,' insisted Neilson.

'I noticed,' said Bobby.

The four soldiers were from a recently closed down A-team camp out near the Cambodian border. The other two were Harry and Doc, both lifers in their late-twenties or early-thirties.

They turned out to be good guys, and Bobby enjoyed the company. They drank and swapped war stories, but he stayed quiet. He had nothing to say.

'You heard the latest?' asked Neilson. 'The war's over. We lost.'

'How'd you figure that?' asked Bobby.

'We leave, the NVA stays. It's that simple,' chipped in Doc.

No one disputed what they knew to be the truth.

'How old are you, kid?' challenged Lew while they waited for another round of beers.

'Twenty–one.'

'Fuck! How we gonna win this war with kids?'

Bobby didn't rise to the bait.

'What you boys do up there in Kontum?' asked Doc.

'We train Montagnards for the Mike Force.' Bobby repeated the CCC cover story.

Doc and Neilson smiled and shook their heads.

'So you ain't in SOG?' asked Doc. A smile played on his lips. He and Neilson obviously knew the truth. Most of the lifers in SF did.

'SOG? That's just running recon. It ain't no big thing,' sneered Lew.

'So why don't you volunteer, Lew?' asked Doc.

'I might just do that,' said Lew, leaning back in his chair. 'Whadaya reckon there, Lake? How about a real pro coming and showing you boys how it's done?'

'I wouldn't run with you,' replied Bobby bluntly.

'Oh, yeah. Why not?'

''Cos you're too fat, man. You get hit and I'm sure as hell not carrying you.'

Even Lew laughed.

★

Next morning, very hung-over, Bobby packed his kit and headed out to Tan Son Nhut. At the Air America terminal he hitched a ride back with a helicopter pilot who was taking a Huey out to Vung Tau where the beach club was.

The only other people in the restaurant that evening were a Vietnamese Air Force Major, in uniform, and his wife. She wore dark glasses even though it was dark outside. Her table manners were appalling and she ate so noisily that even the Major seemed embarrassed.

The meal, of prawns and rice, was one of the better local dishes Bobby had tasted since he had been in the country.

Sipping his wine, he stared out at the surf, just visible in the dark beyond the sand. Compared to the Wild West atmosphere of the club at Kontum, this place seemed fantastically civilised. Sure, the rattan furniture was in need of repair, and the photographs on the wall were faded and speckled with mildew, but it was quiet and it was away from the war.

Bobby felt as if the great coiled spring inside him was beginning to ease. For the first time in his life he had eaten alone in public. The whole experience felt unreal, a bit like playing at grown-ups.

The manager approached with an elegant

woman dressed in Capri pants and a shirt tied at the waist.

'Monsieur Lake.'

Bobby stood.

The manager spoke in French. 'May I introduce Madame Trahn? Like you, she finds herself alone this evening. I thought you might appreciate the company.'

'I'm sure Madame Trahn has no problem finding company,' said Bobby, initially somewhat lost for words.

Madame Trahn was exceptionally good-looking. She was tall for a Vietnamese and had pronounced European features. Bobby remembered Simmons mentioning that there were extremely expensive half-caste prostitutes to be found near Vung Tau.

'Please,' said Bobby, gesturing to the chair opposite. Realising he wasn't going to pull it out for her, Madame Trahn moved the chair slowly back and sat down. Bobby felt himself begin to glow with embarrassment. The Vietnamese Major's wife observed the new arrival from over the top of her dark glasses.

'I'm Bobby Lake,' he said in French.

Madame Trahn smiled. 'Louise, but everyone calls me Lou,' she replied in English. Her accent was French with no trace of Vietnamese.

'So what brings you to this place?'

'I think it is beautiful down here, don't you agree?'

'I don't know Vietnam that well.'

'You surprise me.'

'That obvious, huh?'

'Not that obvious. Your French is very good for an American.'

'Thank you.'

'May I have a drink?'

Bobby was about to reply, 'Fuck, yes, you can have a drink,' but caught himself in time. 'What'll you have?'

'It's OK. He knows,' said Louise, making the faintest of gestures to the barman. Within seconds he brought her Vodka Martini.

'You are a Green Beret, no?'

'Why do you say that?'

'Mr Lim told me. He said you have come here before with your friends.'

'He's a regular mine of information,' said Bobby.

'So where are your friends this evening?'

'My friends are dead. Dead or wounded.'

Neither of them wanted to talk about the war. They talked about movies, music, and what Vietnam was like before the French left.

This is going to be very expensive, thought Bobby. Louise was like no woman he had ever met.

Her age was impossible to guess. She was vastly knowledgeable and well-read. She had a subtle confidence about her, which hinted at something mysterious, untamed and forbidden. She was a game only the big boys played, and only if she let them. Bobby was completely out of his league.

'Are you here alone?' he asked.

'What makes you think that?'

'Well, someone like you must have better things to do than spend time with someone like me.'

Louise smiled, and played with the end of her scarf. 'And who exactly is someone like you?'

'I'm nothing special. I'm not even an officer.'

'Good. I am nothing special, and I am not an officer either, so we are the same, no?'

'I guess.' Bobby took another gulp of wine.

'Is everything all right? You seem very nervous,' asked Louise.

He put down his glass and made a mental note to drink less and to try and act cool.

'Is it the war?'

'Probably.'

'Well, relax, Bobby. I will not hurt you.' He felt the edge of Louise's foot brush against his shin.

'You couldn't hurt me,' quipped Bobby.

'Oh, I think I could.' Louise smiled. 'I think I could.'

*

Two hours later, she glanced at her watch.

'I must go,' she said. 'Thank you for a lovely evening, Bobby. It has been good to meet you.'

'But I thought . . .'

'You thought what?'

'I'm here for a couple of days. Will I see you again?'

'What did you think? Did you think I was here on business?' She raised her fine painted eyebrows.

Bobby wished the ground would open up and swallow him.

Louise stood waiting for his explanation.

'Can I see you again?'

'You would like to see me even though I am not a whore?' she mused.

'Very much.'

'How long did you say you had been in Vietnam?'

'I didn't.'

'And after a year you will leave, yes?'

Bobby shrugged.

'I live here, Bobby. Do you understand? After all the Americans have gone home, I'll still be here. It would be very difficult.'

He couldn't think of anything to say.

'Where are you staying?'

'The Palms. Just down the road.'

'There are some very nice whores in Vung Tau.

I'm sure Mr Lim can point you in the right direction.'

Bobby sighed. 'It's been great to talk. I'm really sorry. I didn't mean any offence.'

'None taken, Bobby. Goodbye.'

They shook hands.

'Goodbye,' he said.

Bobby took a slug of whiskey from the half-bottle he had bought at the club. He still didn't like the taste.

Well, you really managed to fuck that up! he said to himself.

He was about to turn off his bedside light when there was a knock at the door. He pulled his .45 from under his pillow and cocked the hammer.

'Hello?'

Keeping the pistol behind his back, he opened the door. There was no one there. He looked out into the dimly lit corridor. Louise was standing a few feet away by a window, her back towards him. Without a word, she turned and walked past him into the room.

Louise sat naked on the end of the bed, her knees drawn up against her breasts. With calm deliberation she puffed smoke rings into the air.

'Do you have a girlfriend?' she asked.

'Sort of.'

She stared at the tip of her cigarette. 'My husband was killed during Tet, just over two years ago. He had been in the Army but had got a good job with the Government in Hue. When Hue was overrun, they killed him. I was in France at the time.'

They sat in silence.

'Why did you come here?' asked Bobby, after a while.

Louise ground the cigarette into the little metal ashtray.

'I do not know. Why do we do anything? Why do you do what you do?'

'It's my job. Because I believe in what I do.'

'And what good will that have been when you are back in America and we are all still here, fighting the Communists? You know we'll lose, don't you? What will it all have been for?'

'We haven't left yet,' said Bobby.

'When you do, it will be all over for us.' Louise stretched her svelte body across the foot of the bed.

'What makes you so certain that ARVN will lose?'

'Most people here have nothing. Some have less than nothing. That leaves them very little to fight for.'

'They've got freedom,' said Bobby.

Louise chuckled. 'What is freedom when your

life is slavery? Freedom means nothing to these people. They don't own their own land. They have no stake in this country. Corruption is a way of life. We are living in the last days of Ancient Rome. That's is why I am here with you. I want to have fun before all the lights go out and the barbarians are knocking down the walls.'

'You don't have to stay.'

'I was born here. My father was French and my mother Vietnamese. I married a Vietnamese. I could go to France. Maybe I will some day.'

Bobby reached out his hand and stroked the hair from her shoulder.

'What is she like? Your girlfriend in America.'

'She's just some girl I met before I joined the Army. We write to each other.'

'Like pen pals?'

'I guess you could say that.' Bobby didn't really feel comfortable talking about it.

'But you wish it could be more?'

'Maybe. But she doesn't want to be involved with anyone who's in the Army. She thinks I'm going to get killed anyway.'

'But you write to her and she writes back?'

'Yes.'

'So she will still be sorry when you die. It seems a pity that she won't be able to remember you like this. Like we are now. No?'

13

'We got hit last night,' announced the driver at Kontum as Bobby jumped into the jeep. 'Sappers got in through the shithouse drain. Blew the fuck out of the TOC, and killed a bunch of Yards.'

'My guys OK?'

'I think so. We lost nine or ten altogether, but I don't think any of your boys were hit.'

The camp was in chaos. The TOC was a smouldering ruin, and people who didn't normally walk around armed were now bristling with weaponry. Even the Intel Sergeant was sporting a 9mm Browning in a shoulder holster.

'The fucking security lights had been fucked,' scowled one of the gunfighters, 'and guess what? The fucking satchel charge's got our own fucking explosive in! Steamed it out of our own bombs, clever little fuckers!'

It was too early to start drinking. Bobby went back to the hooch and decided he had to write a letter.

Dear Uncle Ethan,
Things have been pretty bad lately. Carlos Nunez

got killed. I was right there when he died. I saw him go. We got his body back, so I guess that was good. Sergeant Nightingale was also badly wounded, but he'll be OK.

I still can't believe Carlos is gone. It just seems so unfair, and it so easily could have been me. Maybe next time it will be. I run the same risks these guys do and I can't stay lucky forever. I know I can quit, but I don't think I've done enough to deserve to yet. I'm scared but I can still do it. Big Jack, Rhett, and Carlos never quit. I don't think I can either. Maybe I'll just get wounded. Maybe it'll be OK.

I know why Dad went out to save that kid, the time he got killed. I understand that now. It is a frightening thing to care about people. If you don't care, then it's not worth doing, and if you do care, then you've got to do what's right.

I see courage on a daily basis, but I'm not sure I can live up to what a lot of these guys do. Everyone's scared, but they just saddle up and go anyway. It's late here so I've got to go. I'll try and write again soon.

Love,

Bobby

P.S. I'm not going to tell Mom about Carlos, or if I do, I'll make out I was nowhere near when it happened.

★

Later that day, Bobby sat in the shade outside the club, reading *To Kill a Mocking Bird* and sipping a beer. It was too noisy inside. On Easter Sunday, a combined team of RT California and RT New Hampshire had gone out on the trail with the specific mission of capturing a truck driver. They had done it in style, and the third all-day party was still in full swing.

Bobby would have liked to have gone down to Pleiku to see Big Jack, but he had been flown out to Japan while Bobby was still in Saigon.

Gingerly he ran his finger over the healing scar above his eye. It was about two inches long and just clipped the outside of his eyebrow. For him, it was better than any medal and ironically it would get him one, the Purple Heart.

Bored and unable to concentrate on his book, Bobby wandered off around the camp. He'd delay getting drunk till the evening.

Joe Eden was practising his putting on the hard stand of the motor pool. The ground was far from ideal, but it would do.

Lieutenant Joe Eden was SPAF-4. He came from a wealthy New England family and treated the CCC camp like a badly run country club. He was constantly complaining about the food in the mess hall or the drinks selection in the club. He played poker as if he could see through the cards, and was equally adept at chess and Scrabble. Though only twenty-four, he smoked a pipe and had a patrician air that even intimidated some of the senior officers. CCC was not short of eccentrics but Joe stood as testament to the fact that the work attracted a special sort of character. Good at his job and an exceptional pilot, he was well liked if poorly understood.

'Want to try?'

Bobby took a spare ball and one of the clubs and tried a few desultory putts, but quickly decided it wasn't his game. He didn't have the patience.

'You won't make Colonel if you don't play golf,' said Joe.

'That's fine by me. I'm just here to fight.'

'Let's make this a little more interesting,' suggested Joe. 'Whoever lands a ball closest to the club door buys the first drink. Best of three.'

It wasn't exactly a fair contest but Joe knew Bobby would never refuse a challenge.

Joe had an effortless professional swing that sent each ball sailing gracefully towards its distant target. What Bobby's swing lacked in grace, precision and timing, it made up for in aggression and determination.

'Let's go see what we hit,' said Joe.

As they were crossing the road, an irate S2 came storming towards them, holding one of the golf balls.

'Ah, well done, we were just coming to find that.' Joe smiled broadly.

'God damn it, Lieutenant,' scowled the S2, 'you almost took my head off.'

'I'm sorry. Young Lake here has a bit of an over-enthusiastic swing. Look what you nearly did, Lake. I think you should apologise.'

Trying not to laugh, Bobby mumbled an apology.

The S2 eyed both men suspiciously, not sure if he was the butt of some larger joke. Unable to decide, he warned them to go play golf somewhere else and stormed off towards the TOC.

'Ow,' said Joe, offended, as Bobby punched him on the arm.

'Thanks a fucking lot, man.'

'You must admit, though, it was a good shot,' said Joe. 'It might even have been yours.'

'You got something to say?' The Recon Company 1st Sergeant looked up from his desk to see that Bobby was still standing in front of him.

'It just seems logical for me to take over the team, Top,' said Bobby.

'Well, listen up, son. Granger's run nine missions, and you've only run six. What's more, you're too young.' The 1st Sergeant leafed slowly through the paperwork on his desk.

'I'm twenty-one, Top,' protested Bobby, 'and Baker is only twenty and he's a One-zero . . .'

'Yeah, and he acts like it! I ain't arguing this with you. This is how it is! You're the One-one. Granger's the One-zero. Now get the fuck out of my office!'

Rod Granger was a twenty-three-year-old Staff Sergeant from Los Angeles. He was a six-foot, well-built, square-jawed, blue-eyed, good-looking surfer type. A former high school football hero, he was the very image of the archetypal Green Beret.

The One-two was Lieutenant Jim Bishop, a new guy, fresh in from the States.

Bishop was from Topeka, Kansas. He was new to CCC and Vietnam. Also twenty-three, he stood about five foot eight and always had a cigarette smouldering in his mouth. He had thick black hair, a moustache and dark darting eyes. He was a quiet man who kept himself to himself. His father was an Army Colonel and had been dead set against him joining Special Forces. But Bishop had joined anyway.

Granger announced they were getting a new team member, a Vietnamese Lieutenant called Dinh.

'Yards aren't going to like this,' said Bobby.

'I don't give a fuck what the Yards think,' said Granger.

He had come from a Vietnamese team, and had never worked recon with Montagnards. Likewise, Bobby had never worked with the Vietnamese. But he trusted Big Jack's verdict that, though some were smart, fast learners, and a few undoubtedly brave, the majority were lazy and dishonest.

'We got to train the Vietnamese to run recon and Dinh's going to be the shadow One-zero. He'll run as the One-three.'

'LLDB are next to fucking useless,' said Bobby, referring to the fact that Dinh was Vietnamese Special Forces.

'You worked a lot with LLDB?'

'Never have. Never want to.'

'Yeah, well, I have. Dinh is on the team. If he fucks up, he's off. He gets the same chance as everyone else. That OK with you?' Granger made it very clear that he neither sought nor needed Bobby's approval for his decision.

Dinh didn't make a great first impression. First he showed up late and, second, he wore tailored black fatigues and Ray-bans. It was an act you could get away with if you were a gunfighter, but not a cherry. After the quiet humility of the Montagnards, Dinh was cocky and over-familiar.

'Hey, Joe. How ya doing, man?' he said, trying to sound cool.

'I'm good, but you're fucking late.'

On the range, things didn't get any better.

'He can't handle a weapon. He reloads slow and the dough bag's dressed for Hollywood, not recon,' Bobby complained to Granger.

'Well, show him how it's done,' replied Granger irritably. 'You see something wrong, fix it. Don't come bitching to me. I know you're pissed about the fact that you ain't the One-zero, but deal with it, OK?'

The downpour died away, leaving the jungle soaked and dripping.

RT North Dakota was five kilometres deep into Laos and about a thousand metres from a main truck route. Who or what was moving on the route was vital information for the boys in Saigon, because out to the east, in Vietnam, the Special Forces camp at Dak-Pek was under siege. Half the camp had been overrun by the NVA. The surviving Montagnards and Special Forces detachment were slogging it out, face to face, with what was estimated to be a complete enemy regiment.

North Dakota had inserted about mid-afternoon the day before, and were now working their way in towards a point from which they could overlook the trail. This was a high-risk operation. The NVA didn't care for anyone getting within earshot of any of its convoys.

Loc was walking point. The ground in front of him suddenly fell away in a steep twenty-foot bank. It was possible to scramble down, but it would be less than ideal if they had to get back up in a hurry.

He signalled to Granger that he was moving left to look for a better route.

We go this way, Granger signalled back.

Loc shook his head.

Granger simply pointed down the slope.

Against all his instincts Loc obeyed and slowly picked his way down to the bottom. The rest of the team followed. Hih came last and managed to lose his footing and tumble into his comrades to hissed curses.

A little further on, Loc held up his hand then advanced a few feet to examine the faint signs of crushed leaf debris on the jungle floor. A small number of men, maybe eight, had crossed in front of them, perhaps in the last three hours or so. They had clearly come this way before it had rained.

Granger glanced at the tracks, and ordered Loc to continue.

Bobby estimated they were within two hundred metres of the trail. The pace was now painfully slow and deliberate, and everyone's senses strained to increase the collective awareness.

A single shot shattered the silence.

Loc spun round. Dinh's weapon had a faint wisp of smoke curling from the barrel.

'Shit!'

The team double-timed it, back to the bank, before changing direction and taking cover in some thick bush. For an hour they listened for any reaction, but none came.

Granger gripped Dinh by the lapel.

'Do that again and I'll kill you. Hear me?' he hissed. Dinh nodded, his face rigid with fear.

Well, at least the fucker's off the team, thought Bobby.

They spent the night huddled amongst a clump of splintered trees, within five hundred metres of the trail. Huge craters from 1000-pound bombs pockmarked the area.

Just before midnight, the faraway sound of trucks passing was clearly audible.

Granger powered up the radio to try and guide Covey in, but by the time he was overhead, the convoy was long gone.

Next day, they encountered a footpath. It cut across the neck of a bow in the trail which had been caused by repeated bombing. The shortcut saved the weary NVA troops about a thousand metres that they would have had to walk had they followed the road.

Granger moved them north to a point close to where the footpath split off from the trail, up a short steep slope that actually had steps cut into it. From this vantage point there was a good view of the trail. The team burrowed deep into the undergrowth and set up a perimeter of claymores.

A convoy of eight trucks passed by soon after dark. Again Granger alerted Covey.

'Er, Roger that, Happy Cloud,' replied Covey, 'I have Spectre en route to your location.'

The huge, slow-moving Spectre gunships only ever flew at night and their reputation as a cruel nocturnal bird of prey was well earned. Spectre could pour concentrated fire down on a target with incredible accuracy.

B-B-Bap. B-B-Bap. Zzzzzzzz. Zzzzzzz.

The sound of firing rippled through the night as Spectre located the trucks. Far away through the trees, across the other side of a distant ridge, the pulsing light from the burning vehicles was clearly visible.

No one could see the dead and wounded

sprawled around the flaming hulks, but a feeling of satisfaction engulfed the team. Eight trucks wouldn't get to Vietnam. More importantly, eight truck drivers would be unlikely to continue the war.

I hope we killed them, I hope we killed a lot. For a moment Bobby felt surprised and vaguely ashamed that he could think such things, but the sound of Spectre opening up a renewed attack quickly banished his introspection.

'Viet! Viet come,' hissed Loc.

Bobby slipped his spoon back into his ration packet and gripped the claymore trigger.

It was barely light and Rah had spotted a group of about forty NVA soldiers trudging towards them. They had turned off the trail and were now clambering up the footpath that passed within twenty feet of the team.

Bobby could hear the creaking of rucksack straps and clink of weapon magazines against their belt buckles. Beside him, Granger eased himself up on to one knee, and raised his carbine to his shoulder.

He can't be going to fire! He can't, thought Bobby. Surely they were not going to ambush a whole NVA platoon! A regiment might not be far behind them.

Granger fired.

No going back now. All or nothing. Bobby squeezed the claymore trigger.

The other claymores all went off half a second later, tearing into the middle of the column. The survivors at the head and the tail fled in opposite directions.

Muzzle flashes tore holes in the gloom and smoke from the claymores hung in the air.

'Cover me!' Granger yelled, stepping out on to the path, firing bursts left and right. Bobby dashed after him. Granger grabbed hold of the first body he came to and rolled it over.

'What the fuck are you doing?' Bobby yelled above the continuing fire.

'Check those guys out. See if we got a wounded one,' ordered Granger.

Mangled corpses lay twisted and open-eyed. The blast had separated some limbs at the joints. Bobby smelt the odour of the newly dead, the mixed scent of blood, faeces, and burnt cordite.

'Nothing here!'

'Let's go!' yelled Granger, hurling white phosphorous to mask the team's retreat.

For the next twenty minutes they ran, as the survivors shot at anything that moved.

After a while they stopped to pull off the black nylon windcheaters they'd been wearing during the

night and lay a pattern of mines across their back
trail.

Granger made another right-angle turn and led
the team back towards the trail. They halted on the
edge of another heavily cratered area and waited. At
least this was a good position. They were well
concealed in thick bush and if necessary could fall
back to one of the craters.

'What now?' asked Bobby.

'We go on with the mission,' said Granger as if it
were blindingly obvious.

'After that shit you just pulled! We're going back
towards the trail?'

Granger didn't reply.

Just before midday a lone shot came from the
north. It was immediately answered by two other
shots, one to the northwest and another to the
south.

Bobby saw the colour drain from Bishop's face.
Granger pulled out his map and started to study it.

I'd move north right now, Bobby thought. I
wouldn't be looking at any fucking map.

Seconds later, Granger had them moving south.
They scurried through the jungle for about a
hundred metres, then turned east at a more cautious
pace.

Suddenly short sharp bursts of automatic fire

opened up from one or more AKs. Bobby heard the crack-thump of the bullets passing overhead. Voices yelled out in Vietnamese. More voices replied and more shots followed from the right. The NVA had caught a fleeting glimpse of the team and was now blindly peppering the area.

As one, North Dakota let rip with a hail of return fire.

'We need to move!' shouted Bobby, changing magazines. In front of him a bullet smashed through the bark of a tree, showering him with sharp splinters.

'Go! Go!' Granger shouted.

After another hundred metres the team halted. Granger reached into the pocket sewn on to the top flap of Bishop's pack and pulled out a claymore. As Bobby and Hih ran past, Granger placed the claymore, tugged the fuse, and ran.

Forty-five seconds later the mine exploded. Granger corralled his men into an extended line to face their pursuers.

Three or four shapes appeared in the jungle, only to disappear in the heat of muzzle flashes and shredded foliage. As bolts locked back on empty magazines, the team swung round and started running. A few minutes later they tumbled into a shallow crater, and prepared to make a stand.

Bobby heard Bishop calling for extraction.

Maybe he had had enough fun, thought Bobby to himself as he stacked his magazines and grenades.

The first charge was stopped dead by a concentrated hail of fire.

The second attempt to overrun North Dakota petered out into a close-range firefight, which ended when the enemy withdrew leaving both dead and wounded.

Cautiously Bobby peered from the rim of the crater and tried to see whether he could spot movement in the trees beyond the fallen bodies. The NVA would be able to reinforce this area quickly. Maybe it would be better to run, but run where? At least here they had an LZ.

The NVA did try to assemble more troops, but Covey called in a flight of Air Force F-4s and used them to drop a perimeter of 500-pound bombs around the team.

Bobby covered his head as the debris rained down on them.

Within fifteen minutes the gaggle was overhead.

The Cobras turned their rockets and guns on the tree line. Pod-mounted 20mm Vulcan cannon reduced the strongest trees to pulp.

The short-clipped instructions and confirmations hissed from the radio.

'Panther 31, in on the tree line.'

'Roger, 31. Watch those guys to the east.'

'25 is coming round again. Slicks are running in.'

'Roger, 25.'

Two Hueys raced down the far tree line banking steeply, bleeding off speed in the turn, and flaring hard to come to a halt within feet of the crater.

In the rush to make their escape, it was not a perfect split of four per helicopter. Bobby found himself with Rah and Granger on the second machine, as it swung itself through thirty degrees, tipped forward and began to accelerate up over the trees towards Vietnam.

Granger was firing his CAR-15 from the open door. 'Yeehaaah!' he yelled with child-like enthusiasm.

It occurred to Bobby that maybe Granger was blessed; that he was one of those people who could do anything he liked and get away with it. Not for him the cruel consequences of challenging the god of war. Granger would emerge from whatever fuck-up he had caused and never be aware of how close he'd been to disaster. And if he died, mused Bobby, he'd probably get the Congressional Medal of Honour.

'Four or five dead is what the radio said.'

According to Bishop, the Ohio National Guard had shot and killed a group of students.

'Seems they burnt down the ROTC building at

Kent State to protest against the Cambodian invasion. Things got out of hand and – blam! Greased four long hairs.' Bishop didn't seem too bothered.

Bobby couldn't believe what he was hearing; soldiers shooting students? Even if they were pro-Hanoi hippies, this was America, for Christ's sake! He could only imagine what Rachel would say in her next letter, and he wouldn't blame her. These days her letters had ceased to express anything intimate, and revolved mainly around the conduct of the war. It was not worth arguing with her. Everything had become theoretical, not personal. The war Rachel talked about was a million miles away from the one Bobby was fighting.

14

'So Dinh's off the team?' asked Bobby as they left the debriefing.

'No. He stays. He fucked up; he knows it. If it happens again, we'll can him,' said Granger casually.

'Never figured you to kiss anybody's ass.'

Granger stopped, and turned. 'Just who the fuck do you think you are? Newsflash, Lake. Dinh's got more chance of staying on this team than you have right now!'

'Anybody else would be gone. You know it.'

'Oh, yeah? Well, if you think you can't run with Dinh, then go get another team.' Granger began walking. 'Otherwise, just do your job and shut the fuck up.'

'Some guys just love to kick ass.' That was Doug Webber's opinion.

'Sure. But I still don't see why we hit them. We could have watched the trail for another night.' Bobby wiped his mouth and placed his glass back on the bar. The mission was considered to have been a success. Trucks destroyed and a bunch of bad guys dead. Granger was basking in the glory.

'Big Jack wouldn't have done it like that.'

'Big Jack is a damn' good soldier,' said Webber. 'But how many One-zero's are gonna want a One-one on the team who thinks he's hot shit but ain't done squat to prove it?'

Bobby felt a flush rise to his cheeks.

'If you wanna be a One-zero then you've got to take all the crap that recon throws at you and deal with it.'

'Even if the One-zero thinks he's bullet proof?'

'Especially if the fucking One-zero thinks he's bullet proof,' growled Doug. 'The One-one's there to back up everything the One-zero does. You can bitch and question all you like in the planning stage, but once the shit goes down, you back him up one hundred percent or get the fuck off the team! Now that's good advice, soldier, and you owe me a drink.'

Bright Light standby meant hanging around the launch-site compound, with all your equipment packed and ready to go. You could read a book, write letters or listen to the radio, but you never left that compound.

North Dakota was spending a week on Bright Light.

Since Bright Lights were only called in once something had gone wrong, the team went heavy. This meant all twelve men, and extra weapons such as two M-60 machine guns and an RPG rocket launcher. The team carried no rations or sleeping gear, just extra claymores, C-4 blocks and extra ammo. There was nothing subtle about a heavy team.

'That was *Little Arrows* by Leapy Lee,' announced the voice of the Armed Forces radio announcer. It was music that made anyone yearn for combat.

Bobby punched his pack to try and make it a more comfortable pillow as he lay down on the floor of the Bright Light standby hut and closed his eyes.

'Lets go!' yelled Granger just as Bobby was drifting off. 'There's a chopper down eight clicks over the fence.'

A Cobra had gone down while waiting to pull a team out.

'Here's the deal,' Captain Gillman briefed them. 'The pilot's hurt bad and the co-pilot's gone. They tried to drop a STABO to pick him up, but took fire. You guys are the only hope. We got Spads overhead and another two Panthers but they're taking a lot of shit.'

Fifteen minutes later, North Dakota was standing out on the runway, waiting for the three Hueys returning to refuel and pick them up.

'Is everybody ready?' yelled Granger, like a football coach, psyching the team up before a game.

The Montagnards all smiled wide-eyed, toothy smiles and vigorously shook their heads.

'Yaahh! Kill VC!' shouted Dinh.

'Damn right we kill VC,' said Granger. Bishop sucked on his cigarette, and completed his radio check with the launch site, before handing the set over to his One-zero.

The weather didn't look good. It was the start of the monsoon season, and it had rained on and off all day. The cloud base was low and foreboding.

The downdraft from the three Hueys whipped spray off the puddles, creating a cooling breeze which mixed headily with the heat of the turbines and the smell of avgas. Clambering aboard the second helicopter with three of the team, Bobby felt a surge of dread. They were almost certainly flying right into a firefight. He just prayed Granger didn't really believe they were all bullet proof.

Occasional rain showers gusted through the Huey's open doors. It was a twenty-minute flight and, by the time they arrived over the crash site, Bobby was soaked.

The Cobra had gone down in a stream. Bobby could see Covey, the other Cobras and A-1s circling and swooping over the scene. The A-1s had dropped napalm on the opposite bank. It was still burning, and the column of greyish-black smoke gave them a useful marker. As the Cobras passed the smoke, the downwash whipped it into looping coils that hung momentarily in the air, and then vanished into formless mist.

What was left of the smashed Cobra was barely visible from the air. The pilot, unable to walk, had crawled off into the jungle. About one hundred and fifty yards downstream was a rock-strewn sand bar, just wide enough for a Huey.

'Lead says we're going in. OK?' yelled one of the pilots.

Bobby gave an immediate thumbs-up.

The first helicopter hovered low over the sand bar. Dirt erupted around it as enemy gunfire grazed the ground. The team spilled from its sides and dived for cover. The Huey tipped forward and sped away up the streambed, the door gunners raking the surrounding jungle with fire.

The pilot of the second helicopter aborted his approach and Bobby hung on tight as the helicopter banked steeply left.

Two Cobras screamed past. One broke to the right as the other rolled into the attack, firing a salvo of rockets at the enemy.

'Get me in there,' yelled Bobby to the ashen-faced pilot.

'No way! It's too hot.'

'Bullshit! My team's down there!'

There was a loud clank as a round hit the helicopter. Bobby held his breath.

'We're OK,' shouted the pilot, scanning his instruments and checking for signs of damage.

'Good. Now get me in there!'

Both door gunners opened up, fingers locked back on triggers. Bobby was worried the pilot was taking them in too fast, but at the last moment the machine reared into a flare. It settled into a hover three feet above the ground, drifting forward at two or three miles an hour. That was good enough. The team burst from the cabin, thumping down on to the sand bar. Relieved of their weight, the helicopter leapt back into the air, and accelerated away.

Bobby wiped damp sand away from his face. The Cobras had done the trick, and they weren't taking any fire, but he could only see two of the three men he was expecting.

'Where the hell is Dinh?' he asked.

'He stay on *helicop*,' said Rah, as if it were no big deal.

Bobby couldn't believe his ears, but he could be angry later. Right now, he had to tie up with the rest of the team. Granger was waving to them from behind the cover of some larger boulders.

Rah hoisted the sling of the heavy M-60 machine gun over his shoulder and led the way with Bobby close behind.

'Who's missing?' Granger asked.

'Dinh. He stayed on the chopper,' replied Bobby.

Granger didn't respond, and then said, 'The radio took a round when we came in. It's fucked.' The One-zero was completely unperturbed by the narrowness of his escape.

The third Huey dropped off Bishop and the last three Montagnards, and the eleven men pushed on to the crash site. It was starting to drizzle.

The Cobra's shrapnel-riddled tail section had smashed off, and one of the twisted blades was sticking out of the shallow water. Smoke from the napalm strike still hung over the scene like a sorcerer's mist. Granger arranged the team methodically in an all-round defence, while Bobby and Hih checked out the wreckage. The nose section lay half in the water, on its side on the far bank.

Within the smashed Plexiglas of the cockpit lay the co-pilot, one arm trapped inside and the other hanging limply down to the ground. The control panel and gun-aiming yoke had been forced back across his chest, pinning him into his seat. The black sun visor on his helmet was down, obscuring his eyes and making him look more like some sort of broken robot than a human being.

The sound of electrical sparking was unmistakable and a thin wisp of smoke rose from the shorting wires. The rain had obviously seeped through the avionics compartment.

Bobby had to move fast. The wreck would be a magnet for the NVA.

The rear cockpit was empty, the pilot having survived the crash. Bobby kicked away at the remaining Plexiglas and reached into the co-pilot's flight suit to pull off his dog tags. Feeling strangely detached from the grisly process, he also removed the dead man's watch and, with the aid of his own saliva, freed his wedding ring from the cold hand.

'Let's find the other guy,' said Bobby to Hih.

Loc waved to indicate he'd found the pilot's trail.

The injured man had managed to crawl about seventy yards. He was alive but unconscious, slumped against a tree, a .38 revolver and survival radio in his hands.

The pilot didn't so much as flinch when Loc placed his foot firmly on the hand holding the weapon, then slipped it from the limp grasp. Experience had taught Loc to be cautious around injured men with weapons. They might just shoot at the first blurred figure they saw.

Both of the pilot's legs were badly smashed and lacerated, and one was twisted at an odd angle below his knee. His flight suit was black with blood, and he looked deathly pale.

Bishop injected him with morphine. He couldn't walk anyway, and the last thing they needed was the man suddenly coming round, screaming in pain.

The rain started to fall more heavily now.

'We need to get the other body,' grunted Granger to Bobby as he hoisted the injured pilot on to his shoulder.

'He's pretty crunched into that wreckage, I doubt we can get him out,' Bobby shouted over the noise of another Cobra passing low overhead.

'We haven't got time to fuck about. Let's get this guy out of here.'

Back at Dak-To, Bobby spotted Dinh limping from one of the other Hueys.

The Vietnamese was looking around nervously and seeing Bobby closing in on him, made his limp more pronounced.

'Hi, Lake.' Dinh smiled weakly, and then suddenly broke into a run.

Bobby swept the man's legs from under him, and

he fell heavily on to the mud beside the runway. Dinh tried to get up, but fell back again as Bobby kicked him hard in the stomach.

'You little shit!' roared Bobby. Dinh's eyes were wide with terror. He began screaming in high-pitched Vietnamese until silenced by a right hook. Bobby felt Dinh's teeth against his knuckles.

'Whoa! That's enough. Leave the poor guy alone.' The helicopter door gunner grabbed hold of Bobby's arm, only to receive an elbow in the face.

Unlike a lot of door gunners, this guy was big. He stood at least six foot two and was nicknamed Bear by the rest of the guys in the 170th Air Assault Helicopter Company. Blood trickled from his nose. He wiped it away almost absent-mindedly with his fingertip, and then lunged at Bobby.

'Hey! Take it easy, big guy.' Granger wrestled Bear to the ground.

'What the hell is going on here!' yelled Captain Gillman, running over from the launch-site compound.

Bear tore himself free from Granger's loosened grip and climbed to his feet.

'I'm sorry, man,' said Bobby to the scowling door gunner. 'This is team stuff. It's nothing to do with you.'

'Yeah, OK, I guess,' said Bear, and walked back to his Huey, to be greeted by a very frosty glare from his aircraft commander who was not at all impressed by the very conspicuous brawling.

'Why'd you stay on the chopper?' Granger snapped at Dinh who remained where he was, curled on the floor.

'He crazy, crazy,' Dinh mumbled, pointing at Bobby.

'Grab your gear and get out of here. You're off the team,' said Granger. 'Sorry, sir. Won't happen again,' he added to Gillman who nodded curtly and marched back to the compound.

'Happy now?' asked Granger as Bobby turned to go.

'Sure.'

'Get one thing straight, Lake,' Granger said, 'it's me who says who's on or off this team, OK? Not you. I don't give a fuck if you hate my guts, I'm the One-zero. The only reason you're still my One-one is that you cut it out in the woods. But you ever pull that shit again, and I'll kick your ass all the way to Saigon. You read me?'

Bobby nodded. 'Loud and clear.'

Back in the Bright Light hut Bobby nursed a cup of coffee, and watched Bishop trying to light a cigarette with shaking hands.

Bobby took the cigarette out of his mouth and lit it for him.

'Thanks, man.' Bishop took a long appreciative drag.

'You know, this shit ain't for everybody,' said Bobby.

'Good for my career,' said Bishop.

'Really?'

'It's the easiest way to get a CIB,' said Bishop. Officers interested in a career saw a combat infantryman's badge as essential.

'It ain't such a great career move if you're dead.'

The rain had cleared and the sun was low in the sky. Shadows stretched out across the launch site, and the Montagnards settled down to a game of cards.

Granger walked in and sat down on the bench seat that ran along the wall.

'The pilot's going to be OK,' he said in a tired voice. 'We're going back in tomorrow to get the other body.'

'We're gonna need tools to cut him out of that wreck,' said Bobby.

'If we can't get him out, we just take his head.' Granger stared at the floor.

'You have to be kidding?'

'That's the deal,' Granger said grimly. 'If we can't get all of him, we just remove the head. If we don't, then he's MIA, not KIA. Gill tells me they had to do the same thing for an Oscar-deuce pilot who went down last year.'

'We gotta cut his head off?' Bishop grimaced.

'You know another way of doing it?' replied Granger.

'Fuck,' said Bobby. He didn't know what else to say.

'If I don't make it,' Bishop was grim-faced, 'leave me in one piece, OK? Please don't cut my head or anything else off. Just leave me.'

They all looked at each other. Then all three men laughed.

Bobby laughed till he felt the tears rolling down his cheeks. Eventually, it didn't sound like laughing any more and he had to go outside until the tears passed.

The next day all aircraft were grounded by a torrential storm, which also brought minimal visibility. When the weather finally broke the morning after, there was one team waiting to insert and two needing to be pulled out.

It was late-afternoon before North Dakota made it back to the crash site. The NVA had already been over the wreck. They had taken the co-pilot's helmet as a souvenir, and opened up the ammunition bays on the side of the fuselage.

It fell to Granger as the One-zero to perform the

grisly task. The two men had spent all the previous day sharpening their banana knives which were normally used to cut bamboo and vegetation for landing zones.

After the rain, the head was slick and difficult to hold on to. Bobby covered the face using two triangular bandages. To an extent, this depersonalised the task and made the crude surgery easier.

Heads do not come off easily, Bobby discovered. He tried not to look but it seemed unfair to let Granger perform the horror alone. Probably for the same reason, Bishop stood close enough to bear witness and it was he who put the blond-haired man's head in the bag and carried it back to Dak-To.

Bobby was awakened by the sound of machine-gun fire.

'Is that incoming?' Bishop asked.

'Not waiting to find out,' said Granger, swinging his feet from his bed and grabbing his pants.

The attack siren wailed into life. It was official. Beyond the thin walls, Bobby could hear the rest of Recon Company snapping into life.

Bishop was first out of the door with Bobby right behind him. He had flung web gear over his bare torso, and carried his fatigue shirt in one hand and his carbine in the other. At best, this was only a drill. At worst, sappers had got into the camp. Memories were still fresh of the 1 April attack that had resulted in ten Montagnards dead.

They reached North Dakota's alert position in the sandbagged bunkers built into the sand berm wall that surrounded the camp. Loc and most of the Montagnards were already there, itching for a fight.

Bobby dropped his equipment and pulled on his shirt. All around, shadowy figures zigzagged along the trench that ran across the back of the bunkers. The air was filled with the clicking and clacking of weapons being readied. Someone fired some illumination rounds and the drifting parachute flares cast an eerie unnatural light across the ground wire entanglement and to the village beyond the bunker.

Nothing. Silence.

'Anyone know what's up?' Granger asked.

Bobby peered along the trench line, trying to raise the attention of the next team down the wall, RT Colorado.

'Hey! Hey!'

'Hey yourself.'

'What's going on?'

'How the hell should I know?'

'Who the fuck is that?' asked another voice.

'Lake, Bob Lake.'

'Hey, Lake. How's it hanging?'

'OK. You guys know what's going on?'

'Shit. I was gonna ask you the same thing.'

'It's gotta be a drill,' said Bishop, fiddling in his breast pocket for his cigarettes.

Mumbled swearing and some laughter began to ripple along the wall. A lone figure picked his way down the trench, from bunker to bunker.

'You men, stand down,' ordered Lieutenant Cohen when he reached them. Cohen was a new guy with the Hatchet Force. He was sporting a GI steel helmet, an item very rarely seen in Recon and an object of some derision. It was one thing being a new guy but quite another dressing like one.

'What the fuck was that all about?' Bishop asked.

'False alarm. That's all,' said the Lieutenant and continued on down the line.

Recon Company wandered back to its rooms. Knowing they were too wired now to get back to sleep, a small crowd had gathered for a drink and a smoke.

'Some fat fuck Major up from Nha Trang got drunk, went down to the bunker by the gate and fired off the 30-cal,' said one of the gunfighters.

Bobby popped the ring pull and let the cold liquid flow down his throat. The beer tasted good. Bishop lit a cigarette and blew smoke into the night air.

'Here's the plan,' said one of the gunfighters. 'We finish the beer and then we'll go and pop some CS gas on the Major, see how *he* likes being got out of the sack at o-dark-zero in the morning.'

15

Based in Kontum, the 32nd *Biet Dong Quan* (BDQ) Regiment or Army Rangers considered themselves an elite unit within the Vietnamese Army.

It was early evening and a group of five BDQ Rangers were posing and showboating outside a café on the edge of Kontum. They laughed and drank and demanded the company of every single woman who walked by. One of the group was a young Lieutenant. He was a confident and popular kind of guy who had risen fast by being helpful to the right officers. His friends knew that anyone who stuck close to him would be all right. It paid to have him as a friend and, under his leadership, the little group of Rangers saw themselves as the brightest and best.

The young Lieutenant leaned backwards on his chair. One hand in his pocket and the other holding his drink, he tipped his head back too far to notice he was going to overbalance.

The chair tipped back and one leg slipped from the raised platform of the café, spilling the young Lieutenant across the pavement and into the street.

A scooter rickshaw had to brake heavily to avoid running him over.

The rickshaw driver gave the young Lieutenant a piece of his mind, but quickly lost interest in the scolding when he saw the officers's four companions get to their feet.

Across the road were two Montagnards. One was a tallish, slim man, well-turned out. The other was younger and shorter and was wearing a big grin.

'Who the hell do you think you are laughing at, you dirty little beast?' called one of the Rangers.

'I no laugh!' came the reply.

'You'll laugh on the other side of your face when I beat you.'

'I no laugh,' repeated the young Montagnard. His grin remained fixed on his face while his eyes flickered nervously this way and that.

The older Montagnard was urging the young one to start walking.

'You laughing at me?' yelled the Ranger Lieutenant, striding across the road. 'Well, try laughing at this!' And he drew his treasured .38 Special revolver from its low-ride holster and levelled it at the young Montagnard's face.

Hih didn't care for Vietnamese, even though Loc had told him that there were both good and bad. Hih knew the good ones didn't point guns at you.

The Lieutenant's superior smirk evaporated as the Montagnards produced pistols and aimed back at him.

'You shoot, you die,' said Loc.

Who the hell were these guys? the Lieutenant wondered. Were they with the American Special Forces out at the camp down Highway 14? If so, then these were crazy men. He didn't want any trouble. He'd carefully avoided any serious combat. He certainly didn't want to die on the street of some provincial town in the middle of the highlands. He wanted to end his days in Saigon, an old rich man, married to a beautiful girl, many years his junior.

'This man must apologise.' The Lieutenant cleared his throat, trying to keep his voice firm for the benefit of his comrades who remained frozen motionless on the other side of the street. The second that guns were drawn passers-by had run for cover. All eyes were now trained on the Vietnamese officer's moment of truth.

'We go now,' said Loc. 'We go. No trouble.'

Hih lowered his weapon and stepped back. The Lieutenant, sensing that Loc was the cooler of the two Montagnards, also lowered his gun.

Loc holstered his .45 and, gently pushing Hih in front of him, walked away.

'You showed 'em,' called one of the Rangers.

'No good dirty little cowards.'

It was more than Hih could stand. He had never run from a fight.

Bang.

The Ranger Lieutenant staggered backwards, arms flailing, and fell heavily, the outside of his right foot hit by one shot from Hih's .45.

'*Merde!*' hissed Loc. '*Allez vite!*' he shouted to his grinning friend.

> *Riding down the road*
> *In our Mercedes Benz*
> *Killing all the gooks,*
> *Saving all our friends*

The club was in full swing. Recon Company was belting out the latest Christmas carol rewrite that the gunfighters had come up with.

> *Spads are in the air*
> *Covey's on his way*
> *Oh, what fun . . .*

Escaping from the cigar and cigarette smoke and the deafening noise, Bobby decided to join Bishop outside.

'This target we got, India Nine. It's going to be a tough one, right?' said Bishop.

'A lot of people have been in there before us,' said Bobby. 'The gooks aren't dumb. They know we might try again.'

India Nine was a hellhole. One of several targets in and around the area, nicknamed the Bra because Highway 96 ran across the river in two distinct bows, the target file made grim reading. No one looked forward to going in there. Even some of the most hardened gunfighters said they'd rather quit than go back. But that was just talk. None of the hardcore would seriously think of quitting.

More than anything, Bobby worried about going into India Nine with Granger. Another unplanned ambush could mean real trouble.

'*Chef!*'

Bobby snapped his heels together and saluted. He always greeted Loc in the style of a French Colonial officer. It had become a standing joke between them.

'*Bonsoir, Capitaine Loc. Ça va?*' said Bobby, happy to see him.

'*Oui. Ça va bien, merci.*' Loc did not return Bobby's smile. '*Nous avons un grand problème.*' We have a big problem. The Montagnard explained the incident downtown.

'Sounds like a hell of a good shot.' Bobby struggled not to laugh.

'He was probably aiming for the guy's dick,'

snorted Bishop. 'Do they know who you are?'

'We all look same, same.'

'Fucking hell, Loc. Can't you control your men?' Granger was extremely irritated at being dragged away from the club.

Loc was only too well aware that he was responsible, though not at fault. He said nothing. His service in the French Army had taught him that arguing with Sergeants was a losing battle.

'Maybe I'd better go and tell the Top we've got some trouble.' Bobby decided to intervene.

'Could be too late.' Bishop pointed to the glow of headlights approaching the main gate from Kontum.

'Bob, go check it out,' said Granger, losing interest in the confrontation. 'You know where to find me.'

Clyde Emery, the duty NCO for the guard that night, was a calm, softly, spoken man from Georgia. He'd done his time with the Hatchet Force and had signed on for a second tour with the Security Company on account of the fact that he'd promised his new wife he wouldn't die in Vietnam.

Back-lit by the jeep's headlights, an agitated Vietnamese Major was yelling at Emery through the gate, demanding to be let into the camp.

'I'm sorry, sir. I can't do that,' drawled Emery.
More shouting followed.

'Yes, sir. I understand, but I can't let you in.'
Bobby walked up slowly behind Clyde.

Spotting that Bobby was younger and had less seniority than the big, obstinate American he was talking to, the Vietnamese Major tried another approach. 'You! You go get Senior Officer. You go now.'

'Fuck you!' said Bobby.

'Steady there, son,' said Clyde, 'I already sent someone to find the Colonel.'

A truck pulled up behind the Major's jeep, disgorging a dozen or so armed men.

The Major beamed. He had back up. His driver lifted an M-16 from between the seats of the jeep and cocked it.

Clyde unslung and cocked his Swedish-K.

'You wanna tell your boys to relax and step back a bit there, Major?' he said in a quiet but determined tone.

The Major barked a few sharp orders, and his Rangers retreated.

The young Hatchet Force Lieutenant was out to impress. He'd heard there was a problem at the North gate and was keen to have it all dealt with by the time the Colonel got there.

'Who are you?' demanded the Major.

'Lieutenant Cohen.'

The Major looked Cohen up and down with barely disguised disgust. Realising the breach in protocol, Cohen snapped to attention and saluted.

'Jesus,' breathed Bobby in disgust, loud enough for Cohen to hear.

The Major returned the salute in a lazy and dismissive fashion.

'So what seems to be the problem, sir?' inquired Cohen in a less than certain tone.

'One of your dirty little tribesmen has killed one of my men!'

'He was shot in the foot. He's not dead. It's all bullshit. ARVN Rangers started ragging on two of my guys downtown. ARVN drew first. The Yards were just defending themselves, sir,' Bobby explained.

'He lie!' barked the Major.

'Yeah, and you suck dick!'

'That's enough!' snapped Cohen. 'Excuse me for a second, Major,' he added, stepping back from the gate with Clyde. 'What do you recommend, Sergeant Emery?'

'Tell 'em to come back in the morning, sir.'

Cohen did as he was advised.

'No! You bring man here! We take him!' The Major was now apoplectic.

'They ain't coming in here, sir,' Clyde said to

Cohen, 'and they sure as hell ain't taking one of the Yards with them. If we let that happen, then we got a full-blown fuck-up on our hands.'

The sound of boots signalled the arrival of the Colonel and his deputy.

'Good evening, gentlemen,' said the Colonel.

Lieutenant Cohen offered his version of events, which was then corrected by Staff Sergeant Emery.

The Colonel was a skilled politician. He explained that it was security that prevented him from being able to invite the Major in. Would he like to come back tomorrow morning for some coffee? Maybe stay for a bite to eat, and a lunchtime drink at the club? The Major agreed. He knew he was being treated with respect, and that was all it took.

The four men watched the Rangers drive off into the night.

'How's it going, Sergeant Emery?'

'Fine, sir, just fine.' Clyde and the Colonel had known each other a long time.

The Colonel turned to Bobby. 'Lake? North Dakota, right? All set for your next target?'

'Yes, sir. We certainly are.'

'Good. Excellent. Outstanding. Good night, gentlemen.'

As the Colonel turned to go he said, 'Lieutenant, I'd like to see your report on this matter on my desk. First thing in the morning.'

*

The team had ditched their packs a while back. Two men were wounded but still able to move though they couldn't run. The One-zero had circled his men amongst some rocks at the base of a small cliff. Sweat stinging their eyes and hearts beating like steam hammers, they tore the grenades and fresh magazines from their pouches and waited grimly for the enemy to appear.

North Dakota had been waiting to insert on the mission to India Nine when it became obvious that things had gone badly wrong for the Bright Light team. Pinned down on the LZ, they desperately needed assistance and North Dakota were closest.

Bobby swung his legs out of the door, ready to jump clear of the Huey. Watching the war on TV news, troops always seemed to disembark from helicopters at a leisurely pace. It was very different in real life.

On the far side of the LZ, the wreck of a shot-down Huey burned furiously. The Bright Light team were holding a perimeter on the northwestern edge.

As the tree tops rushed past close to the skids Bobby gripped the lash-down ring. The Huey reared on to its tail to slow to a low hover in the clearing.

Bobby and three Montagnards leapt to the ground. Spent cases rained down on them from the door gunner's M-60 as the Huey tipped forward, its blades chopping for lift in the humid, thin mountain air, and swept away over the trees.

The air was thick with smoke and the smell of gunfire. The ground was wet and muddy. Two Vietnamese team members lay, bloody and limp, on the flattened foliage in the middle of the semi-circular perimeter that the team had established. A third badly wounded man was propped against a tree. The ground was strewn with spent brass, bloodied field dressings, orange marker panels and discarded web gear.

'Covering fire!' yelled the Bright Light team leader, as the next Huey began its run into the LZ.

All nine weapons on the perimeter crackled away, sending a crescendo of fire into the jungle.

In the rush to get any helicopter in during the lull caused by an air strike, Bobby found himself on the ground first. Granger followed with the wide-eyed Bishop just behind.

'You guys bring any ammo?' was the first thing the team leader asked. He was a black Captain called Carl Joyner.

'We only got what we're carrying,' said Bobby.

'Shit man! We're almost out!' Joyner was far from most people's stereotypical idea of a black man from Detroit. His politics made Nixon look like a liberal, and he had little time for the perceived plight of his fellow blacks, or anyone else for that matter. In Joyner's eyes there was no black or white in the world, just guys like him, then the fucked-up, lazy and stupid who made up the rest of the known world.

'We'd got about two hundred metres down that way,' he told Granger, 'when we ran into at least one platoon. We lost two guys and one wounded. We didi'd back here and they've rushed us about four times. The fast movers have dumped a shit load of stuff on the motherfuckers, so I reckon they must be hurting right now.'

Another Huey came in to evacuate the wounded and dead. The wounded man went first. He was the priority. Bobby helped carry one of the dead, and throw the body into the cabin. It was an act without dignity.

Joyner's team were Vietnamese, and their point man another former NVA soldier who had changed sides. Joyner wouldn't hear a word against this man and trusted him implicitly. The scout dressed in full NVA uniform boldly strode along in front of the team, warning of any approaching enemy who, if they saw him, would assume he was one of theirs.

On the two occasions the enemy had made that assumption, it had proved a fatal mistake for them.

To cover the breakout, the A-1s spread carpet of cluster bombs directly in front of the two teams.

Bobby brought up North Dakota's rear, situated halfway down the column with Alec Hidaka, the One-one from Joyner's team. Hidaka was a slight wiry man of Japanese descent. He tended to keep himself to himself, but Joyner spoke highly of him, and he had enough experience to be a One-zero.

They moved down the slope and then turned to head up the valley.

The column moved fast, towards their beleaguered comrades, occasionally firing a pen-flare so that Covey could talk them forward.

Below them, in the valley, they could hear a platoon of 37mm-AA guns thumping away. The roar of a fast mover drowned the guns and then came the door-slamming detonation of the bombs. Only one AA gun fired after that.

The column halted while air strikes were called in. Bobby felt the earth-shattering thud of the bombs as he crouched, waiting to move on.

B-B-B-Bap. Contact.

'Go! Go! Go!' came the word from the front of the column and the sixteen men pushed on.

B-B-B-Bap. C-C-Cah, C-C-Cah.

Too late. The front of the column was pinned down in a sudden firefight. Bobby and Hidaka pushed left on the flank, dragging the rear half of the column up the slope with them.

Bobby fired towards the sound of the enemy weapons, and pulled one of the Bright Light's M-60 gunners up with him. The M-60 fired long bursts for about ten seconds and then ran dry. Someone threw a last belt of fifty rounds over to them and Bobby flicked open the cover on the gun and slapped a new belt into the feed tray.

'Get down! Get down!' Joyner's voice was obliterated by the thump of rockets slamming into the hillside, only metres in front of their position, showering rain water from the trees. Bobby pulled himself into the foetal position as the debris rained down. Hidaka cried out as he was hit by something heavy.

'You OK?'

'Yeah. Fine,' he groaned, pushing a six-foot, arm-thick log from across his chest.

'C'mon, cocksuckers. Let's go. Up and at them!' yelled Joyner.

'Let's go!' Granger added his voice to the din.

Bobby stood and fired, as did the M-60 gunner, scything down the foliage in front of him. Bloop! Bobby heard an M-79 off to his right. Bright Light and North Dakota now advanced as a ragged line towards the trapped team, with what was left of the enemy between them.

Bobby took cover as return fire started to slap into trees above his head.

Whack! A round hit the M-60 gunner at the base of his neck. He fell clutching the wound, his fingers submerging in thick red blood.

Bobby fired a sustained burst. 'Get some fucking fire down, for Christ's sake,' he roared, as some of the team seemed to be more intent on taking cover than shooting back.

Turning to the stricken M-60 gunner, Bobby ripped the field dressing from his harness. Hidaka crawled to help.

'I got him,' Hidaka said.

'You guys, come with me!' shouted Bobby to the Vietnamese he could see on his left. Without hesitation the four men scrambled over to him.

Bobby crawled on hands and knees towards the sound of the M-79, pushing through the bushes to find Hih firing furiously and reloading. He grinned at Bobby, then snapped the breach shut and fired another grenade up the hillside. Beyond him, North Dakota was blazing away.

A small, trunk-sized rock about ten yards away would provide good cover. Taking a deep breath, not really believing he was doing it, Bobby lunged forward. The rock was further away than he had estimated, but seconds later he felt its cold moss-covered surface against the side of his sweating cheek.

The four Vietnamese flopped down beside him. Bobby lifted his carbine above the rock and fired an un-aimed burst, then scrambled to his knees and fired another.

He could see Granger, Bishop and the rest of North Dakota shooting up the slope. Immediately below him, Hidaka was pulling the wounded M-60 gunner into cover next to Hih.

Granger's eyes met Bobby's. His brow furrowed, as if to say, what the hell are you doing up there?

For God's sake, Rod, get up here, willed Bobby. Granger had picked a hell of a time to play it safe!

The NVA had got a fix on North Dakota. Rounds shredded the ground around them.

Granger jumped to his feet and charged. Drawing level with Bobby he threw himself flat, firing a long burst before rolling over to take cover behind a thick tree trunk.

Bobby took aim at the shapes he could see moving through the smoke in the torn and tangled vegetation. The enemy fire waned.

Joyner, Bishop and the rest of the team were now crawling up the slope towards them. Thank God.

A round clipped the edge of the rock spitting splinters into the side of his face. Could he lead another charge? he wondered. Would the team follow him, as they had followed Granger?

16

A high shot from an RPG shattered the tree above their heads. Branches and leaves rained down. Bishop was bellowing into the radio handset, one hand clamped over his ear to try and hear the reply above the cacophony.

Again the Cobras came in, their mini-guns and rockets ripping into the enemy. The debris from the rocket impacts fell about the team and smoke billowed down the slope. It was time to move forward.

'Let's go!' cried Bobby, hoping the four Vietnamese would follow.

They broke from both sides of the rock and crashed through the patch of mutilated bamboo to their front. Bobby managed a further ten yards, before throwing himself into cover. He looked around to check who was with him. To his left, he saw Joyner, Hih, and the scout. All three were firing. Even the Vietnamese had made it, but there was no sign of Granger.

Fuck! Rod's chickened out, thought Bobby.

Away to the right, the rest of North Dakota,

Bluh, Truc, Rah and Loc, were sheltering in a shallow crater, trying to hold the flank of the assault against a small number of counterattacking NVA. The ground boiled with bullet strikes. Spurts of mud and vegetation burst and popped all around them.

Bobby paused for a moment to catch his breath. They emerged from the tree line. Here, the ground was more open but steeper. Ahead lay the limestone cliff, with the trapped team at its base.

Bobby fired another burst. His magazine empty, he tore a grenade from the side of his ammo pouch and pitched it towards the enemy.

'Grenade!'

Everyone stopped firing and momentarily took cover until the explosion signalled that it was safe to resume.

Jesus Christ! Bishop was dragging something or someone up the slope. Bobby could not see what or who it was, but Bishop was grimacing as he tried to shield his face from the splash of bullets.

Bobby felt frozen to the spot, urging himself up but unable to do anything. It was certain death down there and he was going to have to watch Bishop die unless he did something!

'For God's sake, Jim, go back!' he yelled.

Screw staying alive. He had to go and help. One, two, three . . .

At that moment, crouching low, someone sprinted over and slid to the ground beside Bishop. He seized the burden, helping drag it to cover. It was the former NVA scout.

Bobby turned back to the firefight. He could tell he had used more than half of his ammunition, but now was not the time to hold back.

A weight fell on his legs and a radio aerial whipped across his face.

'Granger's hit bad,' Bishop said. 'I don't think he'll make it.'

In the Operations room at Dak-To, Captain Gillman listened to events unfold over the radio speaker. The gaggle was on its way back to refuel. With no more teams to insert to support the Bright Light, and the Hatchet Force platoon needing two hours before it was ready, Gillman was going to have to call down to Kontum and tell Recon Company to gather every spare body and fly out into the fight.

There was never any shortage of volunteers. The problem was always getting everyone home.

For a moment or two enemy fire seemed to have tailed off.

'You guys OK?' yelled Joyner. They were close enough to the trapped team to call out.

'No! We're not fucking OK. Where are you?' came the reply.

'About thirty yards away down here!'

'OK. We're coming.'

Eight figures broke from the rocks and made a disorderly dash down the slope. Only half had any web gear. One of their Montagnards was injured but could walk. Another could hobble with assistance.

'Is that everybody?' asked Joyner.

The One-zero nodded.

'OK, now let's get the fuck out of here!' said Joyner.

Granger was alive but only just. A bullet had taken away most of his cheek plus some of his jaw and he wasn't going to use his left eye again. The mud had adhered to all the gore in his hair and what was left of his face. Hidaka had swathed his head in wound dressing and injected morphine.

Bobby helped construct a crude litter so that they could carry the One-zero back to the LZ. Granger's breath came in shallow gasps, and for a moment his one good eye seemed to focus on Bobby's anguished face. But nothing registered.

The ragged band of twenty-four men staggered back through the jungle skirting fresh, still smouldering craters where Covey had directed air strikes ahead of them, to clear a safe passage to the LZ.

The first Huey clattered in to extract Granger and the other three wounded men. Covey had four flights of fast movers stacked up, waiting to pound anyone who even glanced at the LZ. With terrifying and methodical precision, the bombs rained down on to the jungle, systematically sanitising each potential source of threat.

Twenty minutes and several helicopters later, Bobby, Bishop, Joyner and Hidaka climbed aboard a Kingbee and took off towards Vietnam.

Bishop was sitting at a table by himself and drinking as if his life depended on it. He gulped down entire cans of beer, with whiskey chasers, in the hope that drunken oblivion would overtake him, at least for a short while. With Granger on the critical list, North Dakota's mission to India Nine had been postponed until further notice.

'I mean, one minute he was there, OK!' hiccupped Bishop, slamming his can back down on the table. 'And the next minute . . . Blamoh! Half his fucking head is gone!'

Bishop punched himself in the side of the head. 'I mean, what's it supposed to mean?' he demanded of no one in particular. 'What the hell is it all supposed to mean?' he repeated loudly to a group of gunfighters sitting on a table opposite playing poker.

'You might want to calm your boy down,' suggested Doug Webber from his usual bar stool. 'He's liable to piss someone off.'

'Bishop did some brave stuff out there today,' said Bobby.

'Can't ask more than that,' said Doug.

'And another thing,' Bobby continued. 'That gook scout on Joyner's team saved Jim's life. If it weren't for him, we'd be two men down tonight.'

'I still don't trust the little fuckers.'

Bishop lurched in between the two men, spilling Doug's drink.

'Hey, Lake, how's it going?' Bishop slurred.

'Why don't you turn in?' said Bobby. 'Try and get some sleep.'

'Screw that. I want another drink.' Bishop was swaying dangerously.

'Whoa there, boy,' warned Doug, 'take it easy.'

'Why the fuck should I wanna take it easy?'

''Cos I'm telling you, boy,' warned Doug. The gunfighters looked over, and then returned to their cards.

'I ran recon,' said Doug, 'I lost people. Shit, there's a man in this club who lost his whole fucking team. Deal with it or get the fuck out.'

'Granger's not dead,' said Bishop. 'Poor bastard.'

Bobby put a hand on his shoulder.

'Hey, Jim. Call it quits tonight. Go get some sleep.'

Bishop shrugged off the arm, and then slumped to the floor.

'Leave him,' suggested Doug.

Bobby suddenly noticed Bishop was shaking. His head was in his hands but he could not muffle the sobs.

'You wanna give me a hand here?' asked Bobby quietly.

Doug nodded.

'C'mon, Jim,' said Bobby.

Bishop looked up, his face shiny with tears.

'Don't cut my fucking head off. Please don't cut my head off,' he mumbled.

'It's OK, man. Let's go get some air.'

The gunfighters pretended not to notice, but had stopped their game of poker and watched the two men carry Bishop slowly out of the club.

'I've talked to the Colonel and you've got North Dakota if you want it,' said the Recon Company 1st Sergeant.

'I'm the One-zero?'

'That's what I said.'

'What about India Nine?'

'Forget India Nine. It's been given to another team. Rest up for a couple of days, but don't leave the camp. I'll get you a new One-two. Lieutenant Bishop is the One-one. OK?'

'Yes, Top.'

'Check the noticeboard. The results of the promotion board are up. You're an E-5 effective immediately.'

'Yes, Top.' Bobby was surprised. He hadn't even attended the last promotion board up at Da-Nang. It had been during his week off and he'd had better things to do.

Outside in the sunlight, he put on his Ray-bans and wandered over to the mess hall. Over a cup of coffee, he tugged an unopened letter from Rachel from his top pocket.

Dear Bobby,
I am just writing to say that I can't write to you any more. There just isn't any point with all the stuff you guys are doing over there. I have tried not to let the war come between us, but I now see what is happening to this country and guys like you are so much part of the problem and why we are fighting this evil war . . .

Bobby read the letter twice, with a growing feeling of anger and despair. There was no reason to go home any more. No promises to keep. No long embrace at the bus station. He crumpled the paper into a ball and threw it across the hall.

Bishop flopped down on the chair opposite him.

He looked pale and bleary-eyed. Fumbling with a crushed packet of Marlboros he extracted a mangled cigarette.

'I made Sergeant,' Bobby said.

'Great.' Bishop exhaled a long plume of smoke.

'That's the good news. Want to hear the bad?'

'Hit me,' said Bishop.

'I'm the One-zero. You're the One-one. Want the job?'

'Have I got a choice?'

'No one has to do this.'

'Yes, they do.'

Bobby ran his finger round the rim of his coffee mug. He knew exactly what Bishop meant.

'Look,' Bishop cleared his throat, 'that deal in the club last night . . .'

'Forget it.'

Bishop nodded and looked down at the table. 'Thanks, man.' He took another long drag on his cigarette. 'Word from Pleiku is that Rod's gonna make it, but it'll be a while before they can put his face back together.'

Bobby tried not to remember the awful sight.

'I was still on the radio when he ran up the hill. He yelled something to me. I guess he thought I'd turned chicken on him. Next thing I know, he's down. I tried to help, but . . .'

'I'm putting you up for a Bronze Star,' said Bobby. 'That was a real gutsy move.'

Bishop stayed silent for a moment, then said, 'You wanna put me up for it, OK, thanks. But truth is, I don't really care. Time was that was all I wanted, a chest full of medals to go back and show my daddy. Now? Now I just don't give a shit.'

Contrary to popular belief, there were more Canadians serving in the US Army than there were US draft dodgers hiding in Canada.

Dick Nylan had been in country eight months already. He'd come from an A-camp that had been handed over to the Vietnamese and, rather than be posted to the B-team at Kontum, had volunteered for Command and Control in the hope of seeing some action.

Just back from One-zero school, Nylan didn't look like the archetypal Green Beret Airborne warrior. He was about five foot nine and stocky, with a large square head, thick black-rimmed Army issue glasses, a broken nose, and a constant smile.

He maintained an enthusiasm that was both bewildering and infectious.

'STABO rig? Wow. Team patch? Cool. Eldest Son ammunition? Amazing!'

Bobby was glad to have him on the team.

★

Dear Uncle Ethan,
*The good news is I have my own team. The bad
news is Rod Granger, our team leader, got badly
shot up. He'd be dead if it wasn't for Jim Bishop.
He saved his life. It was one of the bravest things
I've ever seen. I watched him do it and I couldn't
help. That scares me more than anything. I know
you told me that being scared is OK, but I'm so
damn' scared of being scared. I don't know how
much longer I can keep this up. I still can't believe
I'm doing what I'm doing. I must be doing OK
because they've given me a team, but it doesn't feel
like I'm anything special. When the hammers go
down, I'm just running on instinct. I'm scared to
stop in case I wake up and can't handle it.*

*Rachel wrote and asked me not to write to her
any more. I guess we've just drifted too far apart.
Seems as if Hanoi's propaganda is really working
great on our campuses.*

*Everyone is bitching about the 150 civilians
killed by the Army at My Lai, and no one ever
mentions the 3000 civilians the VC massacred at
Hue, or the thousands of others they kill every year.
What the hell is wrong with these people? How the
hell is America going to look the world in the eye if
we pull out of here and the NVA win? Where are
we supposed to make the stand? Thailand? India? I
don't think those people love peace. They hate*

America. If I'm truthful, I'm not sure I want to come home. These are my people now. I know Vietnam isn't my home, but I'm amongst people I respect, and who respect me. That's more than I have back in the US. I hope you understand. If you see Rachel, tell her I'm OK.

I hope you are keeping well.

Give Mom my love. I haven't written too much recently.

Love,

Bob

Huddled at the bar, the gunfighters listened to the latest tale of misfortune to befall their friends.

An eight-man recon team had been chased and hunted trying to get into a target just south of Highway 110. No one had been hit, but they'd lost a chopper on the extraction, and the team was badly shaken.

They had been looking for a suspected POW camp. The location and rescue of POWs was one of Command and Control's primary missions, and it was the type of mission everyone wanted to run.

'They knew we were coming, man! I swear it,' said Gerry Bloom, the One-zero of the recon team. 'They were waiting on the LZ. Judging by the amount of cigarette butts we found, they'd been waiting some time. They let us land! Waited for the chopper to go and then they hit us! So we assaulted straight off the LZ and ran through them. Cobras rolled in and fucked 'em up.'

'You're one lucky mother, Gerry.'

'You think? Guess what? We're going back. Day after tomorrow we're fucking going back. Apparently we've still got to try and locate the fucking POW camp. There ain't no fucking POW camp, man. I could tell them that. The whole camp thing is a fucking trap, I know it!'

The rest of the gunfighters said nothing. No one was going to argue.

'We need to find that spy,' said one of the gunfighters. 'Word is that it's an agent in Saigon.'

'A gook?'

'Could be an American,' said Bobby from the other end of the bar.

'What?'

'Why not? You think all the anti-war assholes are at home? You can bet there's some fucking draftee working in MAC-V who'd be only too happy to sell stuff to the other side.'

The gunfighters stared at Bobby Lake with raised eyebrows, but nobody argued.

Three days later, Bobby, Bishop, Nylan and the rest of Recon Company watched the choppers come down from Dak-To, scarred with fresh bullet holes and cabin floors slick with blood. Gerry Bloom was first out. Four dead Montagnards lay on the LZ. The surviving Montagnard, the One-one and One-two were all badly shot up.

'No way you'd get me to go back,' said Bishop, wandering away from the helipad. 'No fucking way!'

'That's it? No more Cambodia?' asked Nylan.

'Nixon wants everyone out of Cambodia and that includes us. Word is they're closing CCS at Ban Me Thout, and their recon teams are coming up here.'

'Fuck!' swore Nylan. 'This war's gonna be over before I get a chance to do shit.'

'Bet you ten bucks we go back into Cambodia,' said Bishop, putting down *Death of a President*. 'Nixon's got to be up to something. The invasion just pushed the NVA west, so they got hold of a whole lot more of Cambodia. They can cross into Laos all along the southern border. They can re-supply Cambodia from the Attopeau area, down the Mekong. Attopeau's outside the Prairie Fire AO, so they've either got to let us work all the way into Laos or they'll have to let us into Cambodia again. If they don't, the NVA'll have a free run. And we ain't gonna win this war by leaving them alone.'

'Still think anybody's serious about winning this war?' asked Bobby, loading magazines.

'What the hell are we all doing here if we ain't?'

'Waiting for Nixon to cut a deal so we can all go home,' said Nylan.

'Well, that's not going to happen anytime soon.' Bishop picked up his book again.

'Bet you a couple of months from now, they'll pull the same deal with Laos. Only folks going into Laos will be ARVN teams,' said Bobby.

'Fine by me,' said Bishop. 'It's not like I give a fuck anyway.'

'Intel says that the gooks are going to try and get it together for another stab at Dak-Pek.' The S-3 indicated the area he was referring to on the map. 'So when and if you get close enough to this route, we want you to stay as long as possible because it might be the only warning we get that another attack is on the way.'

The area was just inside the Laotian border, to the north of where Bobby had run the trail watch with Granger. Route 9662 was still feeding a steady stream of supplies into the fight in the south.

'We don't see anything but rain and low cloud for about the next ten days. We might get a break, we might not,' said the Met Officer.

'Just keep in mind, the weather could keep

Covey on the ground,' the S-3 added. 'You're too far north for Leghorn, and Hillsboro may get socked in as well. Don't go getting your tit in a wringer, and then find you got no air.'

'So it's gonna piss with rain and we can't talk to any fucker. Just great,' muttered Bishop loud enough for everyone to hear.

Despite the fact that it might have looked as though the cards were stacked against him, Bobby felt surprisingly relaxed about his first mission as One-zero. Even though he knew the dangers of road-watch missions, this time his destiny was very much in his own hands.

17

Bobby clambered into the cramped confines of the O-1 Bird Dog while Joe Eden did his pre-flight check, shaking the horizontal stabiliser and kicking the tyres.

About eight months ago, Joe had arrived in the country, fresh out of flight school and with only 200 flying hours total. He now had more than 1,000 under his belt, of which more than 830 had been combat sorties.

It was impossible to get comfortable. There were parachutes, but no one ever wore them. They were used as seat padding. The missions were flown at too low an altitude anyway.

Slung over each shoulder Bobby had claymore satchels, packed with twenty twenty-round magazines and six grenades. On his belt he carried his .45. He didn't want to feel stark naked if they went down in the jungle.

To guard against the odd unlucky shot, Joe had rigged the rigid plate from his aircrew body armour below his seat. At least once it had saved him from serious injury or death. He fired up the engine and the cramped cockpit started to shake in sympathy.

Bobby nestled his carbine at the side of the cabin and made sure he had his 35mm camera and maps easily accessible. He felt the joystick brush his legs as Joe stirred the controls to make sure he had no obstructions.

They climbed out of Kontum and headed northwest, flying with all the windows open. Partly to keep cool, partly so that the ageing and scratched Perspex didn't degrade any photographs. And if they did crash in the jungle, it made it easier to escape the wreckage.

Forty-five minutes later, the O-1 Bird Dog dropped down to five hundred feet and overflew Dak-Pek. The bomb craters, napalm scars and signs of fierce fighting were all too evident, even though most of the camp had now been rebuilt. Looking up at them, a few members of the Special Forces A-team waved.

'I'd rather be running recon than be down there,' said Bobby.

Joe grinned. 'I'd rather be up here.'

The idea of being cooped up behind barbed wire and sandbags, knowing that there were several thousand gooks coming to try and kill you, was not a scenario that appealed to Bobby. Dak-Pek was an alternate launch site for CCC. When the camp had first been attacked, CCC personnel had been withdrawn on orders from HQ, leaving the guys at the A-camp to fight it out hand to hand with the NVA. The decision had left some bad feeling in CCC. No one liked the idea of running from a fight.

Staying at five hundred feet or below, they crossed the border up to the northwest of Dak-Pek.

Using month-old aerial photos of the area, Bobby had chosen several possible LZs. Joe had checked them out and decided two of them were non-starters.

The O-1 dropped down into a bowl between two converging ridges.

Something flashed past the canopy. Bobby recoiled in his seat as the joystick slammed into his thigh and the O-1 broke into a sharp right-hand turn, the engine note increasing as the throttle was slammed forward.

Tracer rounds ripped under the plane.

Joe pushed the O-1 through a gap between two trees on the top of the ridge.

'That's where you wanted your LZ. Correct?' said Joe, levelling out.

'Not any more I don't.'

It was like the roller-coaster ride from hell. The ninety-knot airflow howled past the open window as the little plane banked and skidded over the jungle at less than one hundred feet above the trees.

They found LZs that could be used with ladders, and one that could take a Huey if a tree was blown.

Turning south, they followed a wide meandering stream down towards the border.

'Jesus! Look at that!' exclaimed Joe, throwing the aircraft into a tight turn. Axle-deep in the water and just visible under overhanging branches was the distinctive shape of a truck. Clustered around it soldiers were attempting to push it across the fording point. Nervous faces stared skyward.

'Hold tight. I'm going to bag myself a truck,' said Joe, going into a climbing turn.

As Joe commenced his run, Bobby could see muzzle flashes from the NVA soldiers.

With a loud whoosh, the first of the four white phosphorous target-marking rockets streaked from its tube towards the truck. Another followed less than a second later. There were two soft metallic thuds as enemy rounds hit the fuselage.

Joe veered away.

A geyser of water confirmed that one rocket had hit just in front of the truck, and a thickening plume of white smoke showed that the other had landed in the trees just beyond. Several soldiers were wading across the stream, to take cover on the other side.

Joe roared off down the valley to gain height. 'You want to do this?' he asked.

'Why not?' said Bobby, while actually considering it insane. Every gook for miles around would be grabbing a weapon and racing to defend the truck, which were like sacred cows to the NVA.

As they commenced their next run, Bobby could see an officer urging more men to join the effort to save the truck.

The next two rockets were also wide of the mark. Small arms tracer whipped past the cockpit, and another round impacted somewhere near it.

'Let's see if we can't get a picture of it,' said Joe, taking the aircraft into a climbing turn.

As the truck loomed in the viewfinder, trying to keep as steady as possible, Bobby clicked the shutter.

Joe got on the radio to try and find someone else who could destroy the truck. He might be a great pilot, thought Bobby, but he's one lousy shot. 'They're gonna get it moving real soon,' he said.

Joe didn't reply. He brought the plane round again, and dived towards the river. A group of wide-eyed faces stared up at them.

Oh God! We're gonna ram the truck, thought Bobby. At the last moment, Joe pulled up, missing the truck by feet.

'Got any grenades?' he asked. 'I'm gonna do the same thing again. Drop when it looks right.'

'This is fucking crazy,' said Bobby, pulling a

grenade from the bag and sticking his arm out of the
window. He pulled the pin with his other hand and
waited until the truck filled the windshield. Bobby
released the grenade. The O–1 shuddered as bullets
ripped into the fuselage and wings. Something
flashed between, punching a fist-sized hole in the
overhead Perspex.

Joe kept the aircraft flying east. The last bullet
strikes had snapped him out of his fixation on the
truck.

'OK, that's enough fun for today. We go home
now,' he said, his last phrase mimicking the question
often asked by nervous Vietnamese crewmen.

Before taking the aircraft back to Kontum, they
landed at Dak-To and checked the damage. There
were three holes just behind the cockpit. One
round had gone through the tail fin and another
had tracked across the right wing, leaving a jagged
foot-long tear.

'Anyone ever tell you you're off your head?'
asked Bobby, as Joe lit his pipe and examined the
damage in the wing.

'Only my closest friends.'

'Would your guys be ready to go tomorrow
morning?' asked the 1st Sergeant when Bobby got
back to Kontum.

North Dakota's mission wasn't due until the day after.

'I guess. Why?'

'Turner and Kennedy had some bad chow last night. They've spent all day on the can. They ain't going nowhere, so we got a spare slot for tomorrow. The weather looks like a go, but we could be socked in after that. It's your call.'

Bobby thought for a second. He would have one day less to prime and check the team, but what was he going to say? They'd wait? They weren't ready?

Out on the helipad, Bobby inspected the team: Loc, Bluh, Truc, Rah, Hih, Nylan and Bishop.

Bobby couldn't help but smile at the stocky Canadian, sporting a wide grin beneath his black-rimmed Army-issue glasses and his jungle hat, worn with the front of the brim folded up.

Bishop managed a smile too, but his eyes were dead. Bobby had had to order him to eat breakfast. He'd probably thrown it all up afterwards, but there was no shame in that. Bobby had seen many brave men do the same. Just like everyone else, Jim Bishop was ready to go.

With only about ninety minutes till sunset and a low cloud base, the valley was dark and gloomy. The fading light had bleached the green from the jungle and replaced it all with a mottled grey.

Bobby crouched in the wet grass and watched the second Huey come in. The last four men scrambled down the ladders. Relieved of its burden, the helicopter lifted vertically out of the clearing and vanished beyond the trees. The faraway rumble of thunder momentarily masked the sound of the gaggle circling up wind.

As soon as they found somewhere to spend the night, it began to rain.

The men lay soaking under the sodden jungle canopy. Moonlight filtered through the leaves, casting long slanting beams between the trees. The jungle seemed like some enchanted forest where you might find unicorns or dragons.

Bobby sat up and ran his fingers through his sodden hair. He was too cold and wet to sleep. The rain would have obliterated their trail and so tomorrow at least they'd start with a clean sheet.

The rain stopped just before dawn. They ate in darkness, checked in with Covey at first light, and then began working their way down towards the trail.

After about thirty minutes, Loc held up his hand, tugged his ear and made a walking motion with his fingers.

Bobby could only hear the rustle of leaves and the faint wind in the trees.

'Where?' he mouthed.

Loc pointed, and Bobby signalled to his men that they should move forward.

Halfway down a steep, thickly forested hillside, Loc spotted men moving amongst the trees. They were carrying long black shapes balanced on their shoulders. An officer or NCO stood to one side, urging them on.

Bobby recognised the shapes as 12.7mm machine guns. At least six guns and some thirty men made their way up towards the LZ.

Even if the NVA had heard or seen last night's insertion and knew a team was on the ground, surely they didn't expect the team to return to the same LZ? That would only happen in the direst emergency. Was this just a precautionary measure, or was Bobby witnessing part of a wider operation to kill his team? Could it be that the NVA knew North Dakota was close by?

A cold chill ran through him.

They had come in a day early!

Fuck! Fuck! Fuck! Fuck! thought Bobby. Could the spy in Saigon have ratted them out?

Bobby began to tremble. He squatted down, pretending to consult the map while he marshalled his thoughts.

They don't know we're here. They haven't found us. The spy doesn't know we're here; otherwise they'd have come after us last night. We're OK. We can do this.

The rest of day offered no further glimpse of enemy or the slightest hint of trackers. There was more heavy rainfall in the afternoon, which was always good. It muffled the sound of movement, smudged or washed away track sign and dulled the concentration of anyone who might be lying in ambush.

By nightfall they were close to the trail. SPAF-1 had come overhead just before last light and Bobby had told Nylan to code up their RON position at least five hundred metres north of where they actually were. The only piece of information about teams that was ever transmitted beyond CCC was the RON position and it was possible that, if there were a spy, he might be able to transmit it to the NVA.

The practice was much advocated in the club and while neither Big Jack nor Granger had ever done it, Bobby saw no point in making things easy for the enemy if there really was a rat in Saigon.

The dark came as quickly as it always did.

Soon after midnight, Bobby was nudged awake.

'Listen,' Nylan hissed.

At first Bobby only heard the sound of his own heart. Then he detected movement. The team came alive as if electrified. Rain-soaked hands scrabbled for the claymore triggers and Nylan felt for the on switch of the radio in his rucksack.

A branch snapped. The team strained to see into the darkness.

There was a low grunt followed by a long sigh then a loud sniff.

Loc's shoulders relaxed.

It was an elephant.

After a very slow five minutes, the tension subsided. Only Nylan remained sitting up, listening. Perhaps it was the unicorns walking around the forest.

At about two in the morning, the rain started again.

Waiting in the rain and being permanently wet was a test of character. It could fray already taut nerves and the challenge to stay professional and alert was constant.

Loc was oblivious to any weather, but he knew the *Viet* were mostly city boys and farmers. Away from the security of the farms, rice paddies and factories of North Vietnam, they were lost. While they might be imbued with powerful Communist fervour or a desire for glory and world revolution, they were actually no tougher nor more adept at surviving in the jungle than the Americans, or at least those Americans who were genuinely motivated.

Loc knew that the rain would cause the *Viet* patrols to walk head down through the jungle in the hope of soon being back under their leaf-canopied shelters or huts, perhaps to enjoy a little soup with a cold rice ball, if they were lucky. According to the American Chiefs back at Kontum the *Viet* in Laos were always short of food. This made Loc very happy.

After about an hour of dull grey light, the downpour ceased. This close to the trail, there was a very real danger of meeting enemy patrols. Movement was measured in metres per minute, slower than you might have crept past your parents' bedroom on your way to the fridge for a snack. Every sight or sound, normally ignored, was assessed as a potential threat to the team's security. Nothing concentrates the mind more than fear, and concentration was at an unmatchable high.

A large bird flapped away from its perch, squawking. Loc knew the bird's call was a warning and he thanked the spirit of the forest.

Dick Nylan removed his glasses and, for what

seemed like the umpteenth time, shook a raindrop from the lenses. Nylan had seen combat before, when patrolling from the A-team camp where he had originally been posted. Close to the camp, you had mortar and artillery support. Here, you had fucking nothing, and that made things very scary. Maybe he'd made a big mistake coming to CCC. Hours of tension and lack of sleep were leaving him feeling less than his usual cheerful self.

Nylan looked over at Bishop who was gazing towards the enemy with wide blank eyes, his rain-soaked moustache hanging over his top lip, his face pale and devoid of blood.

Hope I don't ever look that bad, thought Nylan.

Further down the valley, they came to a stream. According to the map, and from what Bobby had seen on his VR flight, somewhere on the other side and up the slope was the trail.

Loc examined fresh boot prints in the soft ground. About ten men had passed by in the last hour. This was not a good place to hang around.

They took a route parallel to the stream course, to find a better point to cross. They didn't want to leave easy-to-spot tracks. But where the stream flowed around a rocky outcrop jutting out of the steeply rising far bank, it was possible to reach the water by stepping on the rocks.

The stream was narrow, slow-flowing but deep.

Loc sank up to his chest before finding shallower water at the far bank. There was little point in trying to keep the team dry when the rain had drenched them for the past day and two nights. As One-zero Bobby now carried the camera which, although protected by a plastic bag, he elected to hold clear of the water. Waist-deep, they waded upstream for about twenty-five metres before climbing out over more rocks.

On the slope, the mud and leaves were slick underfoot. Firm footing was hard to find, but this meant their trail was equally hard to follow. After a climb of about thirty metres, the ground flattened out. Loc eased his way through the thick undergrowth and there, like a miracle before him, was a ten-to-fifteen foot-wide strip of rut-churned, puddle-pocked mud.

On the far side, the trail wound around the edge of a spur of scrubby ground. The main group laid up with their backs to the stream while two men were posted about twenty-five metres away, lying near the edge of the trail.

The undergrowth around them was tangled enough to make any enemy patrol's approach a difficult and noisy exercise. This would give the team ample warning. And they had their escape route back to the water.

During daylight hours, only those on foot used the trail. Clearly most of the NVA had walked for miles and just kept their eyes fixed on the ground, watching each plodding footfall through ankle-deep mud as they snaked nearer to the south, into the welcoming embrace of the US war machine.

At night came the trucks. They usually travelled in small convoys. Early each evening, the trucks travelled between parks. Finding a truck park, like the one Bobby had seen in Cambodia, would be a great prize, but he wasn't going to jeopardise the mission by going and looking. It might be several miles away.

The convoys were tempting targets for air strikes, but no one could be contacted on the radio. As they had been warned at the briefing, the weather was keeping aircraft socked in, and, with low cloud and constant rain, Covey was only overhead in daylight.

Bobby found it as frustrating as hell. There really wasn't any point in conducting a trail watch unless you could target what you spotted. Their only option was to report last night's traffic each morning when they checked in, and hope that the trucks might be attacked further to the south or east.

Though well hidden in their patch of undergrowth, the men remained constantly wet and at the mercy of every insect that found them. Every item of clothing and equipment became sticky with mud, and the only relief night brought was a slight drop in temperature. No one wanted to stay, but that was the mission.

18

Bishop hurled his packet of rehydrated rice at the ground. He had just been about to take a mouthful when a large beetle dropped into his food. He had been within inches of swallowing it. A heavy smoker, he tended to be bitten less than his comrades, but no smoking on a mission, combined with this agonising inactivity, was hard to bear.

Bobby knew everyone was finding it tough. Moving guys back and forth to watch the trail every two hours kept them busy, but it was better not to move at all. They needed to disturb the ground as little as possible.

Loc picked up Bishop's packet of rice, and plucked out the beetle.

'*Mange*! Eat,' he said. Bishop took the packet and, after prodding the contents for any other sign of intruders, did what he was told.

On the fourth day, during the early dawn hours, they dropped back down to the stream and moved southeast, parallel to the trail. Just before last light the previous evening, a six-wheeled armoured car and a squad of soldiers on foot had appeared. For one terrifying moment Bobby was convinced their position had been compromised, but the soldiers had walked slowly past them, peering suspiciously into the jungle.

Maybe it had been a routine exercise, but Bobby reckoned it was too much of a risk for them to remain in the same place.

He decided to lead his men south before switching back to proceed parallel to the trail and stream.

Nylan felt stiff and weak. His eyes were almost closed by the swelling from incessant insect bites. Bishop was glad just to be moving again. He could hang on for one more day, then they were due to be extracted. He would have survived one more time over the fence. Which meant he was one mission closer to quitting.

Hih itched for action. He didn't like all this creeping about. He wanted to kill *Viets*.

Bobby and Loc both heard the noise at the same time. It sounded as if someone was clearing ground or chopping bamboo.

The team edged slowly forward, working through the dense jungle.

A tall bamboo in front of them shook with the blows of a machete, then fell backwards out of sight.

A man appeared and continued his methodical cutting. He didn't see Loc or Bobby, both of whom had him fastened in the sights of their carbines. If he even glanced in their direction, then it would be over for him. Gathering up the freshly cut bamboo he disappeared from sight.

The team worked round to a different vantage point.

Then the sound of cutting stopped. Loc and Bobby slid off their rucksacks and began crawling down the slope, which was thick with the smell of rotting leaves and mud. Bobby slithered after Loc, behind a large tree with broad prominent roots spreading from its base.

The clearing beyond was only some twenty-five metres across, and the tall overhanging trees made it near-impossible to spot from the air the three hut-like structures. One was almost complete, while the others were just bamboo frames.

All were sunk into the ground with large mounds of earth piled to one side. These were probably going to be used to store ammunition. The roofs were half-thatched with broad fresh green leaves that had not yet lost their colour.

Bobby and Loc sank back as a soldier came into view. He wore NVA uniform and was followed by a skinny-looking, short, dark-skinned man wearing nothing but a ragged shirt and a loincloth. The man in uniform waved his arms, and the man in the shirt nodded vigorously and bowed his head in submission.

A whistle shrieked and more men appeared.

The guards were NVA but the workers were Montagnards. In both Laos and Vietnam, the majority of Montagnards hated the NVA, and with good reason. The NVA either killed them or pushed them into forced labour, doing either construction work or man-packing heavy loads along the foot trails into the south. When the NVA ran short of food, and they always did, their men were the last to feel the effects of rationing.

Bobby toyed with the idea of killing the NVA and freeing the Montagnards. Maybe even getting them lifted back to Vietnam. It was a nice idea, but out of the question.

He snapped away with his camera, confident that the shutter clicks would be obliterated amongst the renewed chopping and digging.

After they had crawled back to join the others, Bobby sketched what he had seen in his notebook. They were due for extraction the following morning, so the team would need to get moving towards the LZ he had chosen on his VR flight.

After a hundred metres they spotted the thatched roof of another hut.

Once again Bobby carefully circled the team while he and Loc worked their way forwards through the thick undergrowth. They had to shift each stem or vine by hand. Twenty metres took nearly half an hour.

Four huts, on two-foot stilts, lined each side of a widened footpath. Loc put his head against the rear wall of the one closest to them and shook his head. This one was either empty or everyone was asleep. Freshly cut firewood was stacked under a tarp and there was a faint smell of cooking. A sodden blue and red North Vietnamese flag dangled from a pole beside one of the huts. Bobby debated with himself about grabbing the flag; that really would be a hell of a trophy for the club, but again, the risk was too great.

Working their way round to the right of the hut, the two men came to a footpath which snaked into the clearing from the south. Loc checked the path for tracks and detected nothing significant. But on the far side was a real prize, a bundle of telephone wires lashed to an upright stake.

Yeehah! Locating communications wires was a key part of every C&C mission. Wires could be tapped and the conversations recorded for analysis by MAC-V back in Saigon. In the club, the gunfighters reckoned that wiretaps were the greatest single source of intelligence that C&C

gathered. Better even than prisoners, some said.

Bobby took out his camera.

Why the hell was Bob taking these chances? Bishop wondered. Their mission was to watch the trail. They'd done that. So let's go home, for Christ's sake.

Bobby and Loc returned all smiles.

'I want to order up a re-supply and some wiretap gear. That OK with you guys?'

Nylan nodded his assent. He and Bobby turned to Bishop.

'OK by me,' muttered Bishop.

'So we do it,' said Bobby.

It started to rain. Slowly at first, but then in a torrent, filling the jungle with one long hissing crackle which deadened the senses and all natural sounds.

The gaggle departed Dak-To soon after dawn, and flew northwest. It was a wet, grey morning, but Covey reported the target area was clear of low cloud and the operation was a go.

Looking at the other helicopters in the formation, Doug Webber reflected wearily that he had done this too many times before. Next to him, on the floor of the Huey, was a large bundle wrapped in a ground sheet and strapped with heavy black tape.

So Lake's in deep and wants to stay, thought Doug. The boy had become a hardcore gunfighter and recon big dog. Good luck to him.

Twenty-five minutes later they were skimming low over the trees and the ball game had begun.

In the airspace around them the Cobras and A-1s circled, ready for any sign of NVA interference.

The helicopter lowered into the tiny clearing, ladders unrolling from its sides.

Now!

Doug pushed the bundle from the door and watched it fall into the downdraft-flattened grass below.

The helicopter then began what seemed like a painfully slow ascent out of the clearing, as though it was extracting a team.

Nylan keyed the radio.

'Touchdown!'

'Roger that, Blue Cat,' called Covey. 'Good luck.'

After fifteen minutes, Bobby halted the team and waited for another five, to see if the NVA had been fooled. They could hear nothing. The ruse seemed to have succeeded.

Bobby cut open the bundle and organised the rations into eight piles while Bishop looked over the wiretap equipment. It was nothing fancy, merely a commercial General Electric cassette recorder connected to an induction microphone. Within minutes they were ready to move again.

A hundred metres east of where they had discovered the wires, two NVA soldiers came sauntering along the path. One of them stopped to check the line in minute detail, while the other picked up the thick bundle of wires and hitched it on to twigs clear of the ground.

Twenty minutes later, thinking they were now in the clear, the team had nearly been surprised by another group of four soldiers, who were laying yet another wire. A constant trickle of NVA walking back and forth meant that trying the tap in daylight was just too risky.

Lots of trucks were stopping and being reversed. Voices called out in the dark, yelling directions.

'Don't these guys ever sleep?' whispered Nylan.

The stars were visible beyond a few scattered clouds, and the jungle dimmed and brightened as the clouds drifted past the near-full moon.

Nylan powered up the radio, and tried to raise anyone who might be listening. The weather was better tonight. Covey might be out there somewhere. The rest of the team packed up and began moving. If they got the air strike they wanted, then they needed to put some distance between them and the trucks.

Bobby could tell from the sound of the engine that the arriving Covey was an O-2 Sky Master, not an OV-10. Because the OV-10's cockpit lighting caused the canopy to glow like a Chinese lantern, the little 0-2s were used for nocturnal missions. These aircraft also had the advantage of being able to open their side windows and use a night vision scope to look for targets.

The NVA were not deaf. After four shrill whistle blasts, every engine and voice died.

'It's all gone quiet here, Covey. I think they know you're coming.'

'Yeah, Roger that, Blue Cat. I need to fix you guys.'

The team crested the ridge.

Shielding a strobe light with a windcheater, they shone the flashing beacon skyward through the barrel of the M-79.

'Roger, Blue Cat. I see you. Get yourselves under cover.'

Somewhere out in the dark, Covey dropped a ground flare. Nicknamed 'the log', the bulky slow-burning flare would lie on the jungle floor and burn like a campfire. It gave the aircraft a reference point by which to adjust the strikes.

The first A-1s to join the party droned overhead.

The bombs fell far to the east, but near enough for the team to feel the shock wave.

Nylan called the adjustment.

The next bombs were dropped much closer, but still short of the target.

With a skull-splitting thump, one impacted exactly where Bobby estimated the huts and vehicles were. The night was torn open by a huge fireball, blasting through the trees like an angry wind from hell.

The jungle below flashed and glowed. Shadows played around them as more fireballs spread into the dark sky. The bombs must have found truckloads of ammo.

The A-1s attacked again, using napalm, and the smell of the gelled fuel drifted up to the ridge. Running men could be seen silhouetted against the burning debris.

'Blue Cat, this is Covey. We got Spectre 27 here. He wants to know if there's anyone down there still needs killing?' Covey sounded as if he was already bored by the night's proceedings.

'There are some guys you missed,' replied Nylan.

The Spectre's mini-guns and 40mm cannons rained down fire.

'This is so cool!' Bishop stared wide-eyed at the falling flares and an inferno of burning trucks. Another loud explosion caused him to duck. Then he and Nylan began to giggle like schoolgirls.

It was only just light and the sun hadn't even risen.

'We need to go take a look,' whispered Bobby to Bishop.

'You crazy? The place will be crawling with gooks, and real mad gooks at that.'

A strong smell of burning was still heavy in the air.

Bobby wanted to check first-hand the result of the previous night's air strike. Had the huts been destroyed? Could they count how many trucks had been killed? If he didn't find out, another team might have to.

Bishop felt sick to his stomach. Why was Bobby doing this? The bad guys were going to be all over the place. They might be getting a company together just to go hunt the recon team they had to suspect were in the area.

Against a tree right in front of them, an NVA soldier lay clutching a huge gash across his stomach. Loc pushed at the man's head with the muzzle of his carbine, and the body tipped lifelessly to the ground.

Loc picked up the dead man's weapon, and hung

it over his shoulder for disposal at a later time. He then passed the contents of the man's pockets to Bobby.

He decided he didn't want to know too much about this guy who might be just like him. He might have a mother or girlfriend at home, their pictures carried inside his pay book or the envelope of his last letter from home. Their faces might look out accusingly.

The enemy was dead and that was all that was important. Fuck him, fuck his truck and fuck all the other dead gooks out on the trail. Bobby stashed all the items in a pocket on Nylan's rucksack, and went on.

Smoke drifted thickly in the air and filled every depression in the ground. In the distance, a small patch of flames burned bright against the charred-monochrome landscape. Debris hung like discarded clothing from the trees; there was the all-enveloping stench of gasoline. The chassis of a truck lay propped against a tree, like some huge, broken deckchair. The cab, deck and wheels had been ripped off. This was all that was left.

Thrown into the air by the force of an explosion, a body was impaled on a branch. The head and one leg were missing.

Figures were drifting through the smoke, recovering any still-serviceable equipment.

I did this, Bobby thought. I made this happen. This is my work. He felt like a god walking in his own hellish Garden of Eden. The charred forest was like some grotesque monument to his ambition to be a committed One-zero.

A vulture flapped on to a perch in one of the smashed trees and gave two grisly squawks.

An urgent voice pierced the ghostly mist. Another voice called back, and then another. The NVA were looking for survivors.

The LZ would be useable if they blew up two trees.

Bishop had rigged two claymores to each and now sat waiting for the signal.

Covey circled overhead and called out that the first chopper was running in.

Bishop squeezed the claymore triggers and the trees crashed down.

The aircraft descended into the clearing, the ladders unrolling from the doors. Bishop, Hih, Rah and Bluh ran forward.

With the first Huey clear, the second began its descent.

Bobby waited till Nylan, Truc and Loc were climbing before he ascended the ladder, using every ounce of strength to pull himself up to the cabin. Tired and wet, after nearly seven days on the ground, it was not easy.

The young door gunner, on his first C&C extraction, stared at them open-mouthed. Gaunt, coated in mud, and stubble-chinned, they looked like creatures from the underworld.

Bobby lay on the beach, oblivious to the gentle rumble of the surf or the heat of the sun. Was this where he wanted to be?

'We kill many *Viet* muddafucker,' Loc had announced to laughs and cheers as they stood among the crowd that met them on the helipad. The Colonel had shaken Bobby's hand, and bought him a beer. They had celebrated their success at the club in Kontum, and drunk through till dawn with the Covey riders before hitching a ride on a C-130 Blackbird down to Saigon. There was a slight disagreement with the crew chief who didn't like drunken Green Berets playing 'kick the can' up and down the cabin, but they had at least returned to their seats before landing.

At the beach club they had devoured a huge meal and swilled down more beer. They had given their best rendition of 'The Ballad of the Green Berets', and several other lesser-known classics. Nylan's claim to be able to play the piano wasn't proved to anyone's satisfaction, and by nine-thirty they were the last people left in the bar.

Now, warmed by the early-morning sun, Bobby felt as if he was coming back from the dead. What sleep he had managed was full of strange and disturbing dreams. Standing in the devastated truck park in Laos he saw Carlos in the smoke. He'd tried to follow him, but his friend always seemed to slip away. He'd wanted to call out but knew he couldn't or else the NVA might hear.

He jumped as cold water splashed on to him.

'Phewweee! God, I needed that!' exclaimed Bishop, vigorously towelling himself dry before grabbing a beer from the hotel ice bucket and flopping on to the sand beside Bobby.

'This almost makes all the other shit seem worth it,' he said, taking a slug from the can and lying back.

Bobby grunted in acknowledgment.

'I promised myself I'd quit when I got back,' said Bishop.

'I felt the same way,' Bobby confessed.

'Sure you did.'

'I get scared like everyone else, Jim.'

There was a shrill female scream. Nylan was pursuing two bikini-clad Vietnamese girls into the surf.

Bobby looked up. 'Think he can handle it?'

'The man's an animal,' said Bishop. 'You know, Lake, I want to run recon.'

'I know you want to run recon. I want to run

recon. So does Nylan, when he's got time. If we didn't, we wouldn't have volunteered in the first place. Doing it's the tough part.'

'You handle it. I tell you man, I damn' near lost it when you went in for the BDA, I almost fucking shot you.'

Bishop drained his can, and squashed it between his fingers.

'I don't know if I can keep pace with you, Lake. I might be holding you guys back.'

'You aren't holding anybody back. You're doing just fine.'

'Maybe, but I don't know how much longer I can keep it up.'

'Same as the rest of us. One mission at a time.'

Bobby stood up and wandered over the hot sand to the turquoise sea. Nylan was still in the water, except this time he was trying to retrieve his shorts which the women held above their heads as they ran giggling through the shallows.

Diving down under the water for a short while, Bobby felt at peace.

'Tell me something,' Bishop asked, when Bobby returned, 'how badly did you fuck up your life, to end up doing this shit?'

Bobby helped himself to a beer and handed another can to Bishop.

'I figured I was going to come over here and be a hero. I don't mean medals and all that shit, but I wanted to be one of the guys who were going to stand up and be counted. At Harvard, I was hanging out with a whole bunch of guys who thought they were hot shit, going to be President some day, but they didn't want to fight for their country.'

'So, do you feel like a hero now?'

'Not really, but I can point to ten or twelve guys who are.'

'I still say they knew we were coming!'

'Bullshit, Jim,' said Bobby.

'At the debrief, you said, when you saw all those .51 cals being carried up to the LZ, "it was as if they were expecting us". And what about those gooks checking the wires? That was pure coincidence, was it, or did they know we'd ordered up some wiretap kit?'

'You reckon they've really got someone in the camp?' Nylan asked, sitting down beside them, stark naked.

'Someone fucked with those security lights when the camp was attacked. You said yourself, Lake, it could even have been one of us,' said Bishop, hurling a towel at Nylan so that he could cover himself.

'I said it could be an American down in Saigon,' flared Bobby. 'Not someone up at the camp.'

'Could be both.' Nylan seemed totally unconscious of his nudity and began towelling his hair.

'If there is a security problem, and I'm saying
"if", then it's down in Saigon,' said Bobby. 'And
Saigon wouldn't have known we asked for the
wiretap gear.'

'So who screwed with the fucking lights?' asked
Bishop.

'I don't know! One of the gooks who works
there.'

'And he could have told them about the re-
supply.' Bishop was clearly convinced he was
zeroing in on the problem.

'They didn't know about the fucking re-supply,
goddamn it!' exclaimed Bobby. 'They didn't even
know there was a recon team in the area.
Otherwise they wouldn't have sent a big fat juicy
convoy down the trail, just so that we could fuck it
up! Would they?'

Nylan and Bishop couldn't argue with that.

'But there could still be a guy down in Saigon?'
Bishop wasn't abandoning his case.

'Maybe,' Bobby agreed wearily.

'Hey, I've got a plan,' said Nylan. 'We go down
to MAC-V and fuck all the female typists till one of
them reveals who the traitor is.'

'Who'd fuck you anyway?' Bishop snorted. 'You
can't even handle two hookers.'

'Hey! They're nice girls. They want to meet my mother.' Nylan grinned.

'Jeez! They wanna steal your mom's shorts as well?'

'No disrespect, Lieutenant Bishop, but while Lake and I are fucking the typists, someone would have to be blowing all the senior officers. Me and Lake can't do that. Not with us being enlisted men.'

Dear Mom,
How are you? I am fine. It is still raining here, and never seems to stop.

Sorry I haven't written for a while but I have been very busy, and whenever I get time off, I just want to sleep.

I was sorry to hear Brian Olsen got killed. From what I know, flying Navy jets has always been dangerous, not just when there is a war on. Please tell Mrs Olsen I'm sorry.

Thank you for the magazines. From what I read it seems as if we will all be coming home soon. I know you'll be pleased about that. Don't believe everything you read in the papers or see on TV. Most of it just isn't true.

I'll try and write again soon. Say hi to everyone from me.

Your loving son,
Bobby

★

Bobby addressed the envelope and sealed it. He had nothing more to say, at least nothing his mother would understand. He could have told her that he didn't want to come home, but that didn't seem fair.

There was a rumour going around that the 5th Special Forces Group was going to be pulled out some time early next year, so that would be that. Even though Command and Control didn't come under the 5th's chain of command, it didn't seem likely they would stay. Besides, the Vietnamese were due to take over all Command and Control operations fairly soon.

'What a fuck-up that's gonna be!' was Doug Webber's forecast. 'I mean, how the hell is that gonna work? You can't Vietnamise recon. They got no Covey. They got no Cobras. They got no Spectre. They got no CBU for their A-1s. They got no fucking Leghorn or Moonbeam. They got no fucking nothing!'

Recon teams were at the coalface of the whole operation. Someone had to decide where to send them and what to do with the information they brought back. There was a slim chance that the Vietnamese recon teams could pick up the slack if the US ran everything else. But without the US actually continuing the war, the South Vietnamese were doomed. Anyone who had ever spent more than a month involved in the conflict knew it.

'Why don't they just send out a questionnaire to every Dogface in the 'Nam?' asked Carl Joyner. 'Any man who says he wants to go home, then *sayonara*, motherfucker! Leave the fighting to those who want to do it. I want to fight in this war. It's a goddamn' abuse of my civil rights to stop me defending my country. It's an abuse of my fucking civil rights, man, to make me go home.'

It was another hot and humid day, devoid of wind. The sun glowered behind the high cloud, trying to force a way through.

Bobby watched a C-130 climbing out of the haze that hung over Kontum. He turned back to catch the next sandbag that Nylan was hoisting up to him. Heavy rain and lack of maintenance had left North Dakota's section of the wall in poor repair and the Sergeant Major had made it clear he wanted it back up to standard before the day was finished. Bobby was determined to make a real job of it, and the Montagnards didn't seem to mind.

They were in awe of Nylan's physical strength. For a joke, he had lifted Hih above his head. Hih freaked out at first as Nylan whirled him around, but then insisted the stocky Canadian do it to every

Montagnard on the team, which he had. Even Loc, normally aloof and reserved, joined in the curious routine.

'Hi, Lake.' Ed Andrews was the One-one on another recon team, just up from Ban Me Thout. He'd been running recon for about six months and seemed like a good guy.

'Give me a minute here, guys,' said Bobby, jumping down.

'I hear there could be a slot opening up on your team.' Andrews didn't beat about the bush.

'First I've heard of it.'

'We don't seem to be doing much these days. North Dakota kicks ass. I want in.'

'Well, that's good to hear, man, but we haven't got any free slots unless we lose someone. And I don't plan on letting that happen.'

'Sure, but bear me in mind anyhow. If someone gets their own team or quits . . . I'll see you.'

Bishop was kicking a sandbag into place while holding another, waiting to drop it into position.

'Hey, Bishop. Over here a minute,' called Bobby. 'You been telling anyone you're thinking of quitting?'

'No,' replied Bishop. 'Why?'

'Nothing,' said Bobby. 'Forget it.'

'Believe me, you'll be the first to know. I no bullshit you, GI.'

Bobby felt stupid and embarrassed for having jumped so quickly to the wrong conclusion.

'Incoming.' Bishop nodded towards the approaching Intel Sergeant.

'Sergeant Lake,' said the Intel Sergeant, 'you're wanted at the TOC at fourteen hundred hours, OK?'

'OK,' said Bobby.

'Looks like we just pulled our next mission,' said Bishop with a fatalistic grimace.

The mission was point recon, just south of their last target. Again the weather forecast was bad.

'We'll have to stay hidden,' said Bobby, 'so we go in with a small team, some silenced weapons, and we definitely avoid any form of contact.'

'What's the difference between hiding eight and hiding six?'

'Er . . . two guys?' suggested Nylan.

Bobby smiled.

'If we hit trouble, we might not get air support. I'd feel safer taking a full team. Go in with all twelve; all nine Yards. Take every bit of fire power we got,' Bishop suggested.

'A full team's got more noise, more sign, and more choppers. We can get six guys on one chopper, three Yards and us. What do you think?'

'It's your call, Lake,' said Bishop. 'Not mine.'

'First, we got this here Sten gun.' The Supply Sergeant held up a frail-looking weapon, with a side-protruding magazine and wire frame stock.

'You want my opinion, it's a piece of shit. When the Brits built this fucker they did it in a hurry and it's not real accurate. Only good point is, you can take it all to pieces and keep it in your ruck till you need it. But don't be giving up your carbine for one of these.'

The Supply Sergeant had run recon until getting shot up one too many times dulled his enthusiasm. Nonetheless, he had chosen to stay at CCC and his warning about trading the killing power of the 5.56mm carbine for the 9mm suppressed weapon was based on experience.

'I shot a gook down in Cambodia one time. Put about ten rounds of 9mm into him. Little fuck got up and ran off. Wouldn't have happened if I'd had a carbine. Next, we got your Swedish K. Good gun. Very reliable, but still 9mm.' The Supply Sergeant placed the weapon back on the counter and picked up another.

'This here is the M-3. Heavy sonofabitch. Weighs nearly nine pounds, but it's .45 so it'll put down any sucker. The Yards find it heavy, but if you want my advice this is the one for you.'

Bobby hefted the weapon in his hand. It was well balanced and rugged but, boy, was it heavy.

The Supply Sergeant picked up a short, boxy weapon that lacked the long suppressed barrel of the others.

'This is the Uzi. Them Jew boys out in Israel built this baby and they did a fine job. It's a straight 9mm weapon. Makes lotsa noise. Keeps the bad guys' heads down. Does the job. But like this,' said the Supply Sergeant, screwing on the long thick suppressor, 'you got yourself a quiet gun. So you only attach the suppressor when you need it.'

Bobby selected Uzis for both Loc and himself. They each packed twelve thirty-two-round magazines into modified NVA chest webbing, and carried extra grenades on their belts. Everyone else took CAR-15s except for Hih who retained his favourite old reliable M-79.

Bad weather over the target kept them stranded at the launch site for a day. When the weather cleared, there were already two teams backed up, so it meant going in early which was far from ideal.

Bobby had selected an LZ on his VR with SPAF-2. A narrow grass clearing, on slightly sloping ground, it was just big enough for a Huey.

Low cloud obscured the LZ for about twenty minutes. Covey was just about to declare a scrub when the cloud suddenly lifted.

The chopper slowed, pitching nose high as it lowered over the trees. Bobby heard the 'clank-clank' of rounds hitting the airframe, and shrunk to the floor.

The door gunners opened up, hosing the perimeter of the LZ. The aircraft was banking hard to the left and trying to pick up speed, having aborted its initial approach.

Two rounds punched into the bulkhead behind Bobby's head as he keyed the handset. 'Romeo Papa, this is Echo Delta, go to the alternate. I say again, head for the alternate.'

'Echo Delta, this is Romeo Papa,' called Covey. 'That's a roger. All stations, we're heading to the alternate.'

Echo Delta was the North Dakota's new-style mission callsign. Command believed that NVA now knew who Covey, SPAF and Panther were, and it was time to change. Gone were the strange-sounding names, such as Lazy Shoe or Lost Palm. Now it was all straight, cold, phonetic alphabet bigram.

The gaggle climbed back to altitude while Covey scouted the alternate, three kilometres to the northeast. The cloud was still a problem but they could get in if they hurried.

The team readied themselves, determination etched on every face.

The ground rushed up as Bobby stepped out on to the skid, waiting for the moment when they were low and slow enough to jump.

He fell heavily, the impact winding him. As the great shaking tail boom of the Huey swept over him, he watched the rest of the team drop to the ground.

Nylan grabbed his shoulder. 'You OK?' he yelled.

Bobby was trying to catch his breath when the sound of firing caused Nylan to duck.

Helped by Nylan, Bobby staggered up the slope where Bishop had led the team into the cover of the trees.

Rounds ripped over their heads. The team returned fire. The enemy fire wasn't heavy but it seemed to be coming from all around.

Bobby grabbed the coiled cable of the handset, which was trailing from the radio on his back. Finding the handset, he pressed the talk key. 'This is Echo Delta. They've got us. Look for the smoke!'

Nylan unhooked a smoke grenade from the back pocket of Bobby's rucksack, pulled the pin, and dropped it into the centre of the team. Leaves, twigs and fragments of bark filled the air as the firing intensified.

Red smoke spurted from the body of the grenade.

'Echo Delta, this is Alpha Zulu 2. I see red smoke. I say again, I have red smoke.'

'Roger, red smoke. Everything else is gooks,' said Bobby, jamming the folding stock of the Uzi and squeezing the trigger. The weapon vibrated, but there was little sound. The suppressor would cut both the range and effect of the rounds. He could take it off, but there wasn't time.

Seconds later, the Cobra's first salvos of rockets and mini-gun fire tore through the trees into the enemy.

Further out the A-1s dropped napalm. Black oily smoke billowed through the trees. The smell was as comforting as morning coffee. Napalm meant you had help.

Bobby watched a Huey break off its approach as it started to take rounds.

He ordered the team to cease fire. They weren't taking any more incoming fire, but every helicopter that tried to get near the LZ was being hit. Two more attempts were made, but each time the Huey was driven off. Then Cobras and A-1s would swarm on to the NVA to avenge the aborted approach.

'Blackfoot, this is Casper.' John Pasco came on the air, using codenames instead of callsigns. This was a personal message and it was important. 'The weather's closing in, and we're running short of gas.

Shit or bust. I can't get anyone to cover you. They're all socked in. Copy that?'

'Roger, Casper. Let's do it!' said Bobby. His legs felt like jelly and his mouth was dry. If they didn't get out this try, they were in real trouble.

Another napalm strike went down on the far side of the LZ. Cobras roared in, their mini-guns grinding away at anyone stupid enough to show themselves or unlucky enough to be where the Cobras thought they might be hiding.

Against a sky darkened by smoke and rain-heavy clouds, a lone Huey banked over the trees and began to lower towards them.

'Ditch the packs!' shouted Bobby, but he hung on to the radio. You never dropped the radio.

'Now!'

The team dashed from the trees, as the pilot, new to the task, gingerly lowered his machine.

Nylan pushed Hih up into the cabin, while Bluh was clambering up on the skid. The helicopter was still too high. The door gunner could see the problem and was yelling at the pilot over the intercom.

Bobby helped Bishop into the cabin and Nylan reached down a hand to help him.

'Go! Go! Go!'

The Huey began to rise. The door gunners resumed firing. It didn't matter that they couldn't see a specific target. Keep the bad guys' heads down. The rest of the team joined in. Empty cases clattered on to the cabin floor.

'OK, we got 'em,' called the helicopter pilot over the air.

'Roger that, let's get the fuck out of Dodge,' came the reply.

20

'Tell me they didn't know we were coming?' Bishop said. He, Bobby and Nylan were preparing their equipment for the next attempt in the morning.

'They didn't. It was just dumb luck. The gooks stake out LZs. You know that.'

Bishop looked up from packing his rucksack. 'No one's run this target that much. They had both LZs covered.'

'We'll get in tomorrow.' Bobby didn't want to argue about spies again.

'Whatever you say, man.'

Bobby wandered over to the TOC to pull the target file and see if he could spot another useable LZ from the aerial photographs. By the time he got back, Nylan and Bishop had both turned in. He went to check on the Yards and found Loc sitting outside his hooch, smoking.

'*Tout va bien?*' asked Bobby.

'*Pas mal.*'

'Tomorrow, we go back.'

'We go same, same? Like today?'

'No. New plan. I have number one plan.'

'*Trung-Si.*'

Bobby frowned.

Loc pulled his much-prized .45 from its holster and weighed the weapon in his hand. 'This,' he said, holding the weapon, 'not number one plan.' He tapped his forehead. 'This is number one plan.'

Dear Mom,

I am well. I am sorry I haven't written in a long time but I didn't know how to tell you what I am going to tell you now. I won't lie to you and say that what I am doing is not dangerous. It is very dangerous, but I'm good at it. I'm well trained, and work with people who are the best at what they do.

I know you loved Dad very much. I don't remember him, but I know he'd be proud of me for doing what I'm doing. The most important things in my life are things you could never understand. Maybe one day I'll be able to explain it to you, but I'm not sure you'll really want to know. You've got your dream, and I've got mine. Mine's not perfect but I would not trade what I have here for anything in the life you had planned for me.

Thanks for everything you ever did for me. I wouldn't have made it this far if it weren't for you.

Love,

Bobby

★

No one got much sleep that night. In the morning, Bishop felt the whole world was different. Sounds seemed sharper and the light brighter. He went outside to watch the sunrise. It reminded him he needed to get through this day alive if he wanted to see another.

Even the normally garrulous Nylan was quiet and pensive. Whatever happened today, it was going to be tough.

They flew up to Dak-To in silence.

'This is Zulu Hotel. We're going in.'

Tracer ripped past the open door of the Kingbee, causing Bobby and Nylan to recoil sharply.

'That's fucking blown it!' Nylan swore as the Kingbee swerved away.

The plan had worked fine up until that point. Two Hueys, accompanied by four Cobras, were staging a false insertion at a small clearing just south of the previous day's alternate, while the Kingbee headed for another spot created by two bomb craters that straddled a ridge about a kilometre to the northwest.

There was a call over the radio. 'White Two is hit!' False insertions were no safer than real ones, and thus were not a prized method of deception.

'Copy that. I see them. They're still flying,' replied Covey.

Bobby hooked the handset back on his harness. He didn't need to hear what was going on. 'Keep going!' he yelled, gesticulating to the Vietnamese crew chief who immediately relayed Bobby's signal on the intercom.

The aircraft began to descend on to the crest of the ridge. A rotten branch from a dead tree snapped off as the Kingbee's heavy undercarriage swept past. Seven hundred metres away, across the valley, the unseen crew of a 23mm spotted the Kingbee preparing to land. It only took them seconds to traverse the gun and open fire.

The team bunched in the door, ready to burst out. Trees and foliage disintegrated before their eyes, but strangely the sound of the exploding cannon shells didn't register.

The pilot made a tight left-hand turn and the team toppled into an untidy pile on the cabin floor. Sledgehammer blows buffeted the Kingbee.

There was a terrible scream. Bobby looked over to see Bluh, both hands clamped to his crotch. Next to him lay the door gunner, who had sustained a massive and instantly fatal wound to the chest. The floor of the cabin was slick with blood.

'Morphine! Get some fucking morphine!' Nylan was yelling. Hih and Loc looked on in horror. Bobby could smell burning oil, and, for a second, saw Carlos dying in his arms. He grabbed the handset.

'Zulu Hotel. We're hit! We're hit bad. We've got KIA here.'

'Copy that, Zulu. We see you,' responded Covey. 'Head for home. We'll cover you out.'

'Well, that's it, I guess,' said Captain Gillman, as the medics carried Bluh away.

'We go again,' said Bobby quietly.

'You only got five guys.'

'That's enough.'

'Your call, Sergeant, but I want you to think about that real hard before you do it,' said Gillman.

Bobby caught up with the team wandering back to the launch-site compound. 'We're going again.'

'Today?' Nylan looked amazed.

'If we wait till tomorrow the gooks will know we're coming. They won't expect us to come back today.'

'So now you're saying there *is* a fucking spy?' exclaimed Bishop. 'That's no news to me! I know they were expecting us! Fuck! Let some other guys run this target.'

'It's North Dakota's mission! We run it.'

'You've lost it, man,' said Bishop, shaking his head. 'We just got the crap kicked out of us.'

'You can quit if you want. We'll go with four!'

'Yeah, OK! I'll quit!' shouted Bishop, his face inches from Bobby's. 'But I'll quit when we get back!'

Once more over the target, a pair of A-1s settled the account with the 23mm that had killed the door gunner and badly wounded Bluh. Another pair of A-1s and four Cobras wheeled over the other positions in a high-risk attempt to keep the NVA anti-aircraft guns occupied.

Away from the known LZ the Huey was unmolested as it hovered high above the trees on the far side of the ridge, tracking forward until it was over a small clear patch of elephant grass on the steep slope. Rope bags fell from the cabin. Even before they hit, Bobby, Loc, Nylan and Bishop stepped out on the skids and kicked away, rappelling sixty feet to the ground.

Unclipping their snap links from their harnesses, the four men crouched down to cover out.

Hih arrived in a heap, having forgotten every rappelling lesson he had ever had. Thankfully, he was uninjured, and grinned insanely as Bobby helped him out of his harness.

The Huey accelerated smoothly away into the sky while the team picked their way down the slope and into the trees.

★

About twenty feet in front of him, a tiger stood looking directly at Loc. The Montagnards revered this animal. If you came across one, you treated it with respect and left it alone. Loc stared back at the tiger. It yawned with an air of disinterested arrogance and ambled away into the undergrowth.

Nobody else witnessed the encounter. Loc led the team onward, a soft rain drizzling through the trees. As always he remained alert to the calls of the monkeys and birds, for any sign of alarm at humans trespassing on their territory. At a certain moment he thought he caught the faintest smell of cooking, and uncannily the forest fell silent. The barely visible game trail he had been following snaked forward between two large trees that looked like a natural gateway to the rest of the jungle. Loc, feeling distinctly uneasy, studied the surrounding terrain. Maybe he hadn't chosen this path. Maybe the lie of the land and the vegetation had suggested it. If that was so, others would also be aware of the game trail, and might well lay an ambush just beyond those trees. Perhaps that was what the tiger was warning him of. He listened for another five minutes until Bobby came forward to see what the matter was.

The Montagnard signalled they would take another route.

★

Half an hour later, along the side of the ridge, the bushes swayed slightly in front of him. Loc's heart stood still. Fifteen feet away the tiger idled into view. It was the same young male.

The animal looked him straight in the eye. Loc knew the warning sign and started to back up. The tiger took a tentative step forward, nostrils twitching. The whole team backed away and the tiger halted, tail swishing. But it did not follow.

'I see same tiger before,' Loc told Bobby. '*Aujourd'hui*. Today. This very bad place.'

'Sure, it very bad place. We have to go bad place.'

'Tiger say, maybe we die.'

Bobby recalled Big Jack's words about ignoring Montagnard superstition at your peril, but he had no choice. They had to push on.

Huddled together in a patch of thick wet vegetation, the team dozed fitfully to the sound of constant dripping, and the occasional buzz of insects. Each man squirmed to find some comfort on the uneven jungle floor.

A twig snapped and the whole team was awake.

Something brushed against a bush. Hands gripped weapons and snatched up claymore triggers.

More noise. The movement seemed to be rolling towards them like a tidal wave.

The faintest outline of a human figure materialised before their eyes.

Bishop blew his claymore. The rest followed less than a second later. Bobby and the rest of the team were rocked by a sharp series of back blasts.

The men began pulling on their packs. The sleeping gear was abandoned.

Out in the dark, on the slope below them, muzzle blasts lit the jungle like camera flashes.

'Grab on!' ordered Bobby. Each man reached for the back of his comrade's rucksack.

'GO!'

There was yelling and shouting from the NVA. Panicked firing surrounded them. Officers blew whistles and tried to gain control of the operation. It was just the sort of confusion the team needed as they made their escape.

After five minutes Bobby halted. He didn't know where the hell he was going. They should be climbing. Instead they were still heading downhill.

Nylan fired up the radio and began calling. There was no reply.

'Keep trying,' whispered Bobby.

The enemy had fallen silent. Bobby knew it wouldn't take them long to find North Dakota's overnight position and to start following their trail.

'Zulu Hotel, this is Firefly two-four.'

'I got someone!' hissed Nylan. It took him about ten minutes to guide Firefly two-four overhead. Firefly two-four was the lead of a pair of A-1s out of NKP, Thailand.

'Thank God,' said Bishop, hearing the piston engines growl overhead.

The A-1s loitered for three hours until replaced by a Spectre, which had been truck hunting over Route 92. With the dawn it melted away into a dark and leaden sky.

Captain Bell had already delayed his take-off by thirty minutes because of the rain. John Pasco was that morning's Covey rider. By th_ .me both men closed the canopy on the OV-10, they were soaked. Swearing under his breath, Bell started to work his way through the memorised checklist.

Within a minute or two he had his finger on the starter and watched the engine temperature gauge needle begin to creep up, and the 'start' ignition light blink out. The engine stabilised at the advertised 85 percent.

All checks complete, Bell called the tower for clearance to taxi to the end of the runway.

'Covey 548, this is Pleiku Tower. Airfield is closed at this time.'

The message was clear. Don't go flying. It's a nasty day. Stay on the ground. Stay safe and dry.

'Understood, Pleiku Tower. This is a tactical emergency. We have troops TIC.'

'Roger, Covey 548. 270 is the active, wind is 190 gusting fifteen knots. Cloud base is 500 feet.'

Captain Bell taxied the OV-10 past the revetments containing the Vietnamese Air Force A-1s. The huge piston-engine fighters sat forlornly in the rain.

The OV-10 left the runway after a longer than average ground run owing to the pools of water lying on the concrete. At five hundred feet the aircraft was wrapped in cloud, and Captain Bell started a gentle right-hand turn to head northwest to Laos.

The team ate, one at a time.

'Look at the weather, Lake. No one's gonna fly in this. If we get hit, we ain't got any help.'

'I know.' Bobby felt irritated at Bishop for pointing out the obvious.

'They're on to us. You know that, don't you?'

'We'll lose them. Like we did last night.'

'What makes you think we lost 'em? They're just out there waiting for us to move. Look at the fucking weather, man. What are we going to do if we screw up?'

★

John Pasco gazed out into a world of bright sunlight and snowy clouds.

'Zulu Hotel, this is Golf Lima one.'

Pasco had tried three times already. Maybe North Dakota hadn't made it, maybe the only people listening to the radio were the NVA . . .

'Golf Lima one, this is Zulu Hotel.'

'Hey, buddy. Good to hear you! Over.'

Nylan gave the team's encoded position and situation report.

Pasco flipped back and forth through the codebook decoding the message. It ended with the words: No contact at this time. Continuing mission.

Pasco hit the transmit button. 'Roger, Zulu Hotel. I copy that. Be real careful. Good luck.'

With Loc walking point, North Dakota dropped deeper into the valley. Bobby still wasn't sure of their position. The map and the compass didn't seem to relate physically to the terrain. They were constantly finding their path blocked by dense jungle, and having to work round it. The loss of a night's sleep was taking its toll on their concentration, and everyone was taking the utmost care to move as silently as possible through the thick tangle of undergrowth.

They crested a spur and found themselves in more open forest.

A burst of gunfire rang out, rounds ripping above their heads. A voice shouted. They had been spotted.

The team careered down the slope towards the bottom of the valley. The ground was slippery with rain and mud.

'Loc!' Bobby shouted, skidding to a halt. He made the signal that they should double back.

Loc and the enemy soldier almost collided with each other. The Montagnard stared into the NVA's rain-streaked face. They locked eyes. The man looked tired, wet and depressed. This was not where he wanted to be.

The suppressed Uzi coughed and the Vietnamese fell as if a switch had been flicked. To his left, Nylan glimpsed another soldier walking straight towards him. He locked his sights on the man's face and crushed the trigger. The soldier fell. Another appeared. As Nylan stood to deliver another burst, a round smashed into his left forearm, spinning him round and flinging him to the ground. Hih returned fire, while Bishop delivered a fatal burst into his comrade's intended target.

'Nylan's hit!' he screamed.

Bobby unhooked a white phosphorous grenade from the back of Loc's pack and, having pulled the pin, hurled it up the slope. Seconds later it burst into a sparkling, white cloud.

Bishop helped Nylan to his feet.

'Go! Go!' Bobby directed Loc down the slope.

The enemy let rip at the billowing white cloud, but all the rounds passed high.

'Come on, you fat fuck. Try and walk!' Bishop urged a still-dazed Nylan.

The team hurtled down the slope, and crashed into the stream at the bottom. The vegetation on the flooded far bank was too thick to allow any possibility of climbing out. Loc turned upstream and began wading waist-high through the swollen waters. They were totally exposed.

'Bob!' hissed Bishop. 'We need to fix him up.' Nylan looked deathly pale. Deep in shock, he was losing blood fast. Bobby pointed to some rocks on the near bank. The team clambered out of the water, and Bishop set about applying a series of field dressings to Nylan's forearm. The bullet had ripped a deep, thumb-wide gash. Nylan's face contorted in pain.

Bobby grabbed the radio handset from Nylan's harness. 'Covey, Covey, any fucking Covey,' he hissed.

Nothing.

'Shit!' he muttered, checking the radio for damage.

There was a shout, somewhere above them.

Bobby and Loc raised their Uzis while Bishop

unsnapped a grenade from the side of one of his ammo pouches and signalled Hih to do the same. Further away voices shouted orders. Several tense minutes passed and the voices receded. After thirty minutes it was quiet.

The rain had tailed off now to a drizzle, but the heavy cloud stayed low in the sky.

Bobby felt himself begin to shake. The buzz had begun to wear off. This time I've really done it, he thought. We are deep in the shit and the Cavalry is a long way off.

Just as the light was beginning to fade, the rain stopped, and the radio crackled into life.

'Zulu Hotel, this is Charlie Delta two.'

'Charlie Delta, this is Zulu Hotel.'

'Blackfoot? You guys OK?' asked Joe Eden.

'Not really, Delta,' said Bobby. 'Standby.'

Bobby pulled the message he had coded from his pocket and read it over the air.

Eden confirmed that extraction was impossible with less than an hour or so of daylight left. 'You boys take care now. We'll see you *mañana*. Charlie Delta two, out.'

'Blackfoot out.'

At least these rocks give us reasonable cover, reckoned Bobby. If the weather broke, he would risk going out on strings.

There was a soft sloshing sound nearby. Bishop clamped his hand over Nylan's mouth. His eyes immediately flashed open. Bishop held a finger to his lips. Nylan grimaced and nodded his head.

An NVA soldier was standing up to his crotch in the centre of the stream. He was finding it difficult to walk on the uneven bed. Several more soldiers were close behind him.

The first soldier waded within twenty feet of the team, unaware that four weapons were trained on him.

Bobby was certain the NVA could hear his heart pounding. Slowly the soldier turned and looked straight at him.

Bobby opened fire. The rest of the team followed suit.

21

'Stop!' yelled Bobby.

The sudden hush was broken only by the sound of bolts snapping shut on fresh magazines.

A wild burst of fire ripped over the team. One enemy soldier had made it into cover by the far bank. The bodies of four of his comrades drifted quietly away on the current.

Bishop nestled the stock of his carbine into his shoulder and waited for the soldier to fire again. He did, his muzzle flash blinking on the far bank. Bishop squeezed off a burst. There was a splash, then silence.

Bobby grabbed the handset. 'SPAF-4! Shit's hit the fan. Prairie Fire. Prairie Fire.' Seconds ticked away. He was about to try again when he heard, 'Understood, Zulu. On way.'

'We need to move. They've got a fix on us!' whispered Bishop.

From a little way down the river there was a flash. Everyone ducked as something streaked past in the dark. There was a sharp explosion and the zinging sound of shrapnel cutting the air.

'RPG!' grunted Bishop.

Tracer tore through air. The team pressed hard into the unyielding rocks.

'Think they found us?' Nylan forced a grin.

'Not yet,' replied Bobby.

The firing continued for several minutes, wild and wide of the mark. Then ceased. The team gripped their weapons and waited.

'Yankee! Yankee! Give up, Yankee!' a voice called out.

There was another burst of fire. Tracer flashed across the stream, still wide of the team. Inaccurate and random, it was designed to draw a response from North Dakota.

'Zulu, this is Charlie Delta two.'

'Delta, things look bad. We've got our backs to the wall here.'

'Listen, buddy, you've got to get moving. I'll be overhead. Over.'

'Copy that, Delta. Blackfoot out.'

The O-1 had lifted from Dak-To at last light, after sitting out the worst of the rainstorm. Joe Eden could stay airborne for about another three hours.

The aircraft punched out of the rain into a moonlit canyon of towering clouds. The scene had a surreal beauty. Eden checked his watch and racked his brain as to how he could help beleaguered North Dakota. Seconds later he was back in the clouds.

He knew he was helpless to assist. North Dakota was alone. Joe had heard at least one man scream his last words over the air, and knew if it happened again he was just going to have to live with it.

Bobby stepped out from the rocks. If anyone could see him, they would fire now, but the only sound in the dark was the murmur of the water. He waded a short way up the stream. Nothing.

With thudding hearts, the rest of the team followed his example.

'Give up, Yankee. We no hurt you. We have food and medicine. You give up,' a voice called. 'Give up, Yankee. Come out with white flag waving.'

Bobby choked back a hysterical laugh. Where the hell was anyone going to get a white flag?

'Last chance, Yankee. We kill you soon. You give up now.'

Fuck you, thought Bobby. Fuck you and the horse you rode in on.

They had made less than twenty metres when the sound of movement on the far bank was clearly audible. The team froze, weapons trained on the bushes ten metres away across the inky water. Slowly, they backed under the overhanging foliage.

Bobby found himself sitting on the streambed, chest-deep in the chilly water. He resisted the urge to submerge himself completely. The PRC-25 radio was advertised as waterproof, but now was a bad time to test it and everyone knew the handset had to be kept dry to stand a chance of working.

A flash of tracer tore into the position they had just vacated.

Bobby felt his stomach clench. If they hadn't moved moments earlier, they'd probably be dead now.

The firing continued, followed by the splashing of the NVA as they charged across the stream towards the rocks. There was some angry shouting. The Americans had escaped from under their noses.

Methodically, a group of enemy soldiers began searching the near bank, coming closer with every second. Bobby didn't know what to do. Maybe he could use the suppressed Uzi to even the odds a shade, before the rest of the team let fly.

As the last man in the trail, Hih was sitting cross-legged in the water. Like the others, he was partially hidden by overhanging bushes. The leading enemy soldier was creeping nearer, stabbing at the bank, with his AK. Another few feet and he would step on Hih.

The Montagnard didn't need to aim. The blast of the 40mm-canister round flung the NVA back amongst his comrades. Bishop emptied his entire magazine into the mass of bodies.

'Go! Go!' Bobby cried.

The team forged upstream, enemy fire showering them with water.

Loc found a gap in the bushes and scrambled up the bank. Bobby followed as the Montagnard ran forward to cover the rest.

The NVA continued to blaze at shadows, unaware of the team's new location.

Out in the jungle a dog barked.

Oh, God. Not dogs. Dogs could track in the dark.

They had to move again.

Inching slowly away up the slope, the team turned north.

'*Ei be do!*' a voice hissed urgently from a thicket.

The entire team froze in mid-step.

Loc scanned the dark for a sign of the soldier who had called out the challenge.

'*Ei be do!*'

Bobby and Loc both pulled grenades from their pouches. Neither man gave any thought to the implication of their actions. It was instinct and training. Having tugged out the pins, they let the firing levers fly off, counted for two beats, letting the fuses burn like Big Jack had taught them, then gently lobbed the grenades towards the thicket.

There were two loud detonations, and a scream of pain. An angry riposte of firing broke out to the right.

The team scrambled into the cover of nearby tree trunks. Bishop and Hih both quickly returned fire as Bobby ripped the pin from the fragmentation grenade and hurled it towards the muzzle flashes. The grenade exploded with a sharp bang. There was a momentary pause from the NVA.

'Move!'

They managed another twenty metres before the enemy began shooting from further up the slope, sending hundreds of rounds through the surrounding foliage. Dropping to the ground, the team moved forward on hands and knees.

'This way!' urged Bishop, pointing to the left.

There was a yelling and whistle blasts to cease fire. The jungle fell dark again.

'Bishop! For fuck's sake, slow up!' Nylan grunted. Crawling was extremely difficult and painful with only one arm.

A dog barked again. It was close this time.

Five minutes later, as they lurked shivering and wet in the darkness, voices drifted towards them, and Bobby's heart sank to hear the panting and whining of the dog.

The team split up and took cover behind some trees.

The sound got closer. Bobby estimated the position, and then tossed another grenade. The others followed suit.

The grenades exploded, and were replied to with angry bursts of tracer lashing out into the trees about them.

The team broke cover and headed back up the slope. Behind them, the sound of firing continued as well as the high-pitched barking of the dog.

'Bishop. Take the radio,' panted Bobby as they made another dash to change position. He ripped the rucksack from his back. 'I need you to take over the team. Head back to the LZ up on the ridge, where we lost Bluh. If you can't make that, go out on strings as soon as you can.'

'What about you?'

'I'll catch you up. I'll have my Urc. I can talk on that.'

'You're really into this hero shit, aren't you?'

Bobby passed over the map. 'Got any better ideas?' he asked unhooking two white phosphorous grenades from the back of Hih's and Bishop's packs.

Bishop didn't reply.

'OK, let's do it.'

Bobby turned to the Montagnards. '*Trung-Si*

Bishop, *il est chef*. Same, same *Trung-Si* Lake. You go now.'

There were no goodbyes, no good lucks. Within seconds Bobby was alone in the dark. He sat with his back to a tree trunk facing down the hillside. He felt strangely calm. All he had to do was kill the dog, then he could catch them up. He'd just wait for the NVA to walk right over him. He had a suppressed weapon and they didn't know where he was. The odds were in his favour.

At the sound of some scuffing and panting, Bobby pushed the stock of the Uzi into his shoulder. A shadowy figure reached out for a sapling branch to pull himself upwards.

Bobby heard his rounds smash through the soldier's chest-mounted magazines and saw the Vietnamese drop to his knees and topple back down the slope into the path of his comrades.

The dog barked madly, straining at the leash. Bobby fired a sustained burst before dropping the Uzi into his lap and grasping hold of one of the white phosphorous grenades.

The grenade exploded like a beautiful firework, tens of tiny stars leaping up into the dark. Bobby heard a choking cry, followed by an agonised yelp.

He rolled from cover. Saw his own flickering shadow cast in the glow of the burning phosphorous. Tracer flashed to either side of him, kicking up mud. Bobby lunged back behind the tree trunk as rounds splintered the wood.

Losing his footing, he fell heavily and rolled downhill through the wet leaves. For a moment he lay stunned, the Uzi still attached to him by its sling.

Bobby unscrewed the suppressor and flung it away. He fired another burst.

There was a chorus of shouts, and more firing. The NVA were still moving up the slope.

Bobby fired again. 'Over here, motherfuckers! Over here!' he yelled.

The magazine ran dry. He swapped and let rip once more.

Tracer rounds lashed the air over his head.

Bobby headed down the slope, yelling as he ran.

He turned to fire another burst. A heavy blow smashed into his thigh, and Bobby went down. He tried to stand, but couldn't. One leg wouldn't work. Dragging himself down the slope on one elbow, he found the cover of a tree trunk.

His leg was beginning to hurt like hell. He could feel hot blood soaking his pants. Pulling out a field dressing Bobby applied it to the wound, wrapping the bandage tapes around his thigh as tightly as he could. His hands were shaking so badly, he could barely tie off the ends into a knot.

I fucked up. My team's running. I'm hit. The mission's failed. I can't walk. I'll die here.

Bobby consciously began to breathe deeply. His hands became steadier and he unscrewed the top of his canteen and took a long drink of the tepid water.

Stop talking like a pussy and start thinking like a gunfighter, he told himself.

He tried once more to stand but only one leg would take any weight. He sure as hell wasn't going to try and hop anywhere. The only option was to crawl.

Slowly and very painfully, he edged back up the slope.

So this was what it was like to be an American hero. Wet, ragged, and wounded, crawling through the jungle at night while everyone you grew up with sat in bars or in their front rooms and watched the war on TV.

Uncle Ethan's words came flooding back. 'Listen to me, kid. I bet you, right now, there's some poor son-of-a-bitch bleeding to death in a ditch who would give anything not to be there.'

Bobby wanted desperately to live. But that overwhelming knowledge made him feel like a coward. He still had his Uzi. If he couldn't make it to the LZ, he wouldn't die alone.

The leg wouldn't stop bleeding. He tightened the dressing and pressed his bandana into the wound. There was so much blood. He felt sick and dizzy. His vision blurred and he seemed to be falling.

The O-1 circled in the black, swirling clouds. Rain lashed the canopy. Joe Eden was on instruments and had been for the past hour. The storm was worsening and the aircraft difficult to control.

He had received no word from North Dakota for over an hour.

The O-1 suddenly dropped into another air pocket making Eden weightless before the aircraft hit another gust and forced him hard back into his seat.

He couldn't keep flying like this. He wasn't used to flying on instruments, and the concentration was exhausting.

He was going to have to leave soon, and he hadn't been able to get a single Spectre out of Thailand. NKP was all socked in with the same storm.

Joe decided give it another couple of tries, but then he could do no more.

Bishop heard the radio crackle and pressed the handset to his ear.

The rain streamed down while the team took a brief rest just over the top of the ridge at the side of the valley. There was no sign of their pursuers and less than a kilometre to go before they reached the LZ.

'SPAF, this is Wizard. Over.'

'Hey, Wizard. How you guys holding up? Over.'

'We've lost one. Over.'

There was a long pause before Eden came back.

'Roger, Wizard. Who you missing? Over.'

'Blackfoot. We've waited for an hour now. I don't think he's gonna catch up. You heard anything? Over.'

'Negative, Wizard. You wanna tell me where you're heading? Over.'

'Roger, SPAF. Wait.' Bishop got Hih to hold a nylon windcheater over him as he used his penlight to code up the estimated co-ordinates. When he'd done, he read them over the air to Eden.

Joe confirmed he'd copied correctly, and that he'd be back at first light.

'Keep the faith, Wizard. I'm sure Blackfoot is OK. SPAF, out.'

Eden had managed to scrawl Bishop's message on his kneepad. He didn't even know if it would be legible once back on the ground, but he sure as hell couldn't decode it in the air and fly the plane at the same time. They were being thrown around like a bee in a wind tunnel.

He turned due east and tried to hold a steady course. He needed to know exactly where he was. The nearest fields were Dak-To or Kontum but neither was open at night. After about five minutes, he dialled up the area air traffic control.

'Peacock, this is Charlie Delta two.'

'Roger, Charlie Delta two, this is Peacock. Read you weak. Over.'

'I'm somewhere north of Dak-To. Any help you can give, I need. Over.'

'Roger, Charlie Delta two, squawk 7174. Press for ident.'

Eden dialled up the transponder code and pressed the identification button. Far away in some dark control room, the radar operator saw a blip flashing 7174.

'Charlie Delta two, this is Peacock. Turn to 045 now. Over.'

'Roger, Peacock, 045.'

The O-1 forged on for a couple more minutes. The air became calmer and suddenly the clouds parted and the aircraft was straight and level in clear night air.

Far to the north Joe could see lights. He flipped the map over to study the correct section.

Well, if I've got this right, then that's Da-Nang, he thought to himself. Thank you, God.

★

As if someone had turned off a tap, the rain stopped. But down under the tree canopy water continued to drip down through the branches and leaves.

The team lay back to back. Sodden and exhausted, no one wanted to move.

Maybe Bobby was already at the LZ, Bishop hoped, or he might be sheltering close by. Once they started moving they'd have to be careful not to run into him in the dark. He'd be taking the same route they would.

Bishop checked his watch. It was time to move. They needed to be on the LZ ready for sun-up at 06.30.

He stood slowly, signalling the rest of the team to follow suit. Nylan was quiet and slow. He gripped his useless arm across his chest, his carbine slung round his neck.

Hih looked over at Bishop, imploring him silently to go back and find Bobby.

Bishop shook his head.

22

Captain Gillman watched the gaggle descend into Dak-To.

He knew Bobby Lake was missing, probably dead.

Gillman was sorry, but he had long ago developed the critical ability to mourn another man's passing without letting it affect him in any way.

A haggard-looking Bishop climbed from the helicopter's cabin and walked slowly towards him. The Chase medic helped Nylan to a stretcher, his blood-soaked arm in an improvised sling.

Bishop lit a cigarette.

'Lake's dead,' he said to Gillman. 'There was nothing I could do. He told us to go. He never caught up. He's dead and we're not. Stupidest fucking brave shit I ever saw.'

'He not dead.'

Gillman and Bishop looked over at Loc, who was squatting a few feet away, drawing in the mud with a stick. '*Trung-Si* Lake number one. *Il n'est pas mort.* He not dead.'

★

With a few hours' sleep and a fresh load of fuel, Joe Eden had lifted from Da-Nang at first light and returned to the target, intent on finding Sergeant Robert Lake.

He flung the aircraft over, pulling back on the stick so the ground rotated in his view beneath the wing.

His eyes combed every inch of ground for any sign of a panel, or a body, lying in the open. He felt himself willing a pen-flare to fire or to see the flash from a signalling mirror blinking from under the tree canopy. But there was nothing.

Despite the S-3's best efforts, the news from Kontum was not good. The Bright Light team was on hold until they could get some positive proof that Bobby Lake was alive and worth risking lives for.

A torrent of expletives burst from the men huddled in the doorway of the launch site's commo shack.

'Don't give me any shit, Captain,' the S-3 had growled to Gillman over the radio. 'That's the way it is. I don't like it and you don't like it, but if you can't handle it, go play tiddlywinks.'

'Let's just fucking go!' suggested the One-one on the Bright Light team.

An uneasy silence engulfed the assembled men.

No one wanted to disagree, but they all knew that you couldn't just up and launch the Bright Light without the proper chain of command. They might be gunfighters, but they weren't cowboys.

'Did I hear that right?' asked Joe Eden over the radio.

'Affirmative, Lima Victor One,' replied Covey, relaying the message that the Bright Light team was on hold.

This is like a bad joke, thought Joe, cranking his little plane into another violent turn.

Come on, Bob. You've got a radio. Fucking use it. Give me a sign, urged Joe.

The O-1 pulled up over the spur and turned west. Joe had been down that valley four times now and not one round had been fired at him. Maybe there was no one down there. Intelligence reports suggested that the NVA often cleared out of an area in the event of either air strikes or Hatchet Force platoons looking to avenge lost comrades.

Beep. Beep. Beep.

'Covey, this is SPAF,' blurted Joe, abandoning the characterless biagram callsigns. 'You hear that?'

'Sure do.'

The beeper stopped.

Joe swung the O-1 round and hit the transmit button.

'Beeper Beeper. Come up voice. This is Lima Victor One, come up voice.'

Nothing happened. Anyone calling on an URC–10 was supposed to transmit the tone signal then wait for a reply from a passing aircraft before establishing voice communication.

'Beeper Beeper. Come up voice.'

Still nothing.

Five thousand feet above Eden, Covey was signalling Dak-To that they had heard the signal tone from an URC–10. Someone on the ground needed help.

'Jesus Christ, sir. Yes, the gooks might be using his radio to lure us in, but so what!' exploded the S–3 into the telephone handset. It was common knowledge that the NVA had captured at least twenty URC–10 from aircrew and recon teams.

'How the fuck are we going to know unless we go and see, sir?'

The Commo Sergeant looked on amazed at the S–3's outburst. He was fairly sure the S–3 was talking to the Colonel.

'With respect, sir,' the S–3 continued, 'voice contact means shit. There's a million good reasons why he might not be able to talk. The radio might be busted. Maybe he's only got tone and no voice. Maybe he's taken a bullet in the fucking teeth.'

The S-3 paused again to listen to the reply.

'Well, I'll tell you what I think, sir. I think it sends a fucking poor message to anyone running recon. I think it sounds like cowardice, sir! Those boys have got to know that we'll shit thunderbolts to get them back, not run scared over being the last man dead in this shitty little country.'

There was another pause while he listened, fuming, to the reply.

'I don't give a fuck, sir!' He slammed the phone down.

Chances were, thought the Sergeant, the S-3 had just got himself relieved and was also going to get himself court-martialled, which would be a pity because he was a hell of a good officer.

The S-3 smashed his fist into the wall, the corner of his eye flickering with the pain.

'Launch the Bright Light,' he said, examining his grazed knuckles.

Alec Hidaka had been Carl Joyner's One-one before getting his own team, and now found himself back on Bright Light duty.

Hidaka stood conferring with Bishop about Bobby's probable position. UHF direction-finding equipment on Covey's OV-10 was only accurate to about five hundred metres.

'My guess is that he's in here somewhere, to the

west of the stream.'

'We'll find him,' said Hidaka, studying the map.
'Go get some rest, Jim.'

'Screw that. I'm coming with you.'

'You don't look so good.'

'I just popped some Green Hornets. I'm good to
go,' said Bishop, draining the last drops from a can
of Coke.

'We got Loc to guide us back in. You sit this one
out.'

Bishop's shoulders sagged for a moment. It was
as if Hidaka's reluctance to take him was a personal
rejection. Then he straightened up. 'Till we find
Lake, I'm North Dakota's One-zero. I can't quit. I
need to do this.'

'You all bombed up?' asked Hidaka.

Bishop patted his ammunition pouches to signify
he'd recharged all his magazines and picked up four
fresh grenades.

'OK. Saddle up, round eye. Let's go.'

'Covey, this is Jigsaw Lead.'

Covey took his eyes off the approaching
helicopters and looked up. The fast movers were
checking in on the UHF net.

'Go ahead, Jigsaw Lead.'

'Covey, we are at the RP. Jigsaw flight is four,
Fox-fours. We're packing six snake eyes a piece.'

377

Five-hundred-pound bombs weren't ideal for the task he had in mind, but this was the only flight that Leghorn had been able to divert in.

'Roger that, Jigsaw. You guys been briefed?'

'Negative, Covey. We're a little in the dark here.'

'OK. We have a Bright Light going in on the valley to your south. We need you to blow an LZ for them. I'll mark it. You can run in from any direction you want. Target elevation is 2,000 feet approximately. Best bailout area is anywhere on the home side of the fence. Call FAC in sight. Drop singles unless I say otherwise. Also, I've two Zorros inbound from NKP but they ain't checked in yet. Lima Victor One is an Army 0-1 and he'll take over if I get hit. Hold high and dry for now.'

'Roger, Covey. Jigsaw Lead out.'

Covey switched back to the FM radio.

'All stations, this is November Mike One. Let's play ball. Lima Victor, I have you in sight. Heads up, I'm coming down.'

'Lima Victor. Roger. I see you.'

Covey rolled the OV-10 on to its back and dived towards the trees. From the corner of his eye, he caught sight of the O-1 flying along the ridge to the east of the valley. Joe Eden was still trying to raise Bobby on voice.

Covey fired a single white phosphorous rocket into the jungle. The spot was midway up the western side of the valley and eight hundred metres north of where Bobby might be.

'Jigsaw Lead, this is Covey. Do you see the marker?'

'This is Jigsaw Lead. Wait.'

The Flight Leader rolled his aircraft over to look down for the tell-tale plume of white smoke in the jungle.

'Roger, Covey. I see it.'

'Jigsaw Lead, you're cleared in hot. Call FAC in sight.'

It took six bombs to cut down a patch of jungle that one Huey could get into and hover.

The team was spread out across three helicopters. Each machine approached the clearing in turn. The Bright Light team, accompanied by Bishop and Loc, climbed down the ladders and took cover amongst the wreckage of the trees.

High above, in SPAF-4, Joe Eden tapped the fuel gauge. He'd been airborne for well over two hours. He could stay up for two more, but you needed to keep a close eye on the juice. A hole in the tank could leave you without a safety margin.

'Lima Victor, this is November Mike. You heard anything more?'

'Negative, November Mike. It's all quiet.'

★

Despite the pills Bishop had given him, Loc felt tired. He knew he was relying on the skills of the Bright Light scout, who was fresh and alert. Loc felt stiffness in his thighs and the age in his bones.

Suddenly the scout staggered and fell back. Loc could see the exit wounds, where bullets had punched through the man's body.

He hurled himself into the damp leaves as more bullets tore past him. Rolling on to his side, Loc emptied his Uzi towards the sound of firing. The weapon's roar was almost alarming. Loc had discarded the suppressor back at Dak-To. There was no need for silence now.

'Get everyone up here!' Hidaka yelled to Bishop and the One-one. Then grabbed the radio handset. 'November Mike, this is Delta Kilo. Contact. Wait out.'

One of the team's two M-60s began a maniacal chatter of heavy fire towards the enemy.

Shooting on the move, Bright Light crept forward, and formed an all-round defence about the body of the dead scout. Hidaka stripped the still figure of all weapons and ammunition, sharing it around.

Covey checked in to make sure everything was OK.

'Roger that, Delta Kilo. Be aware, I had to let

the fast movers go. I have two Zorros on station now. Good luck.'

The enemy had fallen back, no match for the aggressive firepower of the Bright Light.

Loc soon spotted their tracks from the previous night and swung east. Clearly North Dakota had not been followed. There were no other tracks over theirs.

This was the place. This was where he last saw Bobby.

At the base of a bullet-scarred tree, a 9mm brass case lay on a bed of dead leaves. Sniffing the case, Loc could tell it had been fired last night.

Bishop spotted the fly-off lever from a white phosphorous grenade. The NVA had lost people here. Rain had washed away most of the blood but coils of sodden bloodied bandage lay amongst the burnt vegetation. Hidaka found an abandoned NVA belt lying among the leaves. 7.62mm cases from NVA AKs lay all around.

Hidaka reached for the radio and contacted Covey.

If Bobby had got away from here, he'd have followed the team, thought Bishop. But if he followed us, why didn't he catch us up? He had to be wounded.

A little further down the slope, Loc had noticed

some freshly crushed vegetation, and glinting from under the leaves was another 9mm case. No NVA used 9mm. This was Bobby's trail.

Away to the south a shot rang out and someone shouted. The NVA were still in the area and coming straight for them.

Hidaka hurriedly spread the team out in an east-west line, facing south. He, Bishop and Loc stayed back as rear security.

'He down there,' said Loc to Hidaka. 'He come this way. He hurt!'

Before he could ask Loc to elaborate, one of the Montagnards near the eastern end of the line let rip with his M-60.

The fight was on. The roar of weapons seemed unending and the air filled with the fumes from burnt propellant. The enemy fire didn't slacken for a moment. The Montagnard carrying the M-79 suddenly reeled back clutching the side of his chest.

They were in danger of being flanked if this went on any longer.

A volley of white phosphorous grenades was the signal to break contact.

'Follow me.' Hidaka sprinted back about sixty metres, followed by the rest of the team, two men dragging the wounded Montagnard. The NVA were still firing, though, unaware that the team had broken off.

'Covey, this is Delta Kilo. Contact. I need anything you got, about two hundred metres south of where you see my flare.'

'Roger, Delta Kilo. Watching for the flare.'

'Loc says Lake's down there,' Bishop said to Hidaka.

'How the fuck does he know that?'

'I don't know!' exclaimed Bishop. 'He just does!'

'Just give me a second here,' said Hidaka, turning back to the radio.

Covey's marker rocket ripped vertically down through the trees and slammed into the jungle floor, bursting in a cloud of sparkling stars and billowing white smoke.

'Right on, Covey.'

'Roger that, Delta. Get your heads down. Zorro is cleared in hot.'

The growl of the A-1 grew louder.

A drum roll of explosions rang out, punctuated by the sound of the A-1 pulling out from its dive. Bomblets from a cluster munition straddled the NVA location.

'Let's go!' Hidaka said, gesturing north back to the LZ.

'Wait!' said Bishop, tugging his arm. 'That way!' he said, pointing down the slope. 'Lake's down there!'

'Listen, Bishop. I've got one dead, one injured,

and fuck knows how many NVA on our ass. We're
outta here!'

Joe Eden banked the O-1 on its wingtip and
watched the A-1 scream past in the valley below.
The Bright Light team was in contact, and it didn't
sound good.

Beep. Beep. Beep.

Jesus!

Covey made the call before Joe could even hit
the transmit button.

'Covey can hear a beeper,' said Hidaka. He turned
to Loc. 'Let's go.'

Loc led off down the slope.

An RPG detonated in the branches above the
team, the spray of shrapnel felling Loc, Hidaka,
Bishop and one of the Montagnards.

'How bad you hit?' yelled Hidaka above the
gunfire.

'I'm OK!' gasped Bishop, looking at Hidaka's
blood-covered face. He had shrapnel wounds across
his forehead and chest. Bishop could see Loc
returning fire, dark stains spreading across his back.
Bishop glanced at his left arm; the OG material was
dark and shiny. He knew he'd been hit, but it didn't
feel that bad.

Bishop heard someone fall behind him. One

of the Montagnards, wounded in the upper arm, was sprawled on his side, his face contorted in pain.

At least he can still walk, thought Bishop, crawling into cover behind a large tree trunk and beginning to return fire. To his left, Hidaka was calling in another air strike.

Bishop fired till his magazine ran dry. 'Come on, you fuckers. Come and get me. Come and get me, you shit-eating gooks!'

Bishop wiped the tears from his eyes. Why was he crying and who was that shouting?

The team fell back to give the A-1s more room to work. Hidaka circled everyone into a tight perimeter, another fallen tree providing reasonable cover on the south side. The seriously wounded Montagnard was dumped in the centre and stripped of his ammo.

'We fight here!' shouted Hidaka. He knew another team was inbound from Dak-To. They were going to stay put. The Montagnards began pulling belts of ammunition and claymores from their rucksacks.

The sound of an A-1 pulling out was drowned by the whoosh of napalm igniting a fifty-metre strip of forest to the south. Everyone knew the air strikes might kill Bobby, but that was still better than him being captured.

The firing began again almost immediately.

'Lake! Lake! Where the fuck are you?'

Hidaka grabbed Bishop. Had he gone insane?

Bishop stared back, wild eyed. 'What else can we do?'

Hidaka joined in. The One-one added his voice and then the Montagnards.

A claymore detonated. A reckless charge of NVA was mown down, but one man got so close that he toppled over one of the Montagnards. An M-79 gunner pulled his .45 and shot the NVA soldier in the head.

Bishop watched the Montagnard strip the enemy corpse of his magazines and grenades. This was no longer shocking. This was now normal, and Bishop hated that.

'Cover him!' shouted Hidaka. One of the team was breaking out of the position but Bishop didn't pay any attention. Anything beyond his field of fire might as well be on the moon.

A figure in a dark green tunic burst from the bushes, rifle blazing, screaming at the top of his lungs.

'Motherfucker!' Bishop's finger crushed the trigger of his carbine, and the figure crumpled to the ground.

A surge of anger shook Bishop to the core. How dare they try and kill him!

'Lake! We're here, Lake! Lake! For God's sake, Lake!'

Hidaka grabbed hold of Bishop. 'Look! Look!' he screamed.

Loc was pulling a body from the jungle.

EPILOGUE

I'm still scared, so I can't be dead.

Bobby had lain, curled under a bush, drifting in and out of consciousness, the Urc clutched in his trembling hand.

Then the shooting had begun. The NVA had swarmed around him, and at one point he dreamed of death from a friendly air strike, rather than capture.

Through the mist of pain and despair, he'd heard American weapons. Someone shouted his name. In desperation he'd begun to crawl, then hands had fallen upon him. He had wanted to strike out until he realised they were friendly.

As he was carried through the jungle, a black tide of panic rolled over him. They won't get me out! I don't deserve this. I was ready to die, but too scared to actually do it. I shouldn't have used the Urc. I should have stayed quiet and died.

Only when he was passed to the swaying deck of the helicopter cabin did he begin to feel safe.

'OK, buddy? We're gonna fix you up. Stay with me now! You'll be OK.' Stitch Ellis tore away clothing in search of veins for an I.V.

A vast wave of emotion surged within Bobby. They can't see me cry, he thought. They'll think I'm a candy ass. He'd screwed up his face to stem the tears but the suppressed weeping shook his body while he gripped hold of Stitch's offered hand.

He didn't know when it happened, but he remembered Bishop's face looking down at him. Bishop was saying something important, but he couldn't make sense of it.

'Thanks, man. Thanks.' He didn't know if Bishop could hear him. He'd reached up to pull him close, but a medic had yanked his arm away.

When all the feelings and memories evaporated, Bobby felt himself calm and at peace. Maybe I did die? This isn't so bad.

'How you doing, soldier?'

Bobby awoke to gaze into the cold uncompromising eyes of the S-3.

'I'm fine, thank you, sir.' The strength and clarity of his own voice surprised him.

'You'll be OK. It's gonna be a while, but they'll fix you up.'

'Did everyone make it?'

'All your guys, but we lost a couple of Yards getting you out.'

Bobby opened his mouth, but no words came.

'We lose people, son. Go looking for a fight and

it'll happen. It's just the way things are.' The S-3 paused for a moment. 'You wanna tell me what the hell you were doing, running with only five guys?'

'We had to run the mission.'

'Yeah? Would you have run with, four, three, two? When do you figure you've made it hard enough on yourself?'

'I knew I could run with five, sir. We damn' nearly made it.'

'You got a real short memory, son! You nearly bought the farm.'

'Everything we do is risky,' said Bobby.

'But not everything we do is dumb. I hear you got all fired up, and started hollering and yelling at the gooks to follow you. That right?'

Bobby stayed silent.

'That right?' persisted the S-3. 'Because I don't need anyone dumb running recon. I got my hands full just dealing with the guys we got. I don't need another dumb fuck pissing on my campfire and making it all a whole lot crazier out there. You read me?'

'I didn't have a choice, sir. I had to put things right. It was my call.'

'What exactly did you have to put right, son? Recon teams get chased everyday. What makes you anything different?'

'I fucked up, sir. I nearly got everyone killed.'

'Is that so? Well, live and learn. Don't pull that shit again. You hear me?'

Bobby nodded, then said, 'They know we're coming, don't they, sir? The NVA, I mean.'

The S-3 looked out of the window. 'It's looked that way for a while. Smart money says there's someone on the inside. Maybe in the STD. Hell, he could even be in the President's office.'

'Well, sir, we need to get that fucker.'

'That ain't gonna happen anytime soon. The Vietnamese won't let us investigate. It'd make them look stupid. They're our allies and Washington don't want to think of them as part of the problem. No one's looking to win this war. They're just looking to get everyone home. They won't do a thing.'

'But the guy's a fucking spy!'

'Which guy? Chances are there's more than one and, unless he fucks up, we'll probably never know who he is. We're just gonna have to learn to deal with it. If you can't handle it, quit!'

'I can't do that.'

'I figured. Well, you ain't gonna be running recon for a while, anyhow. That slug tore up your leg pretty bad. I've got to find three more guys to run North Dakota.'

'Three?'

'Yeah, Lieutenant Bishop quit.'

'Jim Bishop's a good man, sir!' Bobby felt his heart begin to race.

'Thank you Sergeant. I know. He's a brave man, but he knows his limitations, which is more than can be said for some other guys I know.' The S-3 tugged his earlobe. 'Lieutenant Bishop tells me he's gonna write you up for the CMH. Tells me what you did was above and beyond.'

Bobby's brow furrowed. 'It wasn't like that, sir. I just screwed up. I'm no hero.'

'Ain't for you to say.'

'I won't take it. You gotta talk to Bishop, sir. Don't let him do it.'

'It's outa my hands. Makes you feel any better, I don't think you'll get it. It's politics. But you'll probably see a DSC or a Silver Star out of this thing.'

Bobby slowly shook his head, unable to accept what he was hearing.

'Don't be a jerk. Think about Lieutenant Bishop.'

'What?'

'It might help him to know that you really are a hero. That what you did saved his life. People need heroes, son. Even if they're real brave themselves, heroes make them feel good about what they did, and makes all the other shit seem worth it. I'll see you around, Sergeant. Take it easy.'